I0761060

# THE WASHINGTON TRAIL

A SLADE AND CORK MYSTERY

LOU AGUILAR

AETHON THRILLS

aethonbooks.com

Aethon Books
www.aethonbooks.com

Print and eBook cover and interior formatting by Steve Beaulieu.

Published by Aethon Books LLC.

## ACKNOWLEDGMENTS

My thanks to a great friend and computer genius Tom Welsh for helping a luddite like me describe technology like Mr. Spock. And to Denver PD cop Brian Franklin for aiding me to spout police jargon like Joe Friday. Also to ace Aethon Books editor Rob Salerno for correcting my errors and sharpening the rest. And to my brother George and old friend Victor Macia for being so critical of my past work, I had to raise my game on this one.

# CHAPTER 1

Mark Slade distrusted his disguise. Straddling a silver *Cervelo* racing bicycle in a navy-blue Army hoodie, grey sweatpants, wool gloves, and black running shoes, and hunched by an olive-green backpack, he resembled a typical bike courier. Only there were a lot fewer bike messengers in DC now than when he'd been one twelve years ago, the summer between his freshman and sophomore terms at Georgetown. He worried he stuck out like a Pony Express rider beside a telegraph pole in 1862. At least he was still in good cycling shape.

The bike made him seem shorter than his six-foot-two height. The sweat-jacket bulked up an already muscular build, its hood warding off the early January chill while obscuring his dark blonde hair, brown eyes, square jaw shadowed by two-day stubble, and earbuds playing Tears for Fears' "Everybody Wants to Rule the World."

He looked west across 23rd Street at the broad glass office building dominating the L Street intersection, then down at his iPhone. The screen showed two minutes to twelve, nearly lunchtime for downtown office workers, including his quarry, Philip Lassiter. He passed the time appraising lunch-bound office women.

Eying a pair of silk-stockinged limbs as far as the street corner, he almost missed Lassiter. His blow-dried white hair, designer sunglasses, and grey suit jacket were ducking into a grey Jaguar sedan with tinted windows, its right rear door being held open by a husky bald man in a black suit. Slade pegged Yul Brynner as more than a chauffeur. When the Jaguar pulled away, Slade did too, both vehicles heading west on L.

The Jag crossed 24th Street on a yellow light, Slade on the red. Three lanes of traffic crisscrossed behind him. A white SUV in the fourth lane just missed his rear wheel. Its claxon blast followed him until "Blue Monday" by New Order came on in his ears.

He caught up to the Jag on 25th, waiting to make a left but stymied by incessant oncoming traffic. He stopped the bike and put his right foot on the sidewalk. The light turned yellow with cars still approaching. On red, the Jag shot left just ahead of two-way traffic that instantly blocked Slade. He swerved left onto the opposite sidewalk full of pedestrians. Those facing him scrambled out of the way. The rest unwarily impeded his path.

"Look out!" yelled Slade.

People spun and dodged him. One heavy businessman stumbled right into a curbside hotdog cart manned by an elder Filipino. Boiling water splashed his backside and he went into a jig, his yelps mixing with Tagalog invectives as Slade flew past him.

The Jag made a right on K Street, where ceaseless 25th Street traffic kept Slade from crossing behind it. He did so anyway and passed the first lane unscathed. A Honda Civic in the second lane braked short of hitting him, only to get rear-ended by the Ford Escape behind it. The ensuing horn blast halted vehicles in the two southbound lanes, letting him reach the other side.

He caught up to the car at a red light on 26th Street. He knew that one block further, K Street would become the Whitehurst Freeway – a bike-unfriendly road with a single narrow westbound lane, no traffic light, and no shoulder for its entire eight miles. Yet when the Jag got on Whitehurst, Slade went after it.

He rode in seventh gear, legs pumping in smooth, rapid circles, the skin beneath his backpack dampening, the New Order song pacing him. He kept perilously close to the low concrete wall on his right, feeling the vibration of each car that passed him. To his left, the Potomac River flowed in the opposite direction as if amplifying his speed. Ahead of him, the Jaguar took a right bend in the road and vanished.

He increased his output to his cardiovascular extreme, unsustainable for more than three minutes. He rounded the curve and saw the Jaguar. It had stopped three cars back from M Street in the right-turn lane, delayed by a red light. Slade slowed his bike, and his breathing. "Safety Dance" by Men Without Hats started playing on his earbuds.

Straight across M Street, behind an old Shell station, rose the steep narrow staircase made famous by *The Exorcist*. Slade turned right on M – Into a long block of row-shops marking the west start of Georgetown. He halted on the corner to await the Jag. It went past him, plus five storefronts to stop before the *Alegria* Restaurant.

Lassiter exited the car without assistance and held open the door. A Bollywood starlet stepped out of it – or an Indian woman striking enough to be one – in a faux-fur coat, gold skirt, and silver high heels. The couple entered *Alegria*.

Slade cycled past the restaurant then six more shops and dismounted in front of *Comic Planet*. A grim Batman on the door appeared to menace all shoppers. Slade lifted the horseshoe-shaped Kryptonite lock from its perch on the bike's seat tube and hooked it around a parking meter pole and his down tube. After securing the crossbar, he walked into *Comic Planet*.

A wide table full of unprepossessing superheroes appeared to fly at him from comic-book covers, backed by more rows of them all the way to the far wall. Two nerds and a plump blue-haired girl were scouring the issues. Slade moved left toward the purchase counter, where a thin thirty-something clerk with stringy brown hair sat reading a graphic novel.

"Hey, no reading on the job," Slade said.

The clerk looked up and grinned. "Mark Slade. I haven't seen you since Professor X died."

"You know why, Claude. Is Thor still a chick?"

"No, he's back – for now."

"How 'bout Iceman? Still gay?"

"He goes both ways," Claude said sullenly.

"Too diverse for me."

"And half my old regulars," Claude whispered, casting a nervous glance at the blue-haired girl.

"I need to use your bathroom," Slade said.

Claude handed him an Iron Man-logoed keychain with two keys. Slade walked to the rear of the store then into a cramped bathroom. Standing his backpack on the toilet lid, he extracted a blue tweed sports jacket, a light gold dress shirt, and black jeans from the main pouch, then a glasses case from the front pocket. He took off his Army sweat jacket to start changing and wiped away the sweat with the t-shirt he removed.

Three minutes later, he approached the counter wearing the different outfit and the glasses and carrying the backpack.

"What's with the Clark Kent look?" Claude asked when Slade reached him.

"I wanted to fit in here."

Slade put the keychain on the countertop and his backpack beside it.

"Claude, can you keep this back there a few minutes?"

"Only if you buy something."

"Okay. Who's the new hot super-villainess?"

"Hot super-villainesses are sexist," Claude said bitterly.

"Great. All right, I'll take the latest Superman. At least he's still fighting for truth, justice, and the American … what?"

Claude was shaking his head.

"Would you settle for two out of three?"

"Geez."

"His new motto is 'for a better tomorrow'."

"It's off to a bad start," said Slade. "See you in a few."

Stepping outside, he walked back to *Alegria*. In the cantina-style foyer, an attractive brunette hostess with the nametag "Maria" smiled pleasantly at him. Soft flamenco guitar music emanated from a

Moorish archway leading to the dining area.

"Hello, sir," Maria said. "Do you have a reservation?"

"No, ma'am," Slade said in a tremulous, higher-pitched voice.

"How many in your party?"

Slade hung his head. "Just me. The story of my life."

"Aw. We're totally booked I'm afraid."

Slade sighed audibly. Maria looked at him with sympathy.

"Tell you what," she said, pressing a button on her stand. "You can have a seat at the service bar. I'll let you know if a table becomes available."

"Thank you," Slade said, brightening.

"Your name?"

"Tom Dunson."

A Latino waiter wearing black pants, a white shirt, and a black clip-on bowtie appeared in the archway.

"Felipe," said Maria. "Show this gentleman to the service bar."

Felipe led Slade under the arch. The soft guitar music became more prominent. Walking beside the right wall, Slade quickly scanned the restaurant. It was packed with affluent people of both sexes being served by waiters uniformed just like Felipe.

Slade recognized a middle-aged network anchorman lecturing two young women. He saw the young Spanish guitarist strumming intensely on a stool by a potted fern. He spotted Lassiter and his Indian starlet at a table near the rear left corner. And he noted Yul Brynner, his chairback against the wall, a cup of coffee in hand. Slade followed Felipe through a swinging door.

Felipe indicated the single stool in front of the service bar. Slade sat down, ignored by the tieless bartender busily fixing drinks for the incoming waiters. His bowtie lay on the bar counter near the backwall liquor rack. Staring at it, Slade felt his brain ping.

A waiter appeared beside him and ordered two daiquiris. The bartender began to mix them. Slade stood up, took off his tweed jacket, and draped it over the stool. He moved behind the waiter toward the liquor rack – and the bowtie on the bar. Pretending to stretch, he snatched the bowtie off the counter, and followed the waiter out the swinging door.

Slade emerged in the main restaurant with glasses off and bowtie on. He knew his blonde hair, yellow shirt, and black denims would make his Latino waiter guise even less convincing than his bike messenger bit, but hoped the dim light would obscure this long enough.

He approached Lassiter's table and by extension Yul Brynner's. Yul watched him near his boss then refocused on his coffee. Slade stepped between Lassiter and his Indian date. Lassiter was finishing a crisp steak, she was poking at a small shrimp salad. Gotta watch that figure, Slade thought, before refocusing on Lassiter.

"How is your meal, senor?" he asked in a Cisco Kid accent.

Lassiter looked up at him in annoyance, the Indian beauty with interest.

"It's fine."

Slade drew a piece of paper the size and shape of a traffic ticket from his back pocket.

"Our dessert menu, senor," he said. "I strongly recommend the *flan*."

He placed the sheet in front of Lassiter. Lassiter picked it up and began reading it. His expression went from perplexed to angry.

"What the hell is this?!" he declared.

The people at the closest tables turned to him. So did Yul Brynner.

"A subpoena," Slade said in his normal voice while removing the bowtie. "You're ordered to appear in DC Superior Court on April 6$^{th}$. Sorry about that, amigo."

Lassiter reddened.

"You son of a bitch!"

"Please, Mr. Lassiter, there's a lady present," Slade said.

He winked at the woman. She looked down at the table as if to hide a smile. Yul Brynner stood up not smiling. The Spanish guitarist started playing faster. Yul took a step toward Slade but paused when a Hispanic man wearing a dark grey suit jacket and mustache came into view, closely followed by two burly waiters.

"Is there a problem, Mr. Lassiter?" the maître d' asked in a real but faint Spanish accent.

"There sure as hell is! This asshole's working for my ex-wife!"

"She misses you," Slade said. "Your eyes, your smile, your alimony checks."

"Hank!" Lassiter snapped.

Yul Brynner joined him. The Spanish guitarist picked up the tempo.

"Kick his ass!"

Hank stepped in front of Slade, flexing his two-inch height advantage. A right cross came fast at Slade's nose. He ducked it and fired two jabs into Hank's stomach, finding it surprisingly soft. He followed with a right uppercut to the jaw.

Hank staggered back. He shook his head and charged. Slade skipped left and slugged Hank right in the gut. Hank doubled over, holding his stomach. He looked uncertainly at Slade.

"You fool, you've had enough of it," Slade said, quoting the storeowner in *Shane*.

Hank scurried toward the bathroom.

"You're fired!" Lassiter yelled after him.

"He's all right against poseur tough guys," said Slade. "Like the people in your crowd."

He turned around to leave. Four waiters and the maître d' blocked his exit path. He didn't relish hurting good working men – even illegally entered ones. His brain pinged at the thought. He whipped out his wallet to show his Cork Detective Agency ID card with its police-like badge and his photo. Only the maître d' was close enough to read it.

"I-C-E!" Slade shouted. "Everyone stay where you are!"

The waiters hesitated. Slade replaced the wallet in his hand with his cellphone and barked into it.

"Dunson here! All units close in!"

Slade looked at the now anxious waiters and snapped his fingers at the middle one.

"You, there. Let's see your green card."

The addressed waiter turned around and took off running toward the exit.

The maître d' yelled, "*Ramon, no! No es ICE! Es detective privado*!"

But the stampede of waiters had started. They banged into chairs and diners in a frantic rush to escape. Ramon knocked over a wine bottle, drenching the skirt of a well-known Democratic congresswoman, who let out a shriek. Maria appeared in the archway, only to be swept back by the fleeing waiters, now including Felipe.

"*Paren!*" the maître d' yelled at the vanishing waiters.

A short waiter passed between him and Slade, heading to Lassiter's table. He placed a brown bill holder in front of Lassiter, who ignored it while still fuming. Slade picked up the bill holder and opened it. He let out a whistle.

"Ninety-six dollars? This is an outrage. If I were you, I wouldn't pay it."

# CHAPTER 2

Neil Cork held the desktop phone receiver away from his ear to diminish the male voice yelling through it. He took off his square purple glasses and laid them next to the computer keyboard. His blue eyes became duller under a high forehead barely covered by strands of brown hair, much of it lost in the twelve years since graduating from Georgetown. As the phone barrage continued, he swiveled his chair to the left to stare myopically out the window.

Two stories down on Florida Avenue, the evening rush-hour traffic crawled in both directions. Pedestrians in coats traveled faster on the sidewalk, like colorful blurs in the fading sunlight. Several people entered Armand's Pizzeria across the street. Cork pressed the phone against his ear in response to a question.

"Still here, Mr. Rocca."

The audial assault resumed. Cork redonned his glasses, bringing the rectangular office back into focus. The furniture comprised two dark wood executive desks on opposite sides of the room, both angled toward the door. Two green leather armchairs faced each desk. The left corner of the office was vacant, unless you counted John Wayne scowling down at Cork from a wall poster of *The Searchers*.

"I can't do that," Cork said calmly in sharp contrast to the voice on the line. "Slade was doing his legal job. His method may have been unorthodox, but it was your staff that exacerbated the disturbance."

The voice growled something more.

"No, Mr. Rocca. Monetary compensation is out of the question ... Sue us if you like. Good luck getting your waiters to testify in court … Yes, sir, I know who you are. And that you have more than strictly legal recourses. Before you apply them, you may want to vet me with my previous employer. The phone number is area code two-oh-two-FBI-three thousand."

The line became quiet.

"Goodbye, Mr. Rocca."

Cork hung up the receiver. He looked over at his partner's desk and shook his head. He pressed the phone intercom button.

"Kathy, will you come in here a moment?"

The woman who entered could have stepped out of a chorus line. She had brown hair done up in a bun, emerald eyes, and a patrician nose on an oval face. Her high breasts, round hips, and firm legs were well delineated by a gold cashmere sweater and grey wool knee-length skirt. Cork admired her all the way to his desk. When she stopped in front of it, he let out a sigh.

"What is it, Neil?" she asked.

"Another threat. And plenty of time left for more. Slade still hasn't checked in."

"Is he in trouble?"

"With me he is."

"I meant in danger."

"Yes, of losing his mind, and our agency with it. He just closed down the *Alegria* restaurant in Georgetown. Wallace said it looked like a Central American revolution down there. Why'd I hire him, Kathy?"

"You needed a partner, and Mark's your best friend, a war hero, and a good leg man."

"More breast man, judging by his girlfriends. That's a whole other issue. He doesn't realize how much sexual politics have changed in this country in the seven years he spent fighting for it."

"Of course, he does," said Kathy. "He just doesn't care."

"The women he chases after will."

"They haven't complained yet."

Cork failed to suppress a smile.

"Don't you have something to type?"

"No, sir, I earn my keep another way," Kathy said.

She slinked left around the desk to Cork's chair. Cork gulped.

"Surely you're not suggesting – sexual favors?"

Kathy let down her brown hair.

"I'm a married man."

"I won't tell," Kathy said, brushing Cork's upper lip with her forefinger.

He took hold of her shoulders and drew her down toward him.

"If you file a harassment charge, you're fired," said Cork.

The two kissed fervently. A baby's distant wail interrupted them. Cork sighed again.

"Feeding time already?"

"That reminds me," Kathy said, replacing her hair bun. "We have to buy apple juice on the way home."

"Okay."

Kathy blew Cork a kiss and exited to the outer office. She found Mark Slade bent over the small crib behind the reception desk, rubbing her baby's pudgy stomach. He was wearing a grey wool sweater with two white stripes and a pair of black jeans. The child's crying stopped.

"Hmm," said Slade. "Someone left an infant at our office door. Well, they picked the wrong spot for it. A trained detective like me will solve the mystery in no time."

"Hi, Mark."

"Shh, let me concentrate ... Judging by the lovely blue eyes, cute dimples, and dark complexion, I deduce her mother to be a knockout with a great sense of humor."

"And the father?" Kathy asked smilingly.

"Ah, yes, the father." Slade said and gestured over the baby's face. "Note the cruel mouth and stormy eyebrows. Definitely someone to avoid."

"Is Slade out there?!" Cork hollered from his office.

"See what I mean?" Slade said.

"He's just come in," Kathy said loudly enough to be heard in the next room.

"I'll rattle for my bread and water," said Slade, stepping toward the inner office.

He sat down in Cork's right client chair. Cork appeared serene but Slade knew better.

"Did you have a nice lunch?' Cork asked in a casual tone.

"Not bad."

"Where'd you eat?"

"Chinatown."

"Chinatown," said Cork, raising his voice. "That's funny. I didn't hear of any Tong Wars breaking out today. Only about a three-block traffic jam on 'L' Street, a bike attack on hot dog vendors, and a Latin American riot in Georgetown."

"Why blame me?"

"Wallace called. He said they have camera footage of a hooded yet familiar-looking maniacal bike messenger. He thought I might know the fellow. I told him I don't know any bike messengers – though I do know a maniac."

"Look, Neil, all I did was serve Lassiter the subpoena that no one else could."

"Great. And now we can join him in court. Since we're being sued by *Alegria* for disrupting their business."

"They started it."

"Sure, like +that clerk at Nordstrom's last Christmas."

"They were paying us to nail the thief, right?"

"You destroyed a three-thousand-dollar television set tackling him."

"It was showing *The View*," said Slade.

Cork snapped. “Dammit, Mark, this isn’t Kunar Province. It’s the nation’s capital.”

“Right, Afghanistan made more sense.”

“God.”

“You want me to pull out?” Slade asked.

Cork shook his head. “Tempting as that may sound, Washington society would never forgive me for setting you loose on it. At least with me you can break cases along with TV sets. All I ask is that you restrain yourself. Pretend to be normal. You may even fool the right girl someday.”

“Like you did Kathy?”

“Now don’t overreach. It helps to be good looking.”

“Ah,” Slade said then added. “Wait a minute. What do you mean ‘the right girl’? What was wrong with Ellen?”

“Nothing that a crucifix and sunlight won’t fix.”

“Nice lungs though. And Sally?”

“She should’ve worked out her mind along with the rest of her.”

“Great buns though.” Slade started to say something else but stopped himself. Cork seemed to read his mind.

“No, not Nina Holt either. Despite that torch you’re still carrying for her.”Slade winced. Kathy popped into the doorway with her baby daughter smiling at the world.

“Boys, we got a walk-in.”

“This late?” said Cork. “Why not/ We might have some extra bills to pay after Mark’s Georgetown adventure. Send him in.”

“It’s a her with a capital RRRH,” Kathy said, adding in a Scarlett O’Hara impression, “Miss Amy Gallup.”

Slade turned to the doorway just as Kathy beckoned someone beyond it. A stunning young woman swept in. Thick auburn hair fell on both sides of her emerald eyes, fine nose, and full pink lips. A peach cashmere sweater didn’t constrain her bosom, neither did the blue scotch-patterned skirther curvaceous hips. Grey silk tights showcased shapely legs down to her ankle-high brown suede boots. She was carrying a small black purse.

Slade stood up almost in salute. Amy Gallup glanced from him to Cork under long lashes.

"Thanks for seeing me without an appointment," she said in a strong Southern accent more backcountry than genteel. "Hope I'm not interrupting."

"It's a good thing you are," said Slade.

Cork indicated the empty client's chair.

"Have a seat, Ms. – Gallup?"

"Yessir, Amy Gallup."

Amy sat down. So did Slade. He tried to look nonchalant, an act made harder by Amy's now more discernible crossed legs.

"I'm Neil Cork. My partner, Mark Slade. What can we do for you?"

"To tell you the truth, I'm not sure," said Amy. "I just didn't know where else to go."

"North Carolina," Cork said.

"Yessir," Amy said, impressed.

"I learned to distinguish Southern accents during my year at the FBI's Atlanta bureau."

"I'm from Gastonia."

"Site of the only communist uprising in American history," said Cork. "The Loray Mill Strike, 1929."

"Yessir. I heard grandma mention that."

"It was a question on my Bureau entrance exam. So, what brings a nice Southern girl to the heart of the Union?"

Amy hesitated before answering. "My boyfriend doesn't wanna see me anymore."

Slade rolled his eyes but quit before Amy noticed, although Cork did and frowned.

"Why don't you tell us about it," Cork said. "From the beginning."

# CHAPTER 3

"We met at UNC last spring semester," Amy said. "Greg was a senior, me a junior. He's from Raleigh, from one of the rich families there, the Bradfords. Not that that matters to me."

"Course not," said Slade.

Amy and Cork looked at him, Cork with impatience. Amy continued.

"End of last semester, he asked me to move in with him – after I graduate this May. He'd just gotten a job as a Senate aide and wanted a year to move up in it."

"For which Senator?" Cork asked.

"One from our state – Sam Owen."

Cork grimaced, perplexing Amy.

"Neil's not a Sam Owen fan," Slade said. "Too conservative."

"Too regressive," said Cork.

"You're right about that," Amy said. "Just one month into his job, Greg asked me to marry him. Said it was the only way he could live with me and keep on working for the Senator."

"How romantic," said Slade.

"I said yes."

"I take it the wedding is off," Cork said.

Amy looked despondent. "I still can't believe it," she said. "We spent Christmas break at Greg's parents' house in Raleigh, planning our marriage. Where we were gonna live. What kind of job I could get up here. Even… how soon to have a baby. It was wonderful. We kept it going long distance, talking every night. Last Wednesday was my birthday. Greg didn't call me, or answer his phone, or any of my texts. I aimed to tease him about it the next day. Then the day after that, and so on, with not one word from him. I called his parents last weekend. His mom said they'd talked that morning. She said Greg was fine and was sure to get in touch with me. It made me a wreck. He finally did call me, last night. Said he'd changed his mind about us getting married – about us, period. It was like a nightmare. All I could ask him was if there was someone else - another girl. He just wished me the best and hung up. So, I drove up here today to confront him. I went straight to the Capitol Building. Wanted to see if he could be so cold to my face."

Slade and Cork looked expectantly at her.

"Never found out," she said. "He told the guard not to let me through. Like I was some kind of stalker. Just like that, he wiped away my whole future."

"Come on," Slade said. "I know fifty guys who'd wanna share your future."

"Possibly fifty-one," said Cork. "Continue please."

"I went to a bar in Capitol Hill. Had me some wine. On the third glass, I got the crazy notion of hiring a private detective. So, I did a quick search, and liked your motto. 'Got a confidential problem? Put a Cork on it.'"

"I'm flattered," said Cork. "But how can we help you?"

Amy took a deep breath. Slade noted that only the bottom half of her sweater moved, the upper part being stretched to the limit.

"It's Greg," she said. "There's something wrong with him."

"That's obvious," said Slade. "Throwing you over."

Cork winced.

"I'm not just being the jilted girlfriend," Amy said. "I could sense it on the phone. Something's eating at 'im. Something he can't share with me. Something so awful he'd hurt me rather than reveal it. I need to find out what that is. And I'm willing to pay for it."

"We're a little pricey," Cork said. "I can refer you to a cheaper yet excellent agency."

"One that doesn't offer our special discount," said Slade.

"Discount?" Amy asked.

"For beauty. And you more than qualify."

Cork cringed but Amy smiled.

"I'll take it," she said.

"If you'll wait outside for a few minutes," said Cork. "I'll discuss this with my partner."

Amy stood up and walked out the door. Slade admired her exit as much as her entrance.

"Look at the case, Mark, not her," Cork said as the door closed behind Amy.

"What about it?"

"There isn't one."

"Hey, we're private eyes, aren't we?"

"You're stretching the definition," said Cork.

"Come on, Neil. It'll be a cinch. I tail the kid, find out who he's banging, and gently break it to that Southern cookie. What've we got to lose?"

"Time and money, both better spent on real cases. Like the vanishing medical instruments at Sibley Hospital."

"I want this one."

"What you want you can find online," Cork said.

Slade smirked. Cork rubbed his chin for several seconds, his expression softening.

"All right," he said. "You have two days. After that, it's back to the sutures."

"Uh," Slade said with a smile.

Cork pressed the intercom button on his landline phone.

"Kathy, send in our new client."

"Right, boss," replied Kathy's voice.

"Will you tell her or me?" Slade asked.

"I will. It'll cut down on flirtation time."

Amy came in and remained standing. Slade rose to his feet.

"We'll look into your problem," Cork said.

"More your ex-boyfriend's problem," said Slade. "Choosing a B-player over you."

"And if you hate lines like that, I advise you not to hire us," Cork said. "Because I'm putting Slade on your case."

"I think he's already on my case," said Amy.

Slade pretended to sulk.

"But I appreciate it."

Slade beamed.

"Our normal fee is five hundred a day plus expenses," Cork said. "We'll charge you three-hundred total, in advance."

"Why, thank you," Amy said, opening her purse. "Will you take a Carolina bank check?"

"If it pays in Yankee dollars."

Amy drew a checkbook out of her purse.

"Actually, we're a pretty progressive state," she said. "We voted for Obama once."

"And Sam Owen thrice," said Cork.

Amy leaned over Cork's desk next to Slade, who appreciated the closeup. She filled out the top check and handed it to Cork.

"Text Mark a photo of your ex-fiance," he said.

"And store my number," said Slade. "202-761-5459."

Amy sent the text. Slade looked at his cellphone. The screen showed a lean, handsome college boy with overlong brown hair and intense eyes. He stood two inches taller than the 5'6" Amy beside him in a skimpy gold basketball cheerleader outfit with "Tar Heels" emblazoned across the top.

"I see only you in this picture," said Slade.

Amy made a one-syllable laughing sound.

"That's Greg right beside me," she said.

"Oh yeah. Where does he live?"

"Capitol South, near the subway station. He shares an apartment with another congressional aide."

"What kind of car does he drive?"

"None. He said he doesn't need one here. Prefers the subway system and Uber."

Cork stood up and addressedAmy. "If you'll excuse me, Miss Gallup, I have an urgent mission at the supermarket. I leave you in capable hands."

Slade held up his palms.

"Good luck."

Cork walked out the door. Slade turned to Amy.

"How long are you in town?" he asked.

"Till Sunday. I'm skipping all my Friday classes."

"Where you staying?"

"With a girlfriend in Arlington."

"Can I drop you?"

"No, that would make two of you," Amy said, and stiffened. "Did I just make a joke about Greg?"

"You did."

"Maybe I'll get over him."

"Maybe I'll help you," said Slade.

Amy's green eyes locked on him.

"With this investigation I mean," he added.

"Will you walk me to my car?".

"Be my pleasure," said Slade.

The outer office was now vacant like the baby crib in it. Slade took down Amy's maroon velvet jacket from the coat tree and helped her into it. He put on his dark green corduroy with wool collar and opened the door for Amy.

They stepped out to the short landing outside the door marked Cork Detective Agency, the down staircase to their left, an old elevator at the back wall on the right. Slade pulled a pair of keys from his coat pocket.

"I'd better lock up. Be bad for business to have our detective office burgled."

Amy watched Slade locking the office door.

"You seem too young to be a detective," she said.

"I'm really an eccentric millionaire," Slade said, quoting Charles Bronson in *The Magnificent Seven*. "Which is what you'll get looking like that."

"I just lost one. Greg's a millionaire. Or will be when his granddaddy passes."

"He's also a knucklehead. Sorry. I don't know that."

Amy looked thoughtful. Slade escorted her down the staircase.

"Anyway, I plan to make my own million," Amy said.

"Where – Hollywood?"

Amy sighed. "I wish you'd stop complimenting my looks, Mr. Slade. I may sound like a hillbilly – I can't help my accent – but I can speak fluent French, play Mozart on the piano, and analyze the stock market."

"But can you make a good omelet?"

Amy made her one-syllable laughing sound. They exited on Florida Street, into a frosty night illuminated by car beams and store lights. Amy turned right, Slade walking beside her.

"About that omelet," he said. "I'd hate for you to spend your brief stay in DC slaving over a hot stove when there are so many fine restaurants here. I'll even throw in the company. Say tonight around eight?"

"Would we talk about my case?"

"Sure."

"That's funny. We haven't so far."

"I need to go undercover first."

Amy wavered between a smirk and a smile.

"I promised Leslie, my friend, I'd have dinner with her and her boyfriend tonight. How 'bout tomorrow night? By then you might have something to tell me. Something I haven't heard before."

Slade smiled at the jab. Amy stopped next to a white Nissan

Sedan from the mid-10s and remotely clicked the locks. Slade opened the driver's door for her.

She turned to him with an engaging smile. "Goodnight, Mark."

She got into her car and started the engine. Slade watched her drive off.

# CHAPTER 4

It was one of those mornings that gave winter a bad name. Sleet pelted Slade's pale blue 2020 Mustang Fastback as it pulled into the Yates Field House parking lot on the Georgetown University campus. The striking ice blurred the normally spectacular view of the Potomac River and Rosslyn, Virginia beyond from the highest hill in Georgetown.

Slade grabbed his black and gold Adidas gym bag off the passenger seat. Raising the hood of his Army sweat jacket, he rushed past a dozen parked cars to the single building on the lot, a futuristic glass beehive. With four tennis courts, two basketball courts, an Olympic-size swimming pool, an indoor running track, and an enormous workout room, Yates resembled a luxury spa more than a college gym.

Slade flashed his alumni card to the student jock at the front desk and continued to the main exercise area. Finding an untaken space by the back wall, he dropped the gym bag and his sweat jacket beside it. His thick upper arms and large barrel chest bulged under his grey t-shirt.

He clicked his earbuds, which began playing the Cars' "You Might Think." He'd learned to love '80s music in Afghanistan along with the rest of Task Force Black after Sergeant Morgan forced it on them. Sarge had banned rap music from their unit, blaming it for the moral decline of America, specifically his Philadelphia inner-city neighborhood. The New Wave blend of masculine assurance, discernible melody, and poetic lyrics would pump them up before a mission – and drove their Taliban enemy crazy.

Ignoring the weight machines, Slade went straight to the pullup bar. His own 190 pounds better suited his purpose. He did twenty pullups, walked around for two minutes, then did twenty more. He completed the same number of chin-ups to "The Whole of the Moon" by the Waterboys.

He took a furled mat from a rack and carried it to a suitable floor space, near two lithe young women doing yoga-style stretches. He mentally compared each girl to Amy Gallup. She won the college beauty contest in absentia.

Slade did a set of fifty pushups to "Ashes to Ashes" by David Bowie, then sat up on the mat still thinking of Amy. There was more to her than met the eye. What met the ear was +just as pleasant, a husky Southern blend of class and country. Slade did a second set of pushups, followed by fifty stomach crunches to "Twist in My Sobriety" by Tanika Tikaram.

He proceeded to the parallel bars and did twenty dips, spurred by Simple Minds' "Don't You Forget About Me." He thought about Greg Bradford. So what if he had the brooding good lucks some women found attractive and was closer to Amy's age, being one year out of UNC? Could he do two sets of twenty dips? And what kind of idiot would dump a package like Amy? And for whom? Slade intended to find out. He did the last set of dips.

He carried his gym bag to the kickboxing area near the basketball courts, two heavy bags hanging from a low metal scaffold. A fit brunette in a gold tank-top and white sweat-shorts was practicing ineffective kicks on one of them. She reminded Slade of a big reason why he quit the Rangers. Under the current Administration, they'd lowered their physical requirements to admit women and men pretending to be women. Slade valued his life more than gender inclusivity.

He took out a pair of Everlast training gloves from his gym bag. He donned them while approaching the free heavy bag to "I Melt with You" by Modern English. Once in arms' length of the bag, he raised his gloves as if it would punch him back, then began shuffling his feet. He fired three left jabs at the bag then a hard right cross. He alternated left and right blows while gradually increasing power and speed.

Twelve minutes into the simulated fight, he noticed Kickboxer Girl staring at him while sipping from a water bottle. But his co-ed dance card was full, or so he hoped. He finished pounding the bag with a hail of *tsuki* punches as Master Choi taught him in Seoul.

He did a brisk downhill walk to M Street, then across it to the C&O Canal, as always fascinated by its history.

The Chesapeake-and-Ohio Canal paralleled the Potomac River for 185 miles from Georgetown to Cumberland, Maryland. Between 1840 and 1924, mules towed coal barges over the riverside path, trampling the dirt into a hikers' paradise. The hikers in turn trod the path into a runners' dream – although it was a bad dream on wet days like this one.

Slade ran west on the towpath against the river current on his left, the sleet now a light cold rain. He evaded mud puddles by jumping on the rusted railroad track that had made the canal obsolete eight years before its completion. Some forty yards short of the five-mile marker, he broke into a sprint. His return pace was slower yet steadier.

In the Yates locker room shower, he lowered the water temperature all the way. He bore the cold for as long as he could, then dashed into the men's sauna. He sat on his towel on the upper wooden rack. .The coal-generated heat permeating his sore muscles resurrected an unpleasant memory from five years ago.

*He was in the ruins of an Afghan village, Mazraq, kneeling behind a dilapidated stone wall, at the right end of it. His helmet, headset, and body armor made the desert heat more brutal than the morning sun, and clutching the Barrett M95 rifle only increased his sweat. He kept peering left past the wall, at the dirt road stretching all the way north to the Hindu Kush mountains a hundred miles away.*

*If Captain Lambert was right, the enemy would be coming down the road to set up an ambush on Task Force Black, ahead of its passage through Mazraq. His job was to ambush the ambushers. Taking another look up the road, he spoke into his headset mike.*

*"Nothing yet, Dix. Guess Haji didn't fall for the leak. A rare miss for Captain Lam -"*

*He cut himself off, seeing a small cloud of dust approaching fast on the road, and the brown speck at the bottom of it.*

*"Scratch that," he said. "Incoming hostile - Goat Trail north."*

*He prepped his rifle for imminent action, keeping his right eye on the speck. It quickly clarified into a farm truck with five Taliban fighters in the bed and two inside the cabin. Four of the back riders had rifles, the fifth a rocket launcher.*

*The truck rolled straight into his kill zone. He jumped out from behind the wall already in shooting stance. He fired four shots at the truck's windshield, putting as many cracks in it. The farm truck swerved left and crashed into a wrecked house wall.*

*The truck bed riders spilled onto the road. They tried to engage him with their guns but were too shaken to do it right. He picked off the four riflemen first, then the fleeing rocket-launcher launcher.*

*Another speck appeared on the road. This one soon turned into a US Army open jeep driven by Ranger Carter Dixon, Black and burly. Dixon weaved the jeep around the Taliban corpses to stop next to him. He nodded at the rocket launcher on the road beside its former bearer's body.*

*"You owe Lambert an apology."*

*"He called the ambush all right. Knew which of our translators to leak to."*

*"I'll give Abdullah something to translate," Dixon said.*

*"He'll be dead before you have that conversation."*

*He climbed into the jeep. It turned around and began the rugged hour-long trip back to Forward Operating Base Black. He swept his hand over the desolate terrain around them.*

*"Soon, this'll be all yours," he said.*

*"Screw that, Slade," said Dixon. "I'll be stateside too. Got new orders – from Ellen."*

*"Get your ass back to Boisie."*

*"You got it. She said our three kids are the real war on terror, and I'd better join it."*

*"Good, you can be my drill sergeant. Three kids sounds good for Nina and me."*

*"You won't need me, man. Women are born leaders on that front."*

*They reached FOB Black shortly before noon. He and Dixon entered their vacant barracks minus helmets and armor. "Twist in My Sobriety" played, maybe just still in his head. There were parcels on all six bunks, a small one on his cot, a larger one on Dixon's.*

*"I must be seeing things," said Dixon.*

*"Army Mail actually found this place."*

*Each man took a cot and picked up his package. He smiled at the label on his. From: Nina Holt, 1335 Connecticut Ave., Apt. 310, Washington DC 20034. To: Crpl Mark Slade, US Army, Afghanistan. He opened the parcel while Dixon cheerfully took out a stack of magazines, the top one Fisherman's News.*

*He pulled out a small computer drive. He inserted it into his laptop side. On the screen appeared a close-up Nina Holt looking almost exactly as he left her – late twenties, patrician, and rivetingly beautiful. Her lush wavy black hair was cut slightly shorter, her expression more serious than normal. He played her voice low, but Dixon could still hear it.*

*"Hi, sweetheart. I hope you're safe and healthy, and that what I'm about to say won't endanger you any more than you already are over there."*

*Dixon looked up at him over his fishing magazine.*

*"I know how much you hate dancing around the point, so I'll come right out with it. I've been offered a job at a TV station in Pitts-*

*burgh. Local news reporter, but Pennsylvania's a battleground state and it's a presidential election season so the eyes of Washington will be on me. What that means, babe, is for the near future, I'll be totally focused on my career. I know we'd planned to get married next June, before you start officer's school in the fall, but that's no good for me right now. To tell you the truth, neither's a family. Not even with you, Mark, and I love you. It's better for both of us if we went our separate ways. But I want you to know – it's not an easy choice. I left your ring with Neil Cork. I didn't trust the Army with it. Take care of yourself, Mark. I love you. Bye."*

*The screen went dark. So did he. Dixon's voice brought him out of it.*

*"Harsh, man," he said. "I'm sorry."*

*"At least she gave the ring back. The four grand I paid for it should come in handy at Fort Moore."*

*"You're not a lieutenant yet," said Dixon. "I'll take point tomorrow."*

*"No, Dix. I'm still a better shot than you."*

*"You'll be a better target with that chick inside your head."*

*"I'm all right," he said.*

"I'm all right," Slade repeated low.

The two male students in the sauna looked at him. He politely waved them off. Drenched in sweat, he left the sauna, heading for a cold shower.

At one sink in a row of six, he shaved his two-day stubble with the straight razor he'd used in Sandland, only here with the luxury of shaving cream and hot water. He splashed on the *Proraso* aftershave lotion, knowing Jeremiah Johnson would scoff at him.

He stepped out to the lobby wearing a grey wool sweater over his black jeans. A few feet from the exit, his cellphone beeped. It was a text from Amy Gallup. Slade paused to read the message: *Kramerbooks, Dupont Circle, 10 PM.* He rang the office with his phone in speaker mode. Kathy Cork answered.

"Mark, thank God you called! The President is missing! They say you're the only man who can find him!"

"Tell them he must've switched coffins."

"That's cruel," said Kathy. "Funny, but cruel."

"Heard any good accents lately?"

"Y'all mean lahk this, Mahk honey?" Kathy said in a backwoods Southern drawl.

"Music to my ears. I'll be meeting her tonight at Kramerbooks Dupont Circle."

"Woo hoo. Hang on. Hubby wants to talk to you."

"Uh oh."

Cork came on the line.

"How's the case coming?"

"I'm Capitol bound now," said Slade. "Will pick up Greg leaving the Dirksen Building."

"I have some background data on Greg from a friend in Raleigh."

"A Fed in Raleigh?"

"A Fed friend," said Cork. "The Bradfords are indeed as high and mighty as Amy said – Raleigh royalty since the Antebellum days. Tobacco money. Greg's grandfather still runs the company – Colonel Geoff Bradford. They're big on military rank, patriotism in general. Your kind of people."

"That explains Greg working for Sam Owen."

"Yeah. Though according to his record, Greg was quite the lib at UNC, a member of the Guevarans."

"The Guevarans? As in commie psycho killer Che Guevara?"

"A social justice warrior in their view," Cork said. "They're a radical intercollege group, a bit after our time. Clearly too radical for Greg, who quit them in his senior year."

"Just before he joined Owen's team."

"Yes, most convenient. In any case, Greg will inherit a fortune when the Colonel dies. Which may explain your girl's ardor for him."

"She prefers a private eye," said Slade.

"Or perhaps a future Congressman. With his family connections and Senator Owen's support, Greg could have a bright political career ahead of him."

"He won't get my vote."

"Fine, but consider this, Mark. Sam Owen is one of the most powerful men in the country, a high-ranking member of the Senate Intelligence Committee. He can make things very dodgy for us. So, for God's sake, be subtle."

"You got it."

"And I'd like to drop it. But we promised the lovely Miss Gallup we'd help her. I listen to you and a young girl's heartbreak becomes my heartburn. If only she'd been homely."

"Then you would've taken the case. You and your sense of chivalry."

"You're not as dumb as you appear," said Cork. "Anyway, just stick to Plan A. Follow the boy, find out whom he dumped Amy for, and pull out."

"Right, then I'll start Plan B."

"What's Plan – Never mind. Goodbye."

Cork hung up the phone in his office. Kathy stood beside him, leaning against his desk.

"Well?"

"So far, so good," Cork said. "But it's early yet."

"He's got a date with her tonight."

Cork shook his head. "How does he do it? He uses lines that would make Charlie Sheen blush."

"That's just it, sweetheart. Women don't fall for his lines. They fall for his gall in coming out with them. A girl can get awfully tired of the Sensitive Man approach."

"Like Alan Nichols?"

"Poor Alan," Kathy said ruefully.

"He took it pretty hard, your dropping him. Especially for a macho man like me."

"I wouldn't go that far."

"Oh," said Cork. "Maybe you'd prefer a man who does this!"

He pulled Kathy down to his lap. She theatrically beat his chest. He kissed her mouth.

"Brute," she said returning the kiss.

# CHAPTER 5

To a casual onlooker, Mark Slade appeared to be strolling east on D Street toward Second Street in Capitol Hill. But anyone observing him for more than five minutes would have seen him walk the opposite way toward First Street. He'd covered the same one-block distance nineteen times in the darkening hour.

The block park to the south gave him an unimpeded view of the Dirksen Senate Office Building's C Street entrance. It was the closest door to a Metrorail stop, Union Station, two blocks away – or one block from his position. Which meant Greg Bradford would have to walk past him to get to it. Unless he'd bought a car since he last spoke to Amy.

Slade watched more people exit the building. Light rain sprinkled his blue-green Irish Tweed hat, the dry earbuds below it playing more '80s music. During Berlin's "Riding on the Metro," Greg Bradford stepped out into the rain.

He looked leaner than his picture even in a light brown double-breasted wool overcoat . He toted a black briefcase in his right hand and a woman's hand on his left shoulder. The hand belonged to a voluptuous mop-haired brunette in a white down jacket and black skirt.

Brunette and Greg stopped on the sidewalk, promising an early conclusion to the Amy Gallup case. But after a brief exchange, Greg nodded at her and went left toward First Street. Neither Amy nor Brunette, Slade reflected. Tailing Greg might give him an inferiority complex.

Greg made a right on First Street heading right toward Slade. Slade looked down at his cellphone as if interacting with it. When Greg crossed D Street, Slade followed, keeping fifteen yards behind him.

They walked two blocks toward Union Station, Slade mentally patting himself on the back. But instead of crossing Massachusetts Avenue to the massive white marble structure, Greg made a left at the corner and went out of Slade's sight. Slade jogged to the corner just in time to see Greg enter the Hawk and Dove bar.

"Greg, this is the first time I've liked you all day," Slade said.

The Hawk and Dove blended English pub warmth with political Americana. It had an oaken bar, crackling fireplace, and dark wood-panel walls lined with portraits of famous Congressmembers including Slade's historical hero, Davy Crockett (portrayed by his movie hero John Wayne in *The Alamo*).

Slade kept expecting Davy's picture to be taken down by triggered millennials. After all, the man fought Native Americans then Mexicans on "stolen land" Texas. Fortunately for Crockett, the young congressional staffers who filled the bar didn't remember the Alamo.

Greg sat at a two-seat table near the fireplace with his back to the wall. He stared so intently at Slade when he came in, the detective thought he'd been tagged. But even after he cleared the doorway, Greg kept gazing at it, no doubt anticipating someone else. Judging by the two girls he'd casually discarded, Slade figured it must be Scarlett Johansson.

Slade took a stool on the left side of the bar, close to Greg yet conveniently obstructed by a 20-something couple at the end of it. Greg looked about ten years older than his recent picture, with more lines under the eyes. Slade ordered a bottle of Stella Artois, his pleasant reminder of being a teenager in Brussels, where his Army colonel dad was stationed.

On his third sip of beer, he saw Greg stiffen, his eyes still on the door. Slade turned to it. A man stood in the entrance – mid-twenties, flagrantly handsome, longish black hair, and a red scarf that fell below a green cardigan to his skinny jeans. He resembled a male model, but for women's products rather than men's. *Use Obsession and entice a pretty boy like me.* Watching him approach his table, Greg visibly relaxed.

Male Model draped his scarf over the vacant chair's backrest and sat down across from Greg. They started to chat right away, too low for Slade to overhear. He sipped more beer, dismissing a new thought.

A comely waitress brought the pair two martinis. They drank them while they talked, Greg's anxiety resurfacing. Male Model tapped on his cellphone. As Greg finished his martini, Male Model signaled the waitress for the check. Slade placed a ten-dollar bill on the bar and left.

Across Massachusetts Avenue, Union Station glowed dully in the cold mist. Slade looked for one of the taxis approaching it in case Male Model had a car. He flagged down a cab and jumped into it eight yards short of the Hawk and Dove canopy. He noted the driver's turban and beard.

"Wait," Slade said.

The Sikh driver started the meter count. A grey Subaru Outback pulled in front of the bar just as Pretty Boy and Greg exited it. They got in the back seat, and the obvious Uber took off.

"Follow that car," Slade said.

The cabbie silently complied.

"Must be a typical request in Punjab," said Slade.

"Sir?"

"Skip it. You're doing great."

The Subaru rounded the east end of Union Station and made a right on F Street. Both cars turned left on 7th Street then right on

Meridian Road. As his taxi reached the intersection, Slade saw the Subaru slowing down just past the corner.

"Drop me off across the street," Slade said, handing the cabbie a twenty.

The taxi crossed Meridian and stopped. Slade jumped out of it. He stood at the entrance to a well-lit street with vintage two-story rowhouses. The Subaru was stopped before the yellow fifth house on the right, unloadingthe two passengers.

Slade crossed to their side of the street and turned left on the sidewalk. He walked unsteadily toward the pair, like someone with a buzz. They gave him a dismissive glance and started up the house steps, Slade picking up their conversation.

"You've got to tell your people," Greg said, his Southern accent more genteel than Amy's.

"Tonight," said Male Model. "I'll tell that rich bitch it's where every moron can stare at it – and have no clue what they're looking at, because they're fucking blind. The longer it's up, the closer we'll be to Judgment Day. Pretty soon she'll give us everything we want."

They stopped in front of the house door, Male Model producing a set of keys. Slade continued past the steps. Appearing to lose his balance, he leaned against a sidewalk tree - and overheard more talk.

"He'll find out, Paul," said Greg.

"Who – your pig boss?"

"He's been looking at me weirdly all week."

"c'Cause you told him you broke up with your perfect girlfriend."

"I had to!He kept asking about Amy and our wedding date."

"Now he thinks you're screwing wanton women. He's half right."

"It's been creeping me out," said Greg. "I can't sleep at night."

"I can help you with that problem."

Slade heard the door shut. He dashed back to the corner, then left on 7th Street. He made another left into the alley behind the rowhouses.

Slowing to a walk, he looked over the high wood fences and

sighted Paul's yellow-brick home. A lamp shone in the second-floor leftmost window, partly occluded by the branches of an old oak tree. Someone moved past the window, making the lamplight flicker.

Slade glanced at both ends of the alley. Seeing no one, he approached the section of fence nearest the oak tree. He jumped and caught the fence top with his gloves. He pulled himself up to overlook a small square patio with a cushion-less steel bench. Using the oak tree for leverage, he stood on the fence rail and scanned up the tree trunk.

The lowest branch was three feet over his head. He leapt and grabbed it, swinging his body to mount the branch. He climbed the cluster of upper branches and stopped a few feet above window level, the trunk between him and the house.

A thick branch extended from the right side of the oak in plain sight of the window. Slade took the risk and rounded the trunk. Perched on the branch while holding a flimsy one above it, he peered into the window.

The lit lamp stood on a night-table on the window side of a master bed. Paul lay on it shirtless, the quilt up to his waist, looking at his cellphone screen. An inner room light went off and he put down the phone. Greg approached the far side of the bed completely naked.

Slade drew his cellphone and started videorecording. He shot Greg getting on the bed then fervently kissing Paul. He kept recording until Paul turned off the lamp. Slade clambered down the tree in near darkness.

# CHAPTER 6

The escalator ride from Dupont Circle Metrorail Station to Connecticut Avenue north took two minutes and twelve seconds. Slade stood on the same step for the entire climb rather than bounding up the stairs as usual. He spent the time getting ready for Amy Gallup, specifically how he would handle her.

He emerged among the well-lit deco shops, and crossed the street to the biggest one, *Kramerbooks*. At just before ten on a Friday night, the bookstore and its café bustled with patrons seeking knowledge, nourishment, or companionship – many of the Greg Bradford variety. Slade spotted Amy's auburn hair beside a discount books table.

She was looking at an open picture book on Japan. Slade recognized the Imperial Palace on the cover. Walking toward her, he appreciated how well her purple jacket and short grey skirt clung to her form. She could make a gay man straight, he thought. Yet her boyfriend had gone the other way.

A goateed yuppie in a double-breasted black coat beat Slade to her side. Slade paused within earshot to observe their encounter. Yuppie pointed at the a full-page photo of Mount Fujiyama in the book Amy was perusing.

"That picture doesn't do it justice."

"'Scuse me?" said Amy, turning to the man.

She spotted Slade and winked at him.

"Mount Fuji," Yuppie said. "Just before sunset, the colors look much more dazzling. You can see the full effect from a temple on the eastern slope."

"I take it you've been there."

"Yes, twice. Extremely romantic."

"Maybe you should go back a third time," said Amy.

"What do you mean?"

"There's no temple on the eastern slope. Only a lake – Lake Fujiyama."

"Oh, right," said Yuppie. "I meant the west slope."

"Here," said Amy, passing the book to the Yuppie. "You need this more than me."

She moved cheerfully toward Slade.

"How ya doin'?"

"Fine," said Slade. "Only there's no Lake Fujiyama either. It's Lake Yamanaka."

"You been to Japan?"

"Uh-huh. I was stationed in Korea for a year."

Amy nodded at her despondent suitor slinking further away.

"I could tell he'd never seen Mount Fuji."

"But he admires other beautiful sights."

"From afar," said Amy with a smile.

"Have you eaten?"

"No, I was waiting for you."

"Good," said Slade. "I have a yen for Japanese food."

Amy chuckled. They walked to the exit, Slade knowing her good humor wouldn't last through dinner.

# CHAPTER 7

"My parents died when I was twelve," Amy said. "Their car hit an ice patch then a tree."

"I'm sorry," said Slade, meaning it.

They sat on two floor cushions across a low table on the balcony of *Sakura,* an atmospheric Japanese restaurant on Connecticut Avenue, two blocks north of Dupont Circle. Slade was having grilled squid with a Sapporo Premium Lager; Amy stir-fried noodles and Macha tea. Both adroitly handled chopsticks. Slade had said nothing about having solved the case.

"I lived with my grandparents till college, and France my junior year abroad," Amy said.

"Paris?"

"No, Dijon. The French Language School there."

"I picked up a little French in Belgium, where my dad is stationed."

"*C'est miserable,*" Amy said in a snobbish French accent. "Eet is nothing like the mother tongue of France."

"You just gotta learn two words there," Slade said, raising his hands. "*Je* surrender."

"Oh, boo. What made you so darn cynical?"

"Afghanistan."

"Oh."

"Seeing good men die for nothing. And ending with a real blast at Kabul Airport."

Amy gazed solemnly at Slade.

"Were you there that day?"

"Yeah, a total shitshow," Slade said. "Brass ordered us to evac – leave our Afghan guide behind – his wife and daughters to the Taliban. We refused. We were putting 'em on the plane when the bombs went off. Thirteen jarheads dead, including a buddy of mine. I got out before we lost the next war."

"Why'd you go in?"

"Patriotism," Slade said. "We had a great country when I joined up – before the changing of the guard. I was only gonna do one hitch. Ended up doing two."

"How come?"

"Personal reasons."

"A girl," said Amy.

Slade took a swig of beer.

"Who was she, Mark?"

"Someone I keep seeing over and over again."

"In your dreams?"

"On TV. She's a CNN congressional reporter."

"Oh, I bet I know who you mean. She's gorgeous. Can't remember her name."

"Nina Holt," said Slade.

"That's her."

The Japanese waitress appeared by the table in her purple kimono.

"Another drink?" she asked.

"No, thank you," said Amy.

"Change your mind," Slade said.

Amy blinked and said, "Sweet vermouth."

"Saki," said Slade.

The waitress moved away. Amy looked inquisitively at Slade.

"You found out something," she said.

Slade nodded.

"What?"

"Let's wait for our drinks," he said.

They ate in silence, less relaxed than before. The waitress returned with their drinks. Amy took a large swallow of vermouth and stared at Slade.

"There's someone else, isn't there?" she asked.

"Yeah."

"Who?"

"Like I told you yesterday," said Slade. "Any guy who'd throw you over has to have a screw loose. Forget him and go back to NC. Cork's agreed to give you back your dough."

Amy glowered.

"You bastards. I don't want my goddamn money or your sympathy. Why can't you just do what I paid you to do and tell me who Greg's sleeping with?"

Slade fingered his Saki glass.

"I was at a party once," he said. "Friend of mine had a thing for the hostess, only she had a boyfriend. After a few beers, my friend went up to her and said, 'Hey, Dianne. How come all the best-looking girls have boyfriends?' And she said, 'I don't know, Todd. How come all the best-looking guys do too?'"

Amy's jaw dropped.

"You're not saying … Greg? You're crazy."

Slade said nothing.

"You obviously got the wrong person."

Slade shook his head.

"Who told you?" demanded Amy.

"Nobody."

"Then what makes you think he's – ?"

"You don't wanna know."

"Greg's straight dammit. I know he is. We made love often enough. And he relished it!"

"Did you?" asked Slade.

Amy gaped at him.

"Anyway, what difference does it make?" Slade asked. "Gay or straight, he's got a new squeeze just like you figured."

"A woman."

Slade took out his cellphone, tapped three keys, and passed it to Amy. She watched the screen, looking queasier by the second. She dropped the phone on the table. Slade retrieved it. Amy stared demandingly at him.

"His name's Paul Adamo," he said. "He's an artist. A decent one, according to Cork. Paints mostly political stuff. Which may be how he and Greg hooked – uh, met."

Amy's wince had prompted Slade's word change.

"He's got a show this weekend at a gallery near here. That's all we know, Amy."

"That's all?!" Amy snapped. "Don't be so modest! That's plenty for one day's work!"

She sprang to her feet. Slade remained on the floor mat. He watched Amy go down the balcony stairway and out the front door. The waitress reappeared, looking curiously at him.

"I guess she wasn't hungry," he said. "To tell you the truth, neither an I. Check please."

He gulped down his Saki. Tactfully done, he thought. 'Your boyfriend's queer.' What every girl wants to hear. Maybe he should get drunk. The Dubliner was a mile up the street. A frosty walk would do him good. He paid the bill with his American Express card and stood up.

He exited the restaurant and heading north on Connecticut Avenue. Amy's husky voice stopped him in his tracks.

"Mark."

Slade turned around, and was briefly blinded by a pair of bright oncoming headlights. As they sped past him, Amy Gallup emerged from the former blind spot.

"I'm sorry, Mark," she said.

"For what?"

"Haranguing you for doing what I asked you to."

"Happens all the time in this job."

"I guess there was nothing special about my case."

"Except for the client," Slade said. "You, Amy."

Amy stopped close to him, looking up at his face.

"Can I go home with you?" she asked.

"Sure," said Slade, soundingI deceptively casual in the face of his wish come true.

# CHAPTER 8

Slade liked the press of Amy's right thigh against his left leg. They were in the back seat of a Chevy Spark Uber heading north on Columbia Road. Amy brushed aside a lock of hair to look at him.

"I hope I'm not inconveniencing you," she said.

"Not at all."

"You might've had other plans."

"Nothing important."

"Other women."

"It's Friday night," Slade said. "I think I can squeeze you in."

Amy made her curt laughing sound. The Uber entered Adams Morgan, a smorgasbord of modest Latin-African shops and restaurants on both sides of Columbia Road. It turned right on Euclid Street, crossed Champlain Street, and stopped before the fourth building on the right, a century-old brownstone five stories high. A sign over the glass door read *El Cid*.

Slade jumped out of the car and helped Amy exit it. They approached *El Cid*'s three grey steps and unlit porch. A stepladder obstructed their entrance. On it stood a husky Black senior in blue sweatshirt and grey sweatpants unscrewing the ceiling light dome.

"Another short, Jimmy?" Slade asked.

Jimmy looked down, showing his bald crown and bent nose.

“Hey, Mark,” he said, and nodded at the light dome. “Yeah. Needs whole new wiring, but you know Sanchez.”

“Yeah, Sanchez is Spanish for Scrooge.”

Jimmy grinned. “I coulda done this on my regular shift tomorrow, ’cept the widow Macia wouldn’t sleep good tonight.”

“You deserve a raise, Jimmy. Just not out of my rent money.”

Jimmy chuckled, his eyes taking in Amy. “Say, that’s quite a pretty miss you got there.”

Amy smiled.

“Brave, too,” said Slade. “She hasn’t seen my place.”

“Saw Dilcia come by yesterday to clean it.”

“I’ve had a day to mess it up.”

Jimmy smiled and resumed unscrewing the light dome. Slade and Amy went around his ladder and through the front door. They crossed the short standard lobby to the elevator in the right corner. Slade tapped the up button.

“Your custodian seems like a nice man,” Amy said.

“Long as you weren’t in the ring with him.”

“He was a boxer?”

“Pretty famous in his day. Knocked out eight guys in five years.”

“Is that a lot?”

“Probably no match for your record.”

Amy scoffed.

“They called him “Machine Gun” Kelly, ’cause he’d sputter for three rounds then, on a cue from his manager, he’d massacre the other guy. It was a racket they worked out to hype the betting. But Jimmy took too many hits. So now, if you yell ‘Warp speed’ at him, he’ll start swinging away.”

“You’re kidding,” Amy said. “Aren’t you?”

“That’s the rumor. I’ve never put it to the test.”

The elevator doors slid open. They rode up five floors and exited on a dim lit, grey-carpeted hall. They walked ten feet to the first door on the right. Slade put his key in the lock and opened the door. He flicked on the light switch and stepped aside for Amy.

. . .

She took in the bare wood floor, the back of a gold-cushioned pine loveseat and the matching furniture beyond. There was a sofa by the left wall, a coffee table in front of it, and a right-angled armchair opposite. Two full waist-high bookshelves spanned the right wall. A compact widescreen TV stood on one, an Alexa cone on the other. A sleek walnut desk and mesh desk chair underlined the rear window, its view blocked by downturned shades. Framed movie posters of *El Dorado* and *Jeremiah Johnson* hung on the right wall; a print of Albert Bierstadt's *The Kern River Valley* hung above the sofa.

In the right corner, past Slade's bicycle, a poker table and four plastic chairs made up the dining set. The doorless kitchen entrance was six feet to their left. On Amy's left, the bedroom door was closed, much to Slade's relief.

"Sweet place," said Amy.

"Thanks, I lucked out."

Amy unzipped her ski jacket, flattering the pink cashmere sweater underneath. Slade helped her remove the coat. He lay both of theirs on the loveseat and escorted Amy to the wider, less suggestive sofa.

"Please," he said, indicating it.

Amy sat down on the sofa, once again showcasing her superb legs.

"Beer, wine, or whisky?" asked Slade.

"Got any red wine?"

"From California, astate so far left it could count as imported."

He Slade went into the kitchen. He came out a minute later with an uncorked bottle of Carlo Rossi, two empty juice glasses, and two napkins. Amy was studying the two movie posters on the wall in front of her. Slade placed the kitchen items on the coffee table.

"Sorry, I don't have any wineglasses."

"I'll rough it," Amy said.

Slade sat down on her right, close yet not intimately so. He poured the wine. Amy nodded at the left side poster on the wall.

"'*El Dorado*'."

"Good Western."

"I've heard of it."

"More likely the poem by Edgar Allan Poe," said Slade. "Altered for the movie's theme song."

"How does it go?"

Slade sang softly but in tune.

"*In sunshine and shadow from darkness till noon*
*Over mountains that reach from the sky to the moon,*
*A man with a dream that will never let go*
*Keeps searching to find El Dorado.*"

"Pretty. You really like Westerns, don't you?"

"Yeah. My dad and I used to watch one every night in Belgium."

"I don't think I've seen one all the way through."

"They don't make 'em anymore," said Slade. "Too triggering."

"Triggering?"

"Yeah," said Slade. "They show a world where a man survives by his own skill, outside any social, civil order. He makes folks nervous by reminding them of the wilderness all around. 'Cause they know, once it starts closing in, all their fancy notions won't save 'em – only him. Since he's part wild himself."

He picked up the two full glasses and handed one to Amy.

"The weenies who run Hollywood can't handle that. Shatters their illusions."

"Such as?"

"Women can do anything men can."

"We can," Amy said. "That Diane girl was right. We can have boyfriends too."

She snickered then sniffled. She put down her glass and leaned forward, both hands on her forehead. Soon, Slade heard low sobbing. He caressed the back of Amy's neck. She turned and threw both arms around him and pressed her face to his chest.

He had decided not to take advantage of her vulnerability. His resolve melted the moment she brought her mouth to his. He kissed her back, savoring her pliant lips and probing tongue.

"Take me to bed," she said. "Please, Mark, take me to bed. I need you!"

Slade stood up and raised her to her feet. He walked her to the bedroom, his right arm around her waist as she stroked his back. He pulled the door open and led her inside. It was his last entirely voluntary act of the night.

# CHAPTER 9

A low cellphone ring awoke Slade. He tried to locate it by the faint sound, hoping he'd brought it into the bedroom. But on the next ring, he could tell it was coming from the living room. And Amy's firm body clenching him in her sleep made it hard for him to get up. The ringing stopped.

Sunlight filtered through the partially open door to his right. Over hiss shoulder, Amy looked exquisite with eyes shut and hair unkempt. He delicately extricated himself from her arm and the brown comforter without waking her. He stood up in his grey briefs and crossed between the foot of the king-size bed and the bathroom door.

He stepped into the living room, found the phone in his coat pocket, and sat down on the loveseat. The screen displayed 6:41 and two missed calls from Cork. The combination could only mean trouble. Slade hit the callback key.

"Paul Adamo's dead," Cork said the instant he came on the line.

"What?!"

Despite his shock, Slade kept his voice down so as not to wake Amy.

"How do you know?"

"Wallace called me. He was shot outside the Winger Gallery round three o'clock this morning."

"Three?! What the hell was he doing there at that hour?!"

"Checking on his paintings, perhaps. His show opens today. Appears to be a straight robbery."

"How awful," Slade said. "I just saw him last night."

"I know."

"Wait a minute. Why would Wallace call you about some dead artist?"

"The gallery owner, Robin Winger, told him I'd been asking her about Adamo. Wallace naturally wanted an explanation."

"What'd you tell him?"

"Everything except the name of our client," said Cork. "We'll have to give her up soon, though. Wallace wants to question us separately. Here's another fine mess you've gotten us into. Will you call Amy Gallup?"

"I don't have to. She's right here."

There was a brief pause on the line before Cork spoke.

"What now?"

"Good question," Slade said. "I'll let you know when I do."

He hung up. Reentering the bedroom, he found Amy in the same position on the bed. He lay down beside her, face up. She stirred and rolled to him with her green eyes now open.

"Good morning," she said sleepily, her left hand stroking his chest.

"It was, and a great night."

Amy stopped her hand strokes, feeling his tension.

"What's wrong, babe?"

"Your ex-boyfriend's boyfriend is dead," said Slade.

He felt Amy's body stiffen against his.

"He was shot last night."

"Greg?!" Amy asked almost as a demand.

"He wasn't with him. Happened early this morning."

"I have to see Greg."

Slade said nothing. Amy's eyes locked on him.

"Don't you see, darlin'? All this time he's been hiding this heavy secret from me. From everyone in our orbit. Must'a been tearing him apart. And now he's got no one to turn to – 'cept me."

"Aren't you forgetting something?" Slade said.

Amy finger brushed his lips. "'Course not, sweetheart. I needed you last night, and you were wonderful. But now Greg needs me. I can't just leave him in pain."

"Like he did you," said Slade.

Amy rolled away from him and off the bed. She walked into the bathroom, leaving the door ajar. Slade heard the shower water running for a while. Amy emerged from the bathroom naked and slightly wet. She stood by her side of the bed and got into the clothes she'd dropped on the floor. Fully dressed, she knelt on the bed and gave Slade a light kiss on the lips.

"I'll call you," she said.

She walked out of the room. Slade heard front door open and shut, then silence.

# CHAPTER 10

The stately marble edifice that was Metropolitan Police Headquarters took up the entire block of Indiana Avenue between Third and Fourth Street. Uniformed police scampered up and down the wide staircase along with detectives, lawyers, and less voluntary visitors, like Mark Slade.

He hoisted his bicycle up the steps to the terrace in front of the entrance, chiding himself for wearing his Army sweat jacket and green backpack. Some alert cop might link him to Thursday's down-town hell ride. Luckily, he had on his Ray-Ban sunglasses to both mask him and dissipate the bright yet cold sunlight.

He hooked his bike to a fence rail with the Kryptonite lock and noticed a patrolman looking his way.

"Think this place can be trusted?" Slade asked him.

The patrolman turned and headed to the building entrance. Slade followed. He passed through a metal detector to the long main corridor, then approached a right-side door marked *Room 1025 – Homicide*. He pushed open the door and went inside.

Navigating the maze of occupied metal desks, he reached the three adjacent back offices. The door on the right had a name on it – *Lt. Carl Wallace*. Slade knocked on it.

"Come in," growled a deep male voice.

Slade entered the tight office containing a dark wood desk and three polyester chairs facing it. A forty-something Black man looked up over his compact desktop terminal at him. He was stocky and hard like a fireplug. He wore a brown sportscoat, a light blue shirt with no tie, and a mustache surrounded by beard stubble.

"Good thing you don't have to shave on Saturdays," Slade said.

"I do shave on Saturday," said Lieutenant Carl Wallace. "Have a seat, Slade."

He pointed to the three visitor chairs. Slade took the inside seat.

"Beats the interrogation box," he said.

"Feel free to confess anyway. That was you downtown on the bike yesterday, wasn't it?"

"I have the right to remain silent."

"Okay," Wallace said. "I got bigger headaches – like Paul Adamo. What the hell was he to you?"

"To me, not a thing. But to my client – the other man."

"Who's your client?"

Slade remained silent.

Wallace snapped, "Come on, Slade."

"Carl, I'll make a deal with you. If this case goes beyond a routine robbery-homicide, I'll spill the beans. But there's a US Senator in the mix. And your department is so deep up the Mayor's butt it could start its own voting bloc."

Wallace frowned. "The brass is – not me," he said.

"I know that," said Slade. "And I'll fill you in either way. Just not yet."

Wallace scratched his chin stubble.

"Maybe you're right, Slade. I'd have to put it in my report, and this place does have a pipeline to City Hall. I'll wait for my team's finding before I grill you and Cork."

"What've they got so far?"

Wallace lifted a printout off his desk and read from it. "Adamo's body was found five-sixteen this morning in a delivery nook behind the Winger Gallery. Coroner said he'd been dead a couple hours. One shot to the base of the skull. Wallet and keys missing - car still there. Robin Wingerhad given him the back door code, already changed."

"Slug?"

"Nine mil."

"And no one heard the shot," said Slade.

Wallace looked at him.

"Right, DC norm," Slade said. "Can I go?"

"For now. But we'll have that Paul Adamo talk real soon."

"I can tell you one thing about him."

"What's that?"

"The value of his paintings just went up," Slade said.

# CHAPTER 11

Slade cycled north northwest toward Dupont Circle listening to "In a Big Country" by Big Country. Reaching the Circle, he rode clockwise around part of Dupont Fountain, then turned left into the narrow street paralleling Connecticut Avenue. On his right stretched the long row of Connecticut Avenue shops, most of them unrecognizable from the back. But a web of crisscrossing yellow crime-scene tape identified the Winger Gallery. Slade dismounted his bike in front of it.

The police tape blocked off a small delivery nook between the alley and the shop's rear metal door, currently shut. The only car in the perimeter was a green Nissan Sentra ribboned with additional police tape. A few feet from the driver's door lay the chalk outline of an absent body. Slade felt a pang of sadness, having seen the actual body very much alive the night before.

Resuming his ride, he made a right at the first cross street then the immediate right on Connecticut Avenue to reapproach Dupont Circle. He stopped before the clearly marked Robin Winger Gallery. He locked his bike to the nearest parking meter.

He entered a white-walled oblong room with midsize paintings, all abstract art of no interest to him. But a standing sign beside the right rear corner doorway drew his attention. The fancy print proclaimed “The Adamo Collection,” followed by “In Memory of Paul Adamo.” Slade passed through the doorless passage.

The back room was identical to the front chamber only with a door at the left end of the far wall marked Emergency Exit Only. Two large colorful paintings dominated the wall, with a vacant space between them clearly reserved for a third picture. Four smaller paintings hung on the side walls. The one nearest the door depicted a bare-chested handsome Eskimo boy on a melting block of ice raising two defiant fists at the hostile sun.

Two nattily dressed young men admired the right painting on the back wall. Neil and Kathy Cork contemplated the left one, her hand on Melanie’s baby stroller handle. She wore a pink puffer jacket and hip-hugging blue jeans, Cork a white wool button sweater and khaki slacks. Approaching his friends, Slade got a closer look at the painting they were viewing.

A flaming orange sun spewed tongues of fire on a green pasture with a cindering American flag. Two semi-naked brown native children, a girl and boy, appeared to be fleeing toward the near end of a green rainbow, its far side obscured by white mist. The title card under the canvas read “Utopia.”

“How unpatriotic,” Slade said, stepping between Cork and Kathy.

“But compelling,” said Cork. “You can almost sense those kids’ despair.”

“Yeah, that they’re about to be scorched by global warming man-made in America.”

“That *is* a bit extreme. What say you, Kate?”

“I feel sorry for the artist,” Kathy said piteously. “He must’ve been seriously tormented.”

She pushed the baby stroller to the front doorway. Two brown faux-leather chairs stood to her left of it, both vacant. Kathy took the middle seat behind the stroller. She began stroking Melanie’s hair as if for her own comfort. An elegant forty-something couple entered past her, approaching Cork and Slade.

The detectives moved to the painting on the right, "The Unholy," according to the title card. It portrayed a plump elder bishop-type in a purple robe on a gold throne, lustfully watching cowled monks drag attractive semi-nude young men toward a pit. Two monstrous tentacles rose from the hole, one crushing the body of a youth, the other about to envelop a second victim.

"Rough times for the LGBTV crowd," Slade said.

"I believe that's the unsubtle message," said Cork.

Looking left, he noticed the title card for the absent middle painting. He sidestepped to it, joined by Slade, who pointed at the bare wall space.

"This is his best work yet."

"A missing painting," said Cork. "It appears Adamo wasn't finished."

"He is now."

"True."

Cork read the title on the placard and said it aloud – Revelation.

"Better it stay hidden," Slade said.

"Did you see Wallace?" asked Cork.

"Yeah. And I was lucky to walk out of there a free man."

"I'd pay your bail since you closed the Amy Gallup case without breaking anything."

Slade sighed.

"Besides your heart," said Cork.

"Joke all you want to, pal. She was the one."

Cork turned away from the wall to face Slade and stiffened without Slade noticing.

"She'll haunt me forever," said Slade. "Her red hair, green eyes, luscious lips …"

"Gold coat, blue-flannel skirt, black boots."

"What?"

"She's haunting *me* now," Cork said, pointing toward the gallery entrance.

Slade turned to see Amy Gallup in the doorway, dressed just as Cork described, arm in arm with a pale Greg Bradford. She didn't see him yet, distracted by Kathy sitting on her right, and the baby stroller. The two women exchanged cordial greetings while Greg bitterly took in the room.

"Is that Greg?" Cork asked Slade.

"Yeah."

Kathy pointed out the two detectives. Seeing Slade, Amy winced, and tried to pull Greg back out of the room. He stood his ground, glowering.

"I'm out of here," Slade said.

"Good idea," said Cork. "Lunch, Golden Grill, twenty minutes."

"See you guys there."

Before Slade could move, the fortyish couple headed to the doorway ahead of him. Greg stepped directly in their way.

"Excuse us," said the male half of the couple.

He and his companion tried circumventing Greg, who again blocked their path.

"Have you seen enough?!" Greg snarled.

Everyone in the room looked at him except baby Melanie. Amy approached him with concern.

"Have you all seen enough?!' he growled again. "I don't think so!"

Amy started worriedly stroking Greg's back.

"It's all right, baby, let's go home," she said.

Greg ignored her, scowling at his uncomfortable audience.

"You people are dead! Your minds are dead! And now Paul's dead – because of you!"

Greg choked up and got visibly angrier.

"They killed him 'cause he cared too much! No one's leaving here! Not till you show his art the respect it deserves! And maybe give some meaning to your worthless lives!"

Behind Greg appeared an elegant grey-haired woman in a white business suit with cellphone in hand. She looked past Greg to Cork, who nodded once to her. Slade presumed her to be Robin Winger, and that she would now call 911.

"You think this is all his work?" Greg said. "You're so wrong.

There's a big surprise coming. And it's gonna shake up this shitty country like nothing ever has."

Melanie made a baby sound, prompting worried looks from Cork and Kathy. Cork took a step toward Greg. Slade put a hand on his shoulder, halting him.

"My speed," Slade said.

He walked around the fortyish couple and right up to Greg, visibly alarming Amy.

"Hey, pal. I'm sorry your boyfriend's dead. But I've seen better art in comic books."

Amy groaned. Greg trembled with rage.

"You son of a bitch!" he screamed.

He charged Slade, placing both hands around his throat. Slade thrust up his forearms and wedged apart the hold. Greg lashed out at him with wild punches which he easily batted away. As the blows kept coming, Slade took a bead on Greg's right jaw and launched a roundhouse punch. Greg fell to the floor, fully conscious. Amy gasped, dropping to her knees beside him.

"What'd you do to him?" she cried.

"Hit the brain link on his chin. He should be okay in a minute."

"You bastard! Stay away from me!"

Cork joined Slade, who was gazing down at Greg and Amy. Greg groggily looked up at the two men.

"Are you – Kudzu?" he muttered.

Slade and Cork exchanged looks, Cork's suddenly much grimmer.

"Who?" Slade asked.

Cork bent down closer to Greg. "Where is Kudzu?" he asked.

"All around," Greg mumbled. "Gotta stop 'em before they –"

"That's him!" declared a woman's voice in the next room.

Robin Winger reappeared beside a Black patrolman. He loomed over Greg and Amy.

"You want an ambulance?" he asked.

"He's fine, officer," said Amy. "His best friend died last night and he's taking it really hard. He didn't mean any trouble."

"The man who painted these," said Cork, his hand sweeping the room.

The policeman turned to Robin Winger. "You pressing charges, ma'am?"

Robin looked at Cork. He shook his head, noticed by a nervous Amy.

"I don't think so."

Amy visibly relaxed.

"Take your boyfriend home and lock 'im in for the night," said the policeman.

"Yessir."

Amy helped Greg to his feet. She looked gratefully at Cork, ignoring Slade. She took Greg by the hand and led him out the door. Slade grimaced.

"Hey, cheer up," said Cork. "You handled him quite well."

"But he took the prize."

"You still have your sanity. Well, most of it anyway. I can't say the same for Greg. Did you hear what he said about Kudzu?"

"Yeah," said Slade. "Who is that?"

"Not a who. It's an ivy, planted in the South during the 1930s to stop soil erosion. But the damn weed was so strong, it just kept growing, till the whole South was covered with it. Still is."

"And Greg seems to think it's reached Washington," Slade said.

# CHAPTER 12

Slade always sat facing the entrance at restaurants. He didn't intend to go out like Wild Bill Hickock, backshot in a Deadwood saloon. The Golden Grill was far from a saloon – as the baby in the high-chair at his table with the Corks proved – but Slade still occupied the vantage seat. He was eating a cheeseburger, Cork a hamburger, and Kathy a tuna-salad sandwich while spoon-feeding Melanie gelatinous baby food. All three adults sipped coffee.

"We need to discuss what just happened," Cork said.

"What's to discuss," said Slade. "She called me a bastard."

"Apart from that."

"Don't be too hard on Amy, Mark," said Kathy. "She's in a tough spot."

"So's Greg Bradford now," Cork said. "There's sure to be talk around the Capitol about his outburst today, and the motivation for it."

"Same-sex sex," said Slade.

"Senator Owen ain't gonna like that," said Cork.

"Honey, it's the Twenties," said Kathy.

"The nineteen-twenties where Owen is concerned. Greg's nascent political career may be over."

"Maybe not," said Slade. "He's still got a queen in the hole."

"Amy Gallup," said Cork.

"Owen really likes her for Greg," Slade said. "Judging by what I overheard last night."

"Amy would make a fine candidate's wife," Kathy said.

"She'd certainly diffuse one of Greg's two drawbacks where the Far Right is concerned," Cork said. "His sexual orientation – "

"As the hottest beard in Washington," Slade said.

"But not the other," said Cork.

"His political orientation," Slade said.

"Exactly. Greg's lover was more than just a pretty face. He was a radical leftist artist."

"*Utopia*," Kathy said. "The name of that disturbing painting."

"Climate doomsday, with America to blame," said Slade.

"And Greg embraced that view along with Adamo," Cork said.

"He should run for office as a Democrat," Slade said.

"Impractical, absent the support of his family dynasty," said Cork. "Better for him to remain a closet liberal. But his lover's death imperiled that. Made him show his true color."

"Blue," said Kathy.

"Minus the red and white," said Slade.

"Yes, he said too much today," Cork said.

"The Kudzu conspiracy," said Slade.

"Sounds like a bad movie," said Kathy.

"Or worse reality I fear," said Cork.

"What are you talking about?" Slade asked.

"A secret Southern rightwing spy cell – code name Kudzu."

"Come on, Neil."

"Hey, I hate conspiracy theories as much as you," Cork said. "But I may have crossed paths with these people."

Slade and Kathy looked at him. He continued.

"My last year with the Bureau, my partner, Alan Nichols, and I got an assignment..."

Slade saw Kathy tense slightly, acknowledging her bad history with Cork's old partner.

"An electrical engineer at Tulane University had vanished – Robert Walsh, an expert on EMP weaponry. He kissed his wife one morning and left for work in his Volkswagen Polo, but he never arrived at the lab. Alan and I retraced his movements, only to learn we were hours behind a parallel investigation by no known government agency. One witness gave me her interviewer's contact card. It had the image of a Kudzu leaf on it, a name, Will Zarco, and a phone number. We traced the number to a staff member on Senator Owen's reelection campaign."

"Your nemesis," said Slade.

"She denied any knowledge of Zarco or Kudzu, or how her number got on that card."

"Did the missing scientist ever turn up?" Kathy asked.

"Oh yes," Cork said. "In a toilet stall at Atlanta International Airport, with his neck broken. He'd missed his connecting Delta flight to Hong Kong."

Kathy's eyes widened.

"He was defecting," Slade said.

"So it would seem," said Cork. "By sheer coincidence, a lovely Chinese student in his class had flown home the week before, with two months left in the semester."

"Honey trap," said Slade.

"Indeed," Cork said. "Sprung by a third party."

"Kudzu," Slade said.

Cork shrugged. "I questioned Senator Owen about it, perhaps too aggressively. We were ordered back to Washington the same night. That was during the previous Administration."

"The good old days," said Slade. "Well, you're your own boss now. With important cases – like the missing bandages at Sibley. I'll start on that one Monday like I promised."

"Not so fast, Mark," Cork said pensively.

Slade looked at him. Kathy concentrated on feeding Melanie.

"You heard what Greg said. There's a surprise coming that will shake the country. To be revealed in Adamo's newest work."

"The missing painting, '*Revelation'*

"Could be the real reason he was shot last night."

"For his painting instead of his money," said Slade. "Damn. Maybe it *is* packing some secret weapon."

"And Kudzu is looking for it – or I should say hunting for it? We had better find that painting before they do. I'm putting you on the case."

"Me?!" Slade exclaimed. "Sam Owen's your vendetta not mine."

"That's precisely why. You'll be far more impartial than I."

"Not necessarily."

"Oh, right – Amy Gallup," said Cork. "Who knows? She might even help you."

"I doubt it. I'll pass, Cork."

"Fine. I'll look into it myself."

Cork noticed Kathy glaring at him and gulped.

"What's the matter, honey?" he asked.

"You," Kathy said. "What are you going to do? Chase after the killer who shot that poor man? When did you ever do anything like that?"

"Why – the Bureau," said Cork.

"The Bureau," Kathy scoffed. "You were in the Bureau when I met you. The only gun you ever used was in that silly paintball war you dragged me to. And you got killed right away."

Slade chuckled. Kathy turned her glare on him.

"And you. Some friend and partner you are. You practically force a case on my husband so you can boink a pretty girl – and when he asks for your help, you refuse him, because she hurt your feelings. Boo hoo. Don't expect any more Thursday night dinners at our house."

"Now wait a minute, Kathy," Slade said.

"I'm serious."

Slade sighed. "What's for dinner next Thursday?"

Kathy smiled. "You'll love it."

Slade turned to Cork. "How do you want me to handle it?"

"With your usual aplomb," Cork said. "That ought to shake loose some bad apples and cause a distur –"

His cellphone pinged. He looked at it.

"It's from Wallace," he said, reading the text. "The bullet that killed Adamo came out through a silencer. Chipped off a piece of it."

"Which makes it a professional hit," Slade said.

"Forget what I asked you to do," said Cork.

"Now I'm more inclined," said Slade.

He pulled out his own cellphone and looked at the screen.

"Hey, voicemail from Amy Gallup."

The Corks appeared curious. Slade laid the phone on the table and hit some keys.

"Mark, I know you hate me," whispered Amy's voice on speaker. "But I'm really scared. I'm at Greg's apartment – three-six-five D Street northeast. He doesn't know I'm calling you. He's going crazy, Mark. Said he's being followed. And he might be right. There's a man sitting in a car across the street. He's been out there a while. I just sent you a picture."

The photo was a high-angle shot of a silver Ford Fusion parked across a residential street in Capitol Hill. Slade enlarged the image of the man behind the wheel. He had short white hair like "B" Western star Jeff Chandler and looked formidable. Slade showed Cork the photo, disturbing him.

"We can alert Wallace," said Cork.

"What's he gonna do, arrest the guy for sitting in his car? I gotta take him, Neil."

"He may be armed."

"I figure he is," said Slade. "You said shake loose some bad apples. Here's one of 'em."

"All right, I'll go with you," Cork said.

"You'd better sign something first," Kathy said.

"The check."

"Our divorce papers – if you go anywhere near that man."

"But Mark –"

“Is a decorated Army Ranger who doesn’t have a wife and child to support.”

“She’s right, Cork,” Slade said. “Besides, you’d cramp my style.”

He grabbed his backpack from beside his chair and stood up. Cork remained seated.

“I’ll check in when it’s over,” Slade said. At Cork’s worried look, he added, “If I can.”

# CHAPTER 13

Slade walked his bike off the last subway car at Capitol South Metrorail Station, "Lips Like Sugar" by Echo and the Bunnymen playing in his earbuds. He approached the elevator behind a young Black couple holding hands. On the ride up, he turned off the music, wanting his senses on full alert. Exiting the elevator on D Street, he mounted his bike.

He pedaled east for two blocks. A few yards short of Third Street, his Cervelo appeared to malfunction, forcing him to dismount. He walked the bike north on the crosswalk, ostensibly testing the break levers but actually scanning D Street on the other side of Third.

There was little moving traffic on the residential block this chilly Saturday afternoon. The silver Ford Fusion in Amy's photo was parked halfway down the north lane, facing Slade, with Jeff Chandler still in the driver's seat. From the angle of the photo, Slade placed Greg's apartment on the second floor of the beige rowhouse across from it.

He walked his bike to the southwest corner of Third Street and remounted it with visible effort. He rode across D Street, making a diagonal beeline for the Fusion. Twenty yards away, he quit pedaling and feigned frantically squeezing the break levers. He could see Jeff Chandler staring at him through the car windshield.

"No breaks!" yelled Slade.

He flew straight at the Fusion's left rear passenger door. At the last moment, he swerved right. His left fist pounded the door to sound as if the bike had struck it. He executed a spectacular spill in the center of the lane.

A westbound car veered around him and the fallen bike, before continuing toward Third Street. The Fusion driver's door opened. Slade rose shakily to his feet and stood up his bike.

"Bummer," he said stoner-like.

Jeff Chandler stepped out of the car. He was in his mid-thirties, as tall as Slade but bulkier in a brown parka and grey pants. He approached the rear door to check for any damage. Slade leaned his bike against a white Chevrolet Volt behind it and shuffled closer to Jeff.

"How's your ride, dude?" he asked dazedly.

Jeff turned to Slade.

"Looks all right," he said in a faint Southern accent, suspiciously adding, "So do you after that fall."

"Yeah, man, that was intense," Slade said, then appeared to get very dizzy. "Woah."

He stumbled against Jeff's chest, grabbing his coat for support. He sank to his knees, his hands sliding all around the parka including both pockets.

"What the hell're you doing?!" Jeff barked, shoving away Slade.

"My most embarrassing pat-down ever," Slade said in his normal voice while standing up straight. "Glad you don't have a gun."

Jeff took a menacing step toward him.

"Who are you?" he demanded.

Slade shook his head. "Only at the point of death," he said, quoting Charles Bronson in *Once Upon a Time in the West*.

"Suits me," Jeff said.

His right fist came fast at Slade's temple. Ready for it, Slade blocked the punch with his left wrist and threw a right hook to Jeff's jaw. His fist struck the left temple as Jeff raised his wrist too late. Slade sent a left cross to his chin but only nicked it as Jeff dodged fast.

Jeff punched him hard in the stomach. Slade absorbed the pain, grateful for his many stomach crunches. He sent a right uppercut to the jaw. Jeff's head rocked back, leaving the chin open to two left jabs then a strong right.

Clearly stung, Jeff took a wild right swing at Slade's head. Slade ducked and fired a right uppercut to the jaw. Jeff stumbled back.

Slade glimpsed a small but growing crowd on the sidewalks. A grey-bearded pedestrian in an old Redskins cap was phone-filming the fight. Jeff advanced on Slade, fists circling. Slade kept up his own fists.

Jeff charged him, launching a volley of punches at his head. Slade blocked and bobbed but two shots got through, striking his lower lip and left cheek. He retaliated with a left-right combination to Jeff's chin and mouth, doing damage.

A grey SUV slowed to a stop across the street. Two fortyish men got out. One of them raised his cellphone.

Jeff threw two punches at Slade's face. Slade blocked them both. He focused on his opponent's jaw, a dark bruise serving as the bulls-eye. He fired a right cross and hit the target. Jeff's legs buckled. He fell to the street on his left side, no longer moving. Slade knelt beside him and pressed two fingers to his neck, checking for a pulse.

"Did you kill him?" asked Cork.

Slade looked up in surprise as his partner stepped out from behind the Fusion.

"Nah," Slade said. "He's got a steady pulse. When'd you get here?"

"Just now," said Cork. "I was unsure of the address. Till I saw a crowd gathering around some sort of fracas, then I knew exactly where you were."

Slade took in the dozen spectators on the sidewalk, doubtless awaiting Round Two.

"You defied Kathy," he said.

"A man's gotta do what a man's gotta do – then sleep on the couch."

A police siren sounded far away but nearing fast. Slade bent over Jeff's torso. He removed a black alligator wallet from the right coat pocket. Going through it, he slid free a driver's license and looked at it.

"Jonathan Woods – Chester, South Carolina. What the hell are we dealing with, Cork – a Confederate second front?"

"The South will rise again," said Cork.

The police siren sounded closer. On the street, Woods stirred awake.

"Hey, Cork," said Slade.

He pulled a business-style card out of the wallet and handed it to Cork. It displayed a green ivy-like leaf next to the name "John Adams" and a phone number, area code 803. Slade recognized the Kudzu leaf, having researched it during his subway ride here. Cork brightened.

"Just like the card I saw before," he said. "I'll wager that phone number is defunct – or soon will be. But this time, we have a member of the gardening society to question."

"We'd better call Wallace," said Slade.

The police siren sounded very close now.+

"I don't believe we'll have to," said Cork. "Help me get him up, will you?"

The partners took hold of the recovering Woods' armpits and pulled him to his feet. A Metropolitan Police car, lights flashing, turned in from Third Street and stopped behind the double-parked SUV. Two patrolmen got out, a stocky veteran and his young partner, the senior man holding a pistol. Slade recognized the nine-millimeter Glock 19.

"Hands up now!" yelled the gun-bearing cop.

Cork and Slade let go of Woods. He crumpled to the ground as they raised their hands.

"I'm Neil Cork – Cork Detective Agency!" Cork shouted. "My partner, Mark Slade! Lieutenant Wallace knows us!"

"He loves us!" added Slade.

The senior cop holstered his gun and unholstered his radio.

"Six-one-two Baker to Homicide Branch. Request Lieutenant Wallace."

"Tell him we have a suspect in the murder of Paul Adamo," said Cork.

The older cop looked at Woods, unsteadily rising to his feet.

"Cuff 'im, Mike," he said.

Officer Mike moved toward Woods while drawing a pair of handcuffs.

"Wallace," said a familiar voice over the radio.

Mike pulled Woods' wrists behind his back, handcuffing him.

"Sir, Joe Behling. Got a couple of PIs here – Cork and Slade – and a third man they say killed Paul Ad – "

"Mark, look out!" screamed Amy Gallup from somewhere unseen. "He's got a gun!"

Slade looked up at the second floor of Greg's rowhouse, scanning all three windows. A rifle barrel jutted out the middle one. Slade tackled Cork on his right. They hit the street just as a gunshot cracked. Woods' chest burst red, splattering blood on Officer Mike behind him.

Slade swept Cork toward the row of parked cars. *Crack!* A cement bit chipped off the spot they'd just vacated. Slade pushed Cork into the gap between an orange Toyota Corolla and a black Chrysler coupe.

Cork started crawling through the gap toward the sidewalk. Slade backed into the same space but remained in a crouch near the street side. *Crack!* The Chrysler's rear window exploded, raining glass on him. He brushed it off and kept watching the street.

Officer Mike had his pistol out and pointed at the rowhouse windows. Behling was barking "Code Three!" into the radio. *Crack!* Officer Mike's chest erupted blood. He fell back, eyes open but unseeing.

"Mike!" cried Behling.

He started running toward his fallen partner, Glock in hand.

Slade yelled, "Get back!"

*Crack!* Behling pitched forward, a red hole in his skull. His gun dropped a foot from his right hand. A woman screamed. The former spectators began fleeing in terror. Another police siren sounded far away. Slade turned to Cork.

"Help is on the way," he said. "Wait here."

"Where're you going?!"

Slade pointed to the rowhouse window.

"To get his attention."

"I'd say you have it already," Cork said nervously.

"So does Amy Gallup. She's in there with him."

Slade ran into the street angling left toward Behling's corpse. He scooped up the loose Glock with his left hand then cut to the right. *Crack!* A concrete chip struck his left heel.

He cut right again, took five steps then dove right onto the street, ending on his back with his feet to the rowhouse. Raising the Glock in a two-hand grip, he fired three shots at the middle window. The window shattered, the rifle barrel no longer in sight.

Slade got up and sprinted across the street to the white front door. He yanked on the bronze handle. It didn't budge. He aimed the Glock at the top door hinge and blasted it, then the lower one. He pulled the door again, budging it open. A sudden lull behind him made him turn around.

An armored black van was approaching from Fourth Street, dispersing armored riflemen out the far side. Each man took cover behind a parked car. The van stopped. Slade read the word *SWAT* on the near side of it. He entered the rowhouse.

A rising staircase took up the entire ground-floor chamber, starting a few feet from the door. Slade warily climbed the lower steps, pointing his pistol at the white wall.

"Greg, don't!" shrieked Amy somewhere upstairs.

A rifle crack cut off her scream. Slade bounded up to the landing and into an open wide living room, ready to shoot left. What he saw made him lower his pistol.

Greg Bradford lay on his back with his head to the glassless window, a bloody pulp for a chin, the AR-15 by his right leg. Amy sat on the floor in the fetal position, her back against the left wall, a purple gash on her right cheek. She moaned softly yet continually.

"Amy," Slade said soothingly.

She turned to him but kept moaning. He stepped over the rifle and past Greg's corpse to the left window. He laid the Glock on the windowsill and moved in front of the middle window, both palms clearly showing.

Down on the street, three rifles pointed at him over parked cars. A grey Sedan was now double-parked behind the SWAT van.

"Hostile down!" Slade shouted.

Cork's head popped up over the Sedan roof, then so did Carl Wallace's. Wallace said something in the van's direction. The SWAT sharpshooters lowered their rifles.

"Mark," Amy gasped, still fetal but no longer moaning.

Slade knelt beside her, taking her left hand in his right.

"I'm right here, babe."

"He hurt me," Amy said, starting to tremble. "With his rifle. Then he … he …"

"You're safe now," said Slade. "Let's go take care of that pretty face."

He swept Amy up in his arms. She clutched his neck as he carried her to the staircase. Bearing her downstairs, he made room for two rifle-toting SWAT men rushing up the steps.

# CHAPTER 14

Emergency Room staffers at Howard University Hospital called it "the calm before the storm." This was early Saturday evening, when the soon-to-be injured from shootings, beatings, and other weekend rituals were still healthy. Only five people sat in the ER waiting area, a bright room with yellow polyester chairs, an analog wall clock indicating eight till six, and the registration-security desk. They were the burly guard at the desk, an academic with a towel around his hand plus his wife and toddler, a busty mulatta policewoman in her late twenties nametagged *R. Valdez*, and, two seats to her right, Mark Slade.

Slade was trying to read the *Washington Post* capsule story on "the Capitol Hill Sniper," but Officer Valdez's sad expression kept distracting him, more than it might have on a less attractive face. She had wordlessly driven him and Amy to the hospital, Amy's facial bruise now being treated by an old GU friend of Slade's. The next destination would be police headquarters – their joint appearance guaranteed by Officer Valdez.

"If you wanna grab a cup of coffee, I won't run away," Slade said.

Officer Valdez brightened slightly. "You promise?"

"Scout's honor."

"You were a Boy Scout?"

"Eagle Scout, baby. Brussels Troop."

"I hear they're letting girls in now."

"Someone's gotta bake the cookies," Slade said.

Officer Valdez almost smiled.

"How do you feel about lady cops?" she asked.

"I think they're vital for Diversity, Equity, and Inclusion."

"Really?"

"No, but you're wearing a gun," said Slade.

Officer Valdez did smile for a few seconds, then her face darkened again.

"So were Behling and Garcetti," she said. "For all the good it did 'em."

"The two cops that got shot today."

The policewoman nodded sadly.

"I dated Behling," she said. "It didn't work out, but we stayed friends."

"I'm sorry, Offi – what's your first name?"

"Raquel. I think I will get that coffee. You want one?"

"No thanks, Raquel."

Officer Valdez stood up and walked to the desk guard, who let her pass. Slade plugged his earbuds jack into his cellphone. "If You Leave" by OMD came on. He leaned back in his chair and shut his eyes. He heard the lyric that now always haunted him: *Seven years went under the bridge like time was standing still….*

"What was it, Mark?" said a breathy feminine voice. "More of your macho bullshit?"

"Hello, Nina," Slade said, opening his eyes.

Nina Holt stood before him looking just as she did on television – green cat eyes, shoulder-length brown hair, and a cute patrician nose that rejected whoever her rosy lips and curvaceous body attracted. Not a classic beauty like Amy, but she had pierced his chest like a Comanche arrow. Once upon a time in the West, he had penetrated her just as deeply.

"If I'd known you'd visit me in the hospital, I'd've checked in long ago," said Slade.

"I always said brain surgery would make you more attractive."

"'Cause then I'd start agreeing with your views."

Nina's mouth formed into something between a smile and a smirk.

"I heard you came back in one piece," she said. "When was that?"

"About a year ago."

"I'm glad, Mark. I was worried about you for the last six, ever since we stopped talking."

"No need for it. Your kiss-off gave me an edge against Taliban killers."

Nina grimaced then suppressed it.

"So, how're you doing?" she asked.

"Terrific."

"I've seen you look better," said Nina, indicating Slade's left eye.

"You should see the other guy."

"I did. He's dead. So are two cops and a young man – Greg Bradford. Before he was a sniper, he was an aide to Senator Owen."

"And you're here to get the full story."

"Lieutenant Wallace told me you're part of it and Cork said where I could find you. It's my job."

Slade said, "And you're great at it -detached, impartial, everything a good reporter should be."

Nina sighed. "Look, Mark. I didn't want to come here. It's difficult for me too. But you and Cork were involved in four shooting deaths, one of them an aide to an important Senator."

"Who your commie network hates."

"I'll admit bringing down Owen would raise my stock at work. But Neil said he won't comment unless you do. God, I hate male bonding."

"Stop trying to join the club."

Nina winced. "Just tell me what you know, and I'll get out of your life.

"You want a story? All right here's one. There was a girl. She was sweet, smart, and feminine. She loved a guy, and he loved her. They planned to get married after his first tour of duty and start a family. While he was in harm's way, she went to Columbia J School. Hooked up with a real fast crowd there. They were going to change the world – a racist, sexist world run by men and ruined by babies. She got into the right racket to do it. All she had to do to was dump the toxic male cramping her style. That she did – and on video – like the pro news chick she became. I still got it somewhere. You can tell a star was born."

Nina scowled, then with apparent effort softened.

"I did love you, Mark," she said softly. "You were everything I wanted in a boy."

"But not in a man."

"That made it more complicated."

"Tell me, Nina, how have you been? Who are you with? Seen any good movies lately?"

Nina's eyes flashed. "None of your goddamn business."

"That's good, baby. Keep playing the tough bitch. Some of your viewers may buy the act. The ones that don't wanna boink you."

Nina's lower lip quivered. She spun around and marched to the exit. Her stormy eyes remained with Slade like the grin on the Cheshire Cat, so did the knot in his stomach.

Amy Gallup stepped out of the inner door pressing an icepack to her right cheek, alongside tall young Black Dr. Ben Hooks. Slade and he had tried out for the Georgetown basketball team and come up short, literally in Slade's case. Slade joined him and Amy.

"Her face should be back to its supermodel caliber in a couple days," Hooks said. "I gave her a prescription for the swelling and –" he paused, noticing Slade's expression. "You okay, man? You look like you've just seen a ghost."

"I did," said Slade. "Nina Holt."

Amy's eyes widened.

"Ouch," said Hooks. "'Fraid I don't have a prescription for that pain."

# CHAPTER 15

The police cruiser sped east on Pennsylvania Avenue past the brightly lit White House gate, Officer Raquel Valdez skillfully driving. Slade and Amy sat in the back seat like two prisoners, except he had his right arm around her shoulders while she leaned into him.

"It's better without the handcuffs," he said. "Funny. Never thought I'd say that to a girl."

Amy half smiled. Slade turned serious.

"Did you talk to your folks back home?"

"Not yet," said Amy.

"You should give 'em a call. Let 'em know you're okay."

"Why would they think different?"

"Your fiancé's about to be world famous as the Capitol Hill Sniper."

"God, you're right," Amy said. "Grandma won't be able to process that. I'll text Ron. He can break it to her gently."

"Ron?"

"Old boyfriend – now just friend."

"How old?"

"My age. We deflowered each other in high school."

"He sure hit a home run first time at bat."

"And he's still swinging for me," Amy said.

"Can't blame 'im for that. You're a tough act to follow."

"He has had a hard time getting over me."

"I know the feeling," said Slade.

Amy clutched his right hand with hers.

"Oh, sweetheart, I felt awful about leaving you," she said. "Even before Greg … lost his mind. I think he sensed that. Could be why he …"

She shivered. Slade squeezed her shoulder.

"He tried to kill you," she said. "And shot those poor people. It coulda been my fault."

"Don't say that to Lieutenant Wallace. Two of them were his men. He's out for blood."

Amy took out her phone and began to text. They soon arrived at the orange-lighted police headquarters. Near the marble steps, a throng of well-dressed men and women watched the cruiser stop just past them. Reporters, Slade not so cleverly deduced from their hand-held mikes and compact TV cameras.

He scanned the group through the rear window but didn't see Nina Holt. He wondered if they'd come to question him and Amy. Better spirit her out on the street side, he thought. Turning to the left car door, he remembered it had no handle, or any way to open it from inside.

"Wait," said Raquel through the partition grate.

A black SUV pulled up behind the patrol car, exciting the reporters. Two formidable-looking men in dark blue wool coats exited the front of the vehicle. One was a ruggedly handsome man despite big ears, on the far side of thirty. His teammate was a boyish-looking East Indian in his late twenties.

They moved to the right rear door, which the Indian opened. A bulky senior citizen stepped out wearing a long black overcoat and brown square glasses. His patchy grey hair came up to the Indian's chin yet he emanatedgreater power. Amy gasped.

"That's Senator Owen."

"Must be North Carolina Day," said Slade.

The reporters swarmed Owen but his two-man escort kept them at bay. He ignored the group all the way up the staircase. They pointed their microphones and mobiles at him while shouting overlapping questions.

"Senator, how long had Greg Bradford worked for you?!"

"Did you know he was mentally disturbed?!"

"What turned him into a killer?!"

"Me," Amy said bitterly.

"No, babe," Slade said. "You were right. Something else was haunting Greg, maybe more than his boyfriend's murder."

Raquel exited the cruiser. Slade heard more questions being yelled at Owen on the terrace, now barely within earshot. The car door on Amy's right swung open, held by Raquel. Amy looked anxiously at Slade.

"Let's get this frigging nightmare over with," he said.

Amy got out of the car. Slade followed her and turned to Raquel, still holding the door.

"I should rent a cell here," he said to her.

The policewoman smiled. Slade took Amy's outstretched hand and led her up the steps.

# CHAPTER 16

Standing outside *Room 1025 – Homicide*, Cork greeted Slade and Amy as they came down the hallway, focusing on Amy.

"Miss Gallup," he said. "Happy to see your face getting back to its lovely appearance."

"Thank you, Neil," said Amy.

"How 'bout my face?" Slade asked.

"Also back to normal. You have my sympathies."

Slade nodded at the door next to them. "Where's Wallace?"

"In the morgue with Senator Owen. He wanted to view Bradford's corpse."

Amy turned slightly pale.

"Forgive me," Cork said to her.

"Do you know where the ladies' room is?" she asked.

"Just past that water fountain."

"'Scuse me," Amy said and started down the hall.

"Anything on Greg's morgue mate – John Woods?" Slade asked.

"Wallace ran his license through the system," said Cork. "Big shock. He's ex-CIA – officially their Accounting Department."

"The only subtracting that guy ever did was people," said Slade, rubbing his jaw where Woods hit him. "What about the Kudzu connection?"

"As I suspected. No such number, no such phone."

"Elvis may sue you."

"Wallace hopes to get more data on the man from Langley."

Slade sneered.

"I know, he'll sooner find out who killed Kennedy," said Cork. "By the way, I told Wallace about Greg and Paul Adamo, in case he asks you."

"Why not? It's a police job now and a media circus. Press give you a hard time?"

"Just one comely reporter of your acquaintance," Cork said. "Persistent witch."

"So, you sicced her on me at the hospital."

"You were longing to see her again – and she you. It was kismet."

"More like kiss-off," Slade said. "Speaking of lost loves – are you still married?"

"I am indeed. Kathy forgave me for defying her once she learned how close she came to becoming a widow. She plans to reward you for saving my life. Thank you, by the way."

"I'll settle for a raise."

"Not a chance. You cost us too much on this case. I'm returning Amy Gallup's deposit."

Cork pulled a folded check from his back pocket. The two friends watched Amy approach, more steadily than she'd walked away.

"You've recovered quite nicely," Cork said to her.

"Hooks called her a model – model patient," said Slade.

"Mark has been really sweet," Amy said.

"Sweet?" Cork repeated mockingly.

"In a rugged kind of way," said Slade.

"Well, lest the senior partner be outdone in the 'sweet' department," Cork said.

He handed Amy the now unfolded check with the Cork Detective

Agency logo at the top – a cork on a churning champagne bottle. Amy contemplated the check in surprise.

"Three hundred dollars," she said.

"Full refund," said Cork.

"But you earned it."

"Not in any way we want to remember," Cork said.

"Or be remembered," said Slade.

Wallace appeared at the end of the hall walking fast toward the group.

"I sure won't forget you boys," Amy said. "Either of you."

"I wish I could," said Wallace, reaching the three. "Inside, you two. Miss Gallup ..."

He pushed open the Homicide section door to let Amy go through, followed by Cork and Slade. They traipsed past the detective cubicles toward Wallace's office.

"Senator Owen?" Cork asked.

"He wanted some alone time with that bastard's body," said Wallace. "As alone as you can be with two watchdogs right outside the door."

"Who are those guys?" asked Slade, quoting Butch and Sundance. "Secret Service?"

"Treasury doesn't protect senators," Cork said. "Except in extreme circumstances."

"They're private," Wallace said. "*Minutemen Security*."

"Think someone's trying to bump off Owen?" Slade asked.

"Whoever drew the short straw," Cork said.

"That would be a leftist, communist, atheist, or feminist."

"Knock it off, you guys," Wallace said.

He opened the door to his office and ushered everyone inside.

# CHAPTER 17

"Capitol Hill Shooting Case – Interview B-Seven. Lieutenant Carl Wallace questioning Amy Gallup and Mark Slade. They were the sole two witnesses inside the premises of homicide suspect Greg Bradford, deceased. Also present is Neil Cork, already interviewed."

Amy took the right guest chair, Slade the middle one, Cork the left. Wallace sat behind his desk holding a remote control. A small black cording machine stood on the desktop, the lens facing the three chairs. Amy appeared nervous but firm. Wallace addressed her.

"Ms. Gallup. I know you just went through a traumatic experience. And you were engaged to the suspect. But you're the only person who can give us vital information."

Amy nodded solemnly.

"Let's go over the chain of events leading up to the first shooting. You called Mark Slade at one-eleven PM. You left a voicemail saying Bradford believed he was being followed. Why would he think that?"

Amy took a deep breath before speaking. "After we left the gallery today, we went to a restaurant, *Il Chalet*. Greg was a wreck 'cause his, uh, friend was killed the night before."

"Paul Adamo," said Wallace.

"Plus, he'd just lost a fight with Mark. Greg knew I'd been with him last night."

"How?"

"He guessed it, from how I spoke to Mark at the gallery."

"She said she never wanted to see me again," said Slade.

Amy mouthed the words "I'm sorry" at him then spoke aloud to Wallace.

"The white-haired man came in right after us, and took a table near the door. Greg saw him and freaked out. He practically dragged me out of the restaurant."

"This man?" Wallace asked.

Wallace held up a blown-up driver's license photo of Jonathan Woods.

"Yessir, that's him," Amy said.

"Go on."

"We took the subway back to Greg's place. The whole ride, he kept muttering about that man. How he'd been following himfor days. I asked him if he knew who he was. All he said was 'Kudzu.'"

Slade and Cork exchanged looks. Wallace glanced at them and refocused on Amy. She continued her account.

"Back at his place, Greg fell asleep on the couch. There was hardly any food in the fridge, and we hadn't eaten at the restaurant, so I walked to the grocery store around the block. Coming back, I saw that man again. He was parked across the street from the apartment in a silver car."

"Did he see you see him?"

"I think so, though I tried to act normal and went inside. Greg was still asleep on the couch – least I thought he was. I went to the window and took a picture of the car, then called Mark. When I turned around, Greg was standing right behind me, glaring at me. I moved past him to the kitchen, a little nervous. While frying up the steak I bought, I heard a commotion on the street. Saw Mark fighting with the man, and knock 'im down. Then Neil showed up, followed by those two policemen."

Wallace winced.

"That's when I got a real bad feeling. I ran into the living room, and saw Greg pointing his rifle out the window. I knew he was gonna shoot Mark. I just grabbed his arm and screamed."

"Her exact words were, 'Mark, look out. He's got a gun,'" Cork said.

"He hit me," Amy said, her voice quivering. "With his rifle, right here."

She stroked the fading bruise mark on her cheek.

"He knocked me down. Then I heard 'im shooting his rifle, over and over again, each time like a nail in my heart."

"Any idea where he got that rifle?" Wallace asked.

"Yessir. Greg was ROTC in school. He hated it. Hated the military. His dad thought it would help his political career. Greg never argued with the Colonel. He was too gentle. That's what first drew me to him in school. This city changed him somehow."

"Perhaps by placing him so close to power yet unable to wield it," Cork said.

"Every man should have a taste of power before he's through," said Slade.

Everyone looked at him.

"John Russell, *Rio Bravo*," Slade said.

There was a knock on the door. Wallace stood up and opened it. The white member of Senator Owen's security team stood in the doorway. He and Wallace had an inaudible exchange. Wallace moved aside as the Senator from North Carolina stepped into the room, looking grim.

# CHAPTER 18

"I've been in politics forty years," Sam Owen said with a genteel Southern accent. "Seen all kinds of wrong. Terrorists called freedom fighters. Rioters called protesters. Baby-murder called a reproductive right. And child mutilation called gender-affirming care. I've pushed back against much of it. But nothing's brought me down so low as seeing that boy on a slab."

"Take my seat, Senator," Wallace said, closing the door behind Owen.

"Thank you, Lieutenant."

Owen sat down behind the desk. Wallace moved to the right of it.

He said, "I took the liberty of calling Colonel Bradford. Let 'im know I just identified his son. Thought it might be easier coming from an old friend."

"I appreciate that, sir," said Wallace. "Always found it the worst part of my job."

"I can see why. Stuart tried to hang tough, but I could feel his pain, even through the phone. He had such high hopes for his boy. His whole dynasty riding on 'im."

Owen scanned the three civilians across the desk from him. Amy looked back respectfully at him, Cork much less so. Owen focused on the girl.

"You're Amy Gallup, aren't you – Greg's betrothed?"

"Yessir," Amy said demurely.

"I'm terribly sorry for your loss. Greg showed me pictures of you two. I was glad to see such lovely flowers blooming in our state. Wish we could've met under happier circumstances."

"Me too, sir."

Owen turned to Cork, his grey eyes narrowing behind his lenses. Cork calmly returned the gaze through his own glasses.

"Neil Cork and Mark Slade," said Wallace. "The two private detectives Greg shot at."

Amy winced. Owen turned his gaze to Slade.

"Slade," he said. "I know a Colonel Jack Slade – our NATO liaison in Brussels."

"My father," said Slade.

"Army could use more like your dad – especially among the present brass of peacocks."

"He's said much the same about you and Congress, sir."

"Has he now?" Owen said with a thin smile. "No wonder he's a colonel."

He turned to Cork, his smile fading.

"We've met before, Mr. Cork."

"Yes, Senator. Your office sandbagged one of my investigations."

"Right, the Walsh case. You were the FBI primary on it. You raised quite a ruckus."

"Not enough to countermand your wishes. It's one reason I work for myself now."

"So Lieutenant Wallace told me. And that you two are mighty fine detectives."

"Why thank you, Carl," Slade said.

Wallace grimaced.

"May I ask how y'all got involved in this sad affair?" Owen inquired.

"You may," said Cork.

He and Owen stared at each other for a lingering moment.

"I hired them, Senator," Amy said. "Greg and I were having some problems."

"I'm sorry to hear it," Owen said. "Nothing to do with his job, I hope."

"No, sir. I wanted to know if he was seeing someone else."

"Was he?" Owen asked with surprising eagerness.

"That's confidential information," Cork said as much to Amy as Owen.

Owen glared at Cork for a second then turned a softer face to Amy.

"Forgive my curiosity, Miss Gallup. You see, I too wanted the best for Greg. And I felt that that included you."

"Thank you," Amy said.

"Did you know he opposed everything you stood for?" Cork asked.

Owen sat back in the chair looking pensive.

"I suspected it for some time," he said. "Last November, I voted against a bill allowing boys into girls' sports. I gave Greg an assignment ahead of my floor speech. State my argument in bullet points even Democrats could understand. He refused and urged me to vote yes. Oh, he tried to shroud it in economic bull-crap about corporations boycotting our state, but it sounded personal to him. I told him to shut up and do his job. For weeks after, he was real mopey, demoralizing my staff. So, I'd decided to let him go. Hardest-working L.A. I ever had. A dear old friend's son. And I was gonna can his butt."

"Of course," said Cork. "Can't have someone working for you who resents your work."

"That goes double for politics," Owen said. "A lot of classified material comes across my desk. I'd rather the Chicoms get their intel from *The Washington Post* instead of my office."

"Like Kudzu for instance," said Cork.

Owen's eyes blinked twice behind his lenses. "A curious plant," he said. "Protects the soil. Maybe too effectively for some invaders."

The desk phone rang, irritating Wallace. He approached the front side of his desk reaching for the receiver.

"Excuse me, Senator," he said picking up the phone. "Dammit, I said no calls … Oh, sorry, sir." His face and tone became angry. "Hell, they can't do that. I got two dead cops and ..." He gritted his teeth. "What about the Adamo connection?" He gripped the receiver. "All right, I'll cooperate … Right, goodbye."

He started to slam the receiver on the hook but touched it down at the last moment. Everyone stared at him.

"FBI's taking over," he said. I'm to pass on all related evidence and information to Inspector Wilcox within the hour."

"Wilcox," Cork said sourly.

"You know the guy?" asked Wallace.

"Unfortunately. He's been a Bureau Yes Man for so long, he probably can't spell 'no.'"

"Hell, no point in wasting everyone's time now," Wallace said. "You're all free to go. I'll see you out, Senator."

Owen stood up. Wallace opened the door for him. The Senator paused in the doorway, turning to Cork.

"Mind how you dig around Kudzu, son. Something of value may wash away."

He walked out the door, followed by Wallace. Slade leaned forward and spoke over Amy's lap to Cork.

"I got a feeling you've just been threatened."

"Didn't think he was giving me gardening tips," said Cork.

# CHAPTER 19

"Go away?!" exclaimed Kathy Cork.

She sat up on her right side of the bed and flicked on the yellow shaded nightstand lamp. The digital clock under it indicated 6:49 in the morning. The rest of the Americana-style master bedroom came into view. Cork lay on his right shoulder looking myopically up at his wife.

"Just for a week or so," he said. "Take Melanie to Chicago to visit your parents."

"We just saw them over Christmas."

"Well now it's almost – St. Patrick's Day. They'll be thrilled."

"They'll be curious. Almost as much as me. What gives, babe?"

"It's just a good time to get away from DC."

Kathy gazed piercingly at her husband.

"You're trying to get rid of me."

"Don't be silly, darling."

"You've got someone on the side."

"Honey …"

"It's one of my friends, isn't it? Annie Wilson – no, Lynn Stewart. You've always had a crush on Lynn. And she, 'Neil's so smart,

Kathy. So smooth. Why can't I find a guy like him?' Looks like she didn't have to. The original came cheap."

"Lynn said that?" Cork asked, pretending to be intrigued.

"Shut up," Kathy said, an impish smile ruining her jealousy act.

Cork patted the bed near his right hip. Kathy lay down in the proffered spot and nestled against him. He turned serious.

"There are dark forces swirling about Mark and me. I'll be better able to handle them if not having to worry about you and Mel."

"Are you in danger?"

"Not like yesterday. More legal jeopardy, if I know our *federal-istas*. Which I do, having been one for eight years. And they've become even more corrupt since I resigned."

"We're a family, sweetheart," Kathy said. "This is our little house on the prairie."

"Must be why Mark feels so at home here. He's always looking out for Indians."

"There are the Rajanis two houses down."

"Won't do. For Mark, the only good Indian is a red Indian. But I'm serious about you and Mellie leaving town for a week."

"Chicago?" Kathy asked.

She reached under the covers to Cork's groin area, eliciting a gasp of pleasure.

"Maybe that's a bit too far," he said. "How 'bout Cape Cod, my sister's cottage?"

Kathy licked his ear.

"Baltimore?" he asked.

Kathy gave him a fervent kiss.

"I've got a cousin in Georgetown," Cork said, and returned his wife's kiss.

# CHAPTER 20

Amy writhed beneath Slade like a trapped lioness, hissing, clawing, and pulling him into her. He felt her everywhere at once, a sweetness permeating his body, which tingled then rippled then surged with pleasure. He tried to hold back but she drew him out, detonating an explosion of ecstasy. He fell on his back, delightfully drained.

"I must be ten pounds lighter," he said.

Amy rolled to him, warming him with her firm body. "I love you," she said.

"You barely know me."

"I know you're funny and brave, and very, very sexy."

"True," said Slade.

"And only you could've gotten me through this."

"I doubt that, baby. You're a pretty strong chick. Inner strength, not the warrior-woman crap sold by Hollywood, and peddled by our woke generals."

"You got a problem with women in the military?"

"Lot more than the Chinese will when they take us on," said Slade.

"Bah."

"Women cause enough trouble out of uniform," said Slade.

"They're a paradox. They like strength in a guy but do their best to weaken him, like a virus."

"Why do you chase us then?"

"I'm searching for a vaccine."

"Boy," Amy said. "That Nina Holt really infected you."

She brought her luscious mouth to Slade's and gave him a deep wet kiss. They maintained the kiss for a long while until he gently pulled away.

"Amy."

"Mmm hmm."

"I want you to go back to Carolina today."

Amy stiffened.

"All right," she said.

She withdrew from Slade and lay her head on the pillow, looking upset.

"Don't be mad."

"I'm not. I'm disappointed."

"Will you head to Chapel Hill or Gastonia?"

"What do you care?"

"I'd like to know where I can find you," Slade said.

Amy looked hopeful.

"You mean it?"

She rolled to Slade again, her face an inch from his right ear.

"You mean it. You really want me to stay."

"Sure."

"Then let me, Mark. Please. I want to."

"I can't handle the distraction. Cork's going after Owen. I gotta watch his back."

"I thought you liked Sam Owen."

"I do. He stood up for us troops when the new regime did us dirt."

"Then why ...?"

"Neil's my partner, and a man's gotta back his partner even if he's going the wrong way. I can scout ahead, keep him from getting scalped."

"Maybe I can help. I knew Greg better than most." Amy rubbed her right cheek and frowned. "Though not as well as I thought."

"I'll call you if I need you. Even if I don't. Besides, we could use the time apart."

"It won't change how I feel about you."

"It'll restore my energy. Like I'll be able to get up."

"You can get up now." Amy licked Slade's ear.

"I'm not that tough," Slade said.

# CHAPTER 21

Slade carried his bike down the *El Cid* porch steps, with Amy Gallup on his left. It was a bright but cold morning. Slade was dressed in his normal winter riding outfit, green backpack included. The nearby St. Matthew's Church bell began to peel ten times, announcing the second Sunday Mass.

Slade reclined his bike on the two lower steps and walked out to the sidewalk beside Amy. They looked left on Euclid Street for her Uber. Not seeing it, they turned to each other.

"Are you sure about this, baby?" Amy asked.

"No, but that church bell is making up my mind."

"About shunning sex?"

"Let's go with a Day of Rest."

"Then let me lead you into temptation," Amy said with a coy smile.

She brought her mouth to Slade's and kissed him. He returned it until the last bell rang. A grey Subaru hatchback pulled to a stop beside them. Slade opened the right rear door. Amy embraced him tightly.

"I love you," she said, and got into the car.

Slade gave her a small wave as the Subaru pulled away. He watched it make a right on 18$^{th}$ Street. He stood his bike up and started riding in the opposite direction, Billy Idol's "White Wedding" playing through his earbuds.

He'd declined Amy's offer of a lift to her friend's place, though Chain Bridge was much closer to his destination, Cork's house in Glen Echo, Maryland. The long, brisk ride would give him time to reflect – on Adamo's death, Greg's death, his and Cork's near death, Kudzu, and a girlfriend even James Bond would envy. What do you do with them between missions, Mr. Bond?

He made a left on Columbia Road and a quick right on Calvert Street, heading west at a good clip. Zipping past the still closed small shops on the north end of Adams Morgan, he saw a yellow streak out of his left eye. He swerved right too late to dodge the opening car door that clipped his shoulder.

His bike shot right toward the sidewalk, its low elevation a high wall to the vehicle. Just before impact, he yanked up on the handlebars. His front tire jumped the ridge, but the back wheel bumped it. The bicycle slid perilously before rising upright onto the sidewalk. Slade kept flying toward a *Starbucks* patio table section where a young couple looked up from their lattes in shock.

Slade took his shoes out of the toeclips and squeezed the break levers. The bike stopped hard, launching him ten feet onto a plastic table. He bounced off the table into a chairback, knocking it to the ground along with himself. He lay on his bulky backpack like an overturned turtle. A young face under brown hair looked down at him in concern.

"Are you alright?" asked the young woman.

Slade sprang to his feet despite the backpack. He rushed to the sidewalk scanning Calvert Street ahead. A yellow sports car was pulling away fast – too fast for a cyclist to overtake, especially a battered one.

"Aw, hell!" Slade said.

He dashed back to where his bike lay flat on the sidewalk. He got it up and mounted it on the run. He clicked the right earbud control. "Underneath the Radar" by Underworld came on.

Paced by the song, he increased speed, the sports car still distancing. He knew it would soon reach the Duke Ellington Bridge – eight hundred feet of unobstructed roadway high over Rock Creek Park – with no chance of his catching up. But then right before the bridge, the sports car stopped at a red light, the only vehicle in the right westbound lane.

Slade increased his speed, hoping to beat the light change to his prey. Thirty yards away, he knew he'd make it. He closed quickly on the car, hoping its occupants wouldn't spot him. There were two of them, he knew, the driver and the bastard passenger who almost killed him with the door.

"Don't turn around, assholes," Slade said pumping the bike pedals.

With his left hand, he drew the Kryptonite lock from the slot. Twelve yards ahead, the traffic light turned green. The sports car began moving as Slade overtook its right tire.

A trim-bearded Arab profile in the window turned his way. A silencer rose behind the window to point at him. Slade swung the Kryptonite lock at it, its crossbar acting as a hammerhead. Glass shattered into bits, pelting the Arab and the curly-haired driver. The sports car swerved left then right, and struckthe bridge railing just behind the speeding Slade.

The gun had raised the stakes, Slade knew, from cat and mouse to life and death. Pedaling hard, he took a backward look. The sports car was stopped at a right angle against the low railing separating the road and walkway. Arab and Curly were no doubt clearing glass shards from their eyes,. Slade calculated they'd be coming after him before he reached the bridge's end - six-hundred feet away with no closer exit.

A hundred feet below him on his right spanned Rock Creek Park in a breathtaking view. Slade hoped it wouldn't be the last breath he took. He swung right through the last gap in the railing into the walkway-bike path. The rail would block a car door from hitting him but not a bullet.

He rode west at full velocity, taking constant looks over his left shoulder. A backward glance at mid-bridge confirmed his fear. The sports car was moving again and closing fast. He somehow increased his speed, knowing it would only buy him a few seconds.

A sight ahead pinged his brain – the oncoming stream of east-bound pedestrians ready to enjoy Sunday in Adams Morgan. Slade rode straight at them. A father and two young daughters cringed before sidestepping out of his improvised bike path.

The sports car appeared lleft of him just outside the railing. It matched his speed, the Arab and his silencer visible at the window. Slade weaved between pedestrians, protected by them while endangering them.

A woman yelled at him as he flew by, in words unsuitable for her children. People dodged his bike all the way to the end of the bridge at Calvert Street and Woodley Place. He made a right on Woodley. Looking back, he saw the sports car do the same, only to get delayed by crossing pedestrians.

"You don't want to break up our friendship," he said, imitating Eli Wallach in *The Good, The Bad, and the Ugly*. "Well, I'll break it."

He flew down the steep two-lane road, Bruce Cockburn's "If I Had a Rocket Launcher" playing in his earbuds. At the bottom of the hill, Woodley Place merged into Rock Creek Park. Then so did Slade. He knew the sports car would be right behind him but his odds would soon improve. The park road was closed to cars on Sunday.

Throngs of adults and kids walked the parkway near the National Zoo, as cyclists zoomed past them on the right-side bike path. Slade cut across a strip of lawn onto the path. He rode toward a chest-high boulder near the black iron zoo gate.

He dismounted his bike on the move. He leaned it against the left side of the boulder and dashed behind the boulder. Keeping an eye on the road and parkway merger, he took off his backpack and unzipped it.

The sports car came downhill fast then breaked hard, blocked by the heavy foot traffic. Arab and Curly jumped out of the car, leaving its blinkers on. Arab wore a long blue parka and jeans, Curly a khaki jacket and jeans. They scanned the passing people with their hands inside their coats.

Curly turned to the boulder and stiffened. He tapped Arab on the shoulder, nodding at Slade's bike against the rock. The pair joined the flow of south-moving pedestrians to approach the boulder. Slade popped up behind the rock and yelled at the crowd.

"The lion is loose! Run for your lives!"

The crowd motion froze, as did Arab and Curly. Everyone stared at Slade and the expression of sheer terror on his face.

"He bit the zookeeper's arm off!" he cried.

A young mother scooped up her toddler and retreated from the zoo fence. A father did the same with his teen daughter. A flight of pedestrians soon followed, clearing the area around Arab, Curly, and a little boy.

"I wanna see the lion," said the boy, just before his mother yanked him away.

The now isolated Arab and Curly glanced around their empty area, then at Slade behind the rock. He returned their look only now without projecting fear. They started moving toward him, each man pulling a black silencer-tipped pistol from inside his coat.

Slade's right hand came up with his own gun – a Combat Magnum revolver Model 66 with silver barrel and black handle. He shot Arab in the forehead and spun his gun to Curly, who aimed too late. Slade fired once at his chest. Four shots struck the boulder as Curly fell back to the grass a few feet from his partner.

A police siren wailed nearby. Slade placed his pistol on top of the boulder and circled it to reach his bicycle. On the bike path, several cyclists stopped to point their cellphones at him and the two dead men. He sat down on the lawn next to the bike and leaned his back against the rock, both hands behind his head. The last part of "If I Had a Rocket Launcher" played in his ears.

*If I had a rocket launcher*
*If I had a rocket launcher*
*If I had a rocket launcher*
*Some son-of-a-bitch would die.*

# CHAPTER 22

"The Gunfight at Rock Creek Park," groaned Cork. "Slade finally did it."

He sank deeper into his brown polyurethane armchair facing the stone fireplace. It was his favorite seat in the living room Kathy had tastefully designed. Steam rose from the tea in his purple mug with the white GU eagle in the right cup holder. On the left armrest lay his cellphone, screen up, Lieutenant Wallace on the line in speaker mode.

"He killed two men. Witnesses said they drew first."

"That makes it all right then," Cork said sarcastically. "The Code of the West!"

"Looks good for self-defense. Slade's still in jail though."

"Great, keep him there."

"Not our jail," Wallace said. "U.S. Park Police, Anacostia Station."

"They'd better watch their horses. Mark's likely to make a jail-break on one of them."

"They use motorcycles now."

"He rides them too," said Cork.

"I know the inspector in charge, Will Nakia. Good man. He said your former outfit put a gag order on his crew. But he did share one item with me. Slade's shooters had gun suppressors."

"Like the man who killed Paul Adamo."

"No longer my case," said Wallace. "Keep me posted, Cork."

The line clicked off. Cork stood up and crossed the living room to the foyer. He pulled his green wool sweater out of the coat closet and put it on. He opened the front door out to his frost-covered small yard. The phone rang in his sweater pocket. He checked the caller ID and stepped back into the house, pushing the door shut. He put the phone back on speaker mode.

"Hey, Alan," he said distractedly.

"Some greeting," said the voice on the line."After all the times I made you look good on the job."

"Sorry, man, something just came up."

"And went down," said Alan. "A firefight in Rock Creek Park involving your partner."

Cork tensed. "You heard."

"The name Mark Slade, linked to the Capitol Hill Sniper – along with yours."

"Wilcox took over that case," said Cork.

"No kidding. He called me into work today. Questioned me for half an hour – about you."

"That's no good."

"Meet me at the old spot in an hour. And try to look different. They may be watching me."

The line clicked off. Cork headed upstairs.

--- --- ---

The outdoor Frank Delano Roosevelt Memorial has four square marble chambers, one for each of FDR's terms, with quotes from the specific term inscribed on the smooth stone walls. Cork entered the Third Term chamber wearing a curly black wig over his prescription sunglasses. Near the bronze statue of the 32$^{nd}$ President, sitting of course, and his Scottish Terrier, Fala, stood Alan Nichols holding a paper coffee cup.

Nichols had gained weight and lost hair in the two years since

Cork last saw him. He wore a long vanilla coat with brown fur and grey slacks. He didn't react when Cork walked right past him to the back wall, not until Cork began reading aloud the words inscribed there.

"They who seek to establish systems of government based on the regimentation of all human beings by a handful of individual rulers call this a New Order. It is not new, and it is not an order."

Cork turned to Nichols, who was staring at him with mouth agape.

"You said look different," Cork said. "I gather I succeeded."

"Where'd you get that wig?"

"It was my mom's chemo wig. I kept it as a memento."

"Right, sorry about Marilyn. She was a great lady."

"She was," said Cork. "You're looking robust, Alan."

"You mean rotund, yeah. And Pam can't cook as good as Kathy. How is Kathy?"

"Fine. She still hates fishing."

"I knew we should've stuck to bowling," said Nichols.

"She's away right now with our daughter."

"Yeah? Where?"

"Out of town,"

Nichols nodded. "Smart move. In your place I'd do the same thing."

"Just where am I, Alan?"

"Right now, way too conspicuous."

Nichols nodded at the white stone bench near the right wall. He and Cork moved to it, Nichols favoring his right leg. They sat down on the slab.

"The ankle still bothering you?" asked Cork.

"Never should've kicked that door in like Mel Gibson."

"For a little Russian hacker."

"I can still predict the weather with it," said Nichols. "You could be hit by lightning any day now. Somebody up there doesn't like you."

"Wilcox?"

"Higher than that."

"The Director?"

"Keep going."

"Not the A.G.?"

"He's running scared, Neil. The big guy's driving him nuts."

"The President. No wonder. He's getting crushed in the polls by the man they tried to destroy, who's out for revenge."

"And Bureau blood," said Nichols.

"To survive, the Regime needs a scandal that will smear the opposition. Like a secret right-wing network working against the government – Kudzu."

"That would help."

"I had one of them, Alan," said Cork. "Right in front of me. He was shot."

"Johnathan Woods. Wilcox was hot to grab him. He blames you for getting him killed."

"Is he crazy? I was shot at too. Slade saved my life, along with his own."

"Wilcox knows that. Shows you how badly he wants to flush Kudzu."

"Hope he has better luck than I did," said Cork. "They're shrouded by Senator Owen, as we learned on the Koenig case."

"Owen has too much clout for our people to harass him. You and Slade, not so much."

"So, the trick for us is to uproot Kudzu just enough to keep Wilcox off our back and Owen off our chest."

"You always were a good analyst, Neil. I can help point you in the right direction."

"Feel free to start now," Cork said. "The team that attacked Slade – you ID them yet?"

"We're working on it."

"Why was Woods tailing Greg Bradford?"

Nichols glanced around the chamber before answering. "We believe Bradford copied something off of Owen's server. Something so clandestine, Owen couldn't notify the proper agencies, including us. Something they call the Apocalypse Mask."

"Sounds apocalyptic."

"'It's the greatest threat America has ever faced.'That's what Owen told a closed session of the Intelligence Committee. He said nothing more about the thing, other than he'd introduce it on the Senate floor – once it was neutralized. He didn't want any leaks."

"What he got was worse," Cork said.

"You're right. Last Monday, all hell broke loose at Owen's office. According to his aides, total strangers were seen going in and out of there and given unprecedented access to the Senator. One of them was the late John Woods."

"Kudzu people."

"Looks that way," said Alan. "We find them, we find what they're after."

"The Apocalypse Mask," said Cork.

"You can help us, Neil – help me. I've got a wife and kid now. I could use the promotion."

Cork nodded. "I'll need Slade on this – and out of the federal prison system."

"I'll see if I can swing it. But if you guys get nailed, I can't help you. And Wilcox likes to impress the boss by putting people in jail."

"Great," said Cork. "I'll be stuck with Slade forever."

Chapter Tw+enty-Four

The US Park Police Criminal Investigation Branch office was a small, square, well-heated room on the third and top floor of Anacostia Station. The rear window provided a darkening view of DC across the Anacostia River. Three pine desks honored the agency's timberland beat, as did the poster on the left wall of Hoh Rain Forest in Olympic National Park.

Only the right desk was occupied, by an attractive young Japanese woman in a blue blazer working the desktop computer. Cork could distinguish the physical differences between Asian peoples thanks to his FBI training at Quantico. This skill had helped him ferret out several Chinese and North Korean agents in the Nation's Capital.

Cork and Inspector Will Nakia stood by the printer now flicking out crime scene photocopies of the two dead men taken shortly after Mark Slade snuffed out their lives.

"The one without the hole in the head should be easier to ID," Nakia said. He was a thirty-something native Indian with a body-builder physique in red-flannel shirt and jeans on what had to be Casual Dress Sunday. He pulled the pages off the printer and handed them to Cork.

"Your friend nailed them both with two shots. One guy barely managed to return fire. Where'd Slade learn to shoot like that – the Army?"

"Tombstone," said Cork, st+udying the pictures.

"Arizona?"

"Hollywood. The Rangers only honed his marksmanship."

"Good enough for a Bronze Star," said Nakia. "My dad was real proud of his from Vietnam."

"Slade's war had the same sad ending."

"And the same bad leaders."

"They're why I quit the Bureau," Cork said.

"Don't blame you. They're going full blast on this case. Their AD told me to shut it down and spring your friend. I said yes, officially."

"And unofficially?"

"I'm pursuing our investigation," Nakia said, turning to his office mate. "Julie, what've you got?"

"Chest Wound was Theodore Paretsky," Detective Julie said, reading her desktop screen. "Born Montreal, Quebec, August 14, 1989. Education – NYU. Occupation – bartender, The Catacombs. Two misdemeanor arrests for trespassing, 2019 and '22. That's what gave us a print match."

"Trespassing?" Cork asked Julie.

She looked at Nakia, who nodded.

"Climate change protests at the Capitol and White House," she said. "Organized by Green Strike."

"I support Green-peace," said Cork.

"They're way too tame for today's eco-warriors," Nakia said.

"Pistol silencers would seem a bit extreme even for them."

"Or Islamic terrorists," said Nakia, turning to Julie. "Anything on Head Wound?"

"No, sir," she said. "You'll be the first to know."

Nakia nodded at her to Cork. "We get wise gals now."

Cork viewed the crime scene photo of a yellow sports car.

"What about the car?" he asked.

"Bogus tag number."

"Suggests a high level of sophistication – and premeditation."

"Yeah," said Nakia. "Wasn't road rage nearly killed your partner. By the way, I'm releasing him into your custody."

"Can I waive that honor?"

Nakia smiled. "Julie, take Mr. Cork to the prisoner and let him out."

"Yes, sir," Julie said, rising to her feet.

Two minutes later, Julie and Cork were buzzed into the detention center on the ground floor. A uniform-stretching Park Ranger led them toward the cell area. They could hear Slade's Dean Martin-style crooning before they saw him.

*"Purple line on the canyon,*
*That's where I long to be,*
*With my three good companions,*
*Just my rifle, my pony and me."*

Cork and Julie reached twin small cells with Slade the only occupant. He sat on a concrete slab in the right cell, singing.

*"Gonna hang my sombrero,*
*On the limb of a tree,*
*Comin' home, sweetheart darlin',*
*With my rifle, my pony, and me.*
*Whippoorwill ..."*

Slade quit singing at the sight of Cork and Julie. The Park Ranger slid open the steel-barred door.

"You're free to go, Mr. Slade," Julie said.

"Good," said Slade. "Saved me the trouble of busting out of here."

Cork grimaced. Walking out of the cell, Slade addressed the Park Ranger.

"Could I see something a little roomier?"

Cork shook his head and Julie smiled. She and the partners followed Park Ranger to the "unwelcome" desk. He disappeared behind it into a walk-in storage closet and came out rolling Slade's Cervelo. Slade inspected his bike as Park Ranger reentered the closet.

"Looks okay," he said.

Park Ranger placed Slade's backpack on the desktop. Slade quickly rummaged through it.

"Where's my gun?" he asked.

"We're withholding it as evidence," Julie said. "You're lucky it was registered, or you'd be in serious trouble."

# CHAPTER 23

Cork drove his black Mercedes SUV west on Canal Road, Slade beside him, his bike in the hatch. The low headlight beams shed light on the rustic two-lane expressway, free of buildings and lights.

"The Apocalypse Mask," Slade said.

"It's the end of the world as we know it."

"Good '80s song. But didn't Owen specify a threat to America?"

"We are the world, Mark."

"Bad '80s song. The country's pretty shaky already, thanks to President Zombie and his Marxist band."

"We're on thin ice ourselves."

"You mean the feds on one side, Kudzu on the other, and us right in the middle, one step away from jail or more bullets?"

"I've been thinking about that," said Cork. "They used a car door on you first. No guarantee of fatality. Which suggests -"

"They'd've settled for a bad spill, and me in traction."

"But you being you, you couldn't let them get away with that, thus forcing their gun hand."

"Reckless of me."

"Though quite in character. I wouldn't be you for anything. But sometimes, when I encounter rudeness, ignorance, or malice, I almost envy you."

"Really?"

"Then I come to my senses."

The friends shared a chuckle. Cork turned serious again.

"Let's assume your assailants' original intent was to incapacitate you for some time. What does that imply?"

"They're on some kind of deadline," said Slade.

"Same as we – to find the Apocalypse Mask."

"And stop the Apocalypse."

"Or cause it," Cork said.

The road ahead appeared suddenly darker. Slade spoke into the gloom.

"Could be either one of 'em with that motive, couldn't it? Kudzu or your old crew."

"That's where we are," Cork said. "I disliked the last President. He was an obnoxious boor, but a duly elected one. What my superiors had us do to neutralize him, in league with the other party – fabricating collusion, spying on his people, outright undermining him – that I couldn't countenance. So, I resigned."

"Now he's a few months away from coming back – and kicking ass."

"The guillotine will fall on the DOJ. They'll do anything to save their necks."

"Even kill?"

Cork hesitated before answering. "I don't know," he said. "That's what scares me."

"And just when you thought you were out, they pull you back in!" declared Slade, imitating Al Pacino in *The Godfather, Part III.*

"I had little choice in the matter. I wanted you out of jail."

Cork veered the Audi right onto MacArthur Boulevard, a major street lit by lampposts, traffic signals, and modest store windows.

"The guys I put down weren't FBI," Slade said. "Unless silencers are standard issue."

"No, nor for Kudzu either. They're too tied to Senator Owen. Woods was unarmed."

"Jesus, Cork. You know what that means?"

"A third faction," said Cork.

"It ain't a two-way gunfight. It's *The Good, the Bad, and the Ugly.*"

"With us as the gravestone."

"So why bury me instead of you? No offense."

"There are three possibilities," Cork said. "One – you were first on their hit list, with me to follow. Two – they dread a loose cannon more than an analytical mind. Three – you know something I don't that may foil their plans."

"I told you everything I know."

"Everything you think you know. Perhaps not everything *they* think you know – or you don't know you know."

"You lost me," said Slade.

"I'm still working it out. Just keep doing what you do – causing havoc. We'll see which tree bears fruit."

"Or hides another shooter."

"That's the downside of my plan," Cork said.

The car passed the white *Welcome to Maryland* sign. MacArthur Boulevard became a snaking suburban road with a chain of hills on the right, houselights flickering atop them.

"Speaking of shooters," said Slade. "Tell me more about the one the Park Police ID'd."

"Theodore Paretsky. When not trying to kill you, he was a climate change activist and a bartender at the Catacombs."

"Must'a been a lousy bartender."

"Why do you say that?"

"He made a bad kamikaze," said Slade.

The car paused at the first Maryland traffic light on Goldsboro Road, now red. A neon marquee on the left proclaimed "Glen Echo Park", the former amusement park turned cultural center famous for its historic hundred-year-old carousel. Slade noted the small rose-brick shopping center across Goldsboro.

“Should we grab some beer? I missed the jailhouse rock.”

“Kathy left me a few bottles before she took off this morning,” said Cork. “And some harder stuff for the Slade-induced headache.”

He turned right on red. The car passed white-pillared houses on the left and rising woods on the right with more houselights beyond, including Cork’s. Fifty yards further, Cork made the first right at a vintage sign for *Tulip Hill.*

The residential street curved rightward and upward between well-lit upscale homes. A dark sedan came down the hill in the other lane then past Cork’s car. Slade spied two large male silhouettes in front, one in back.

At the top of the hill, Cork turned right into the left side driveway of a pleasant single-level stone house. It was the only home around with less than two stories, excluding the partially submerged basement. Slade got out of the car as Cork clicked open the rear hatch.

Slade extracted his bike and backpack from the SUV. Pulling down the hatch, he felt a chill in his spine. He’d learned to trust that sensation in Sandland. Twice it had signaled a hidden shooter targeting him.

He scanned the well-lit residential street and the cars in the driveways. IAn unfamiliar vehicle in this neighborhood would prompt multiple 911 calls, especially at night. Slade rolled his bike to the walkway some twelve feet behind Cork.

He watched Cork climb the three porch steps. Saw him move his keychain toward the lock, halt, then push in the clearly unlocked door. Slade heard the gasp from nine feet ahead. Letting his bike fall on the grass, he ran up the porch steps to join Cork at the doorway.

Even in the semi-darkness, he could see the living room in shambles. The blue sofa by the rear window was de-cushioned. Cork’s faux-leather armchair lay on its left side, the bottom cloth torn to strips. All four drawers of Kathy’s rustic maple cabinet on the carpet, their contents strewn about them. And that was just what Slade could glimpse from the doorway.

“Doesn’t take long for a house to get messy,” he said.

# CHAPTER 24

Slade grabbed the poker from the fireplace. A brooding Cork followed him to the study's double doors, the left one slightly ajar. Slade yanked it open all the way, ready to strike. Seeing no one, he stepped into the windowless library. Cork switched on the ceiling light.

Hardback books, some classically bound, lay spilled on the brown carpet, swept off the wall-to-wall dark wood shelves. Files and documents covered the chestnut desk facing the doorway from the right rear corner. Cork spoke low through gritted teeth.

"They made a thorough search of it. But didn't get what they were looking for."

"The Apocalypse Mask," Slade said equally low.

The partners went out the left rear door. They turned right into a short hallway terminating at the left wall of the house. A cross-corridor ran from the door on the right – to the master bedroom, Slade knew – to another door at the far end. Cork put his hand on the nearer doorknob.

"I'll check this room out by myself," he whispered intensely.

"What if they're still in there?" Slade whispered back.

"The way I feel right now, it'll be a fair fight."

"Here, you might need this," said Slade, handing Cork the poker.

Cork entered the room. Slade moved toward the slightly open door at the other end of the hall, his brain pinging like a sonar strike. He stepped into the dark nursery. Instinct kept him from flicking up the light switch.

Streetlight penetrated the pink lambkin-decorated curtain on the window. Slade took in the baby crib by the left wall and the plastic adult chair beside it. He moved the chair to the window and sat down facing it. Lifting the curtain half an inch, he peered out to the street.

Cork's SUV was parked in the driveway just to his right, by the row of pine hedges demarking the neighbor's yard. Across the street, atop a long ridge, stood two houses, their uphill driveways leading to frontal garage doors. Cork's garage was in the back of the house at the bottom of the driveway, Slade knew, requiring a U-turn to access it.

He placed his cellphone on the windowsill with a quick glance at the time – 9:14 PM. He donned his earbuds and clicked on "Der Kommissar" by Falco. At 9:39, during the Police's "Every Little Thing You Do is Magic," he barely heard Cork's voice.

"Mark."

"In here," Slade said, removing his earbuds.

He turned to see Cork reaching for the light switch.

"Don't."

Cork dropped his hand and approached Slade.

"What's wrong?"

Slade pointed to the window.

"Look up at the roof," he said.

Cork did so. "I don't see anything."

"Wait for it."

Cork continued staring up for half a minute.

"Any second now," Slade said, glancing at his cellphone screen clock then the window. "There."

A kite-size shadow with four protruding propeller bars flew out past the roof overhang. It curved rightward over the driveway to the side of the house then out of sight.

"Drone," Cork said nervously.

"Unarmed."

"You sure?"

"I saw enough armed birds in Sandland," said Slade. "That one's strictly for surveillance. It's how they knew you weren't home, so they could search the house. And when you came back. They pulled up stakes just before we got here. I thought I saw 'em on the drive in – three guys in a dark sedan."

"Who the hell are they?"

"The Good, the Bad, or the Ugly."

"We'd better label them for future reference," Cork said. "The Good – FBI."

Slade smirked.

"I know, I know – a questionable 'good'," Cork said. "The Bad – Kudzu. The Ugly – whoever hired your assailants."

"All three could afford that thing," said Slade, pointing at the window.

"What are we going to do about it?"

"First – calm you down with some Slade tonic."

Twelve minutes later, Slade sat on the re-cushioned living-room sofa in T-shirt and sweatpants with both feet on the wood coffee table, appraising his restoration work. The room looked somewhat normal again – the faux-leather armchair upright, the antique cabinet re-drawered. Cork emerged from the doorless dining room carrying a green liquor bottle and two whiskey glasses. He appraised the room.

"Thanks for the home improvement," he said.

Slade nodded. Cork placed the three items on the coffee table.

"Speaking of," said Slade. "How's the master bedroom?"

"More like mistress bedroom," Cork said, sitting down on Slade's left. "It's Kathy's domain. Thank God she didn't see how they defiled it. Though she'll know, no matter how well I tidy up."

"Good thing you ran her out of town this morning."

"She may soon return the favor," said Cork.

He filled the two glasses with whiskey. Slade approved of the bottle label, Ardberg. They clinked glasses. Cork put his feet on the coffee table. Slade took a sip of Scotch.

"Mm. Good stuff, Cork."

"Aye, laddie."

"So," said Slade. "They don't have the Apocalypse Mask – and trashed your house looking for…? What, physically? Some kind of computer chip?"

"A painting," Cork said. "By Paul Adamo."

Slade paused in mid whiskey sip. "Why do you say that?"

"Combination of things," said Cork. "Starting with Greg's tirade at the gallery yesterday. Remember what he said. 'There's a surprise coming that will shake this shitty country – like nothing ever has."

"And you took that seriously."

"In hindsight, yes, given what followed. You know Kathy's very Catholic, right?"

"She thinks the current Pope's a heretic," said Slade.

"We listen to Father Jack Sterling's podcast at bedtime. A scholarly overview of the Bible, from Genesis to the last book, Revelation - lesser known as the Apocalypse."

"Holy shit."

"Literally," said Cork.

Slade took a whisky gulp.

"My theory as follows," Cork said. "Greg takes the Apocalypse Mask from Senator Owen's private safe. Gives it to Paul Adamo, perhaps at his behest. Adamo, being not only a passionate artist but a radical leftist, grafts both personae into one masterpiece that will, quote, 'shake the world.' Somehow, he fused the Mask into his painting, *Revelation*, which was all set to display at the Winger Gallery. He was delivering a painting there in the wee hours when he was shot."

"So, whoever killed Adamo has the painting," Slade said.

"But the wrong one."

"How do you know?"

Cork did a hand sweep of the house. Slade understood.

"Else why search this place?"

"Only the Ugly knew the true value of the painting," said Cork. "And that's because, according to you, Adamo was negotiating with them."

Slade scanned his memory. "'I'll tell that rich bitch it's where every fool can look at it,' he said. 'The longer it's up, the closer to Judgment Day.'"

"Judgment Day," reflected Cork. " Of course. The deadline isn't *by* some date –"

"It's on that date," said Cork.

"The event which will trigger the Apocalypse."

"And everyone but us seems to know what that is, and when."

"Not for long," said Cork.

He downed his whisky in one swallow, surprising Slade.

"We're going to find that painting, 'Revelation', extractthe Apocalypse Mask, and bring down the whole rotten crowd – the Good, the Bad, and the Ugly."

"Why, Neil," said Slade. "You're sounding like me. Okay, a more Richard Burton version of me."

"Let's get some sleep," Cork said. "We'll hit Adamo's place at dawn."

"I could use a shower first," said Slade. "That jail cell was no Bed and Breakfast."

Cork started to stand up but stopped, looking downcast. He pointed a thumb at the wide window behind him.

"I forgot about that flying eyeball out there."

"I may be able to blind it," said Slade.

"That I'd like to see."

"Not yet, or they'd just send a backup. Right before we leave."

"What do you have in mind?"

"When was the last time you played paintball war?" Slade said.

# CHAPTER 25

Slade stepped through the garage door into the basement. The paintball rifle felt light in his hands – much lighter than the Barrett M95 he'd borne for seven years. He'd loaded it in the garage, where Cork kept it, and by flashlight, to not alert the drone pilot into changing the three-minute orbits. The next pass over the back yard would come at zero-four-forty-nine hours – 4:49 AM cellphone time.

Wearing his conveniently dark Army sweat jacket, Slade moved left through the den to the rear sliding glass door. The interior darkness helped him ignore the mess all around him. Cork's visitors had ransacked the den too.

Slade stood before the door glass, staring up at the moonlit cumulus clouds. Forty-three seconds later, the black drone crossed his view, circling clockwise over the roof. He slid open the back door and shut it behind him.

Wielding the rifle in front of him, he ran past the garage and across the widened driveway . He jumped over the wood post into the neighbor's back yard then darted left beside the pine hedges paralleling Cork's driveway. Midway to the street, he ducked behind one hedge.

He peered over the shrub at the area between Cork's roof and the

SUV. The drone entered the airspace, circling clockwise some sixty feet above the driveway. It flew slowly past the nursery's side window as if basking in its voyeuristic power.

Slade sprang to his full height, aiming the rifle over the hedge. The drone halted in mid-air and began rising fast. Slade fired twice, pelting the aircraft with white paint. He followed with four more shots, splattering the whole drone white. It withdrew across the street toward the left hill house wobbling the whole way. It cleared the roof but smashed into the chimney, and dropped like a dead bird.

Slade approached the street with his weapon lowered. Rounding the hedgerow, he heard the locks click on Cork's SUV. He moved around the vehicle to see its owner approaching from the walkway in a heavy wool sweater. Cork pointed at the gun in Slade's hand.

"Superb paint job."

"Better than Paul Adamo," Slade said, and pointed to the rooftop crash site. "Now that thing won't be going our way."

He opened the SUV's rear right door and threw in the rifle, then climbed into the front passenger seat. Cork behind the wheel. He backed the car out of the driveway and drove it past the hill house on the right. Nothing airlifted off the roof.

# CHAPTER 26

Slade dozed through most of the traffic-free trip east to Capitol Hill. On Meridian Street, Cork drove slowly past Adamo's rowhouse. He and the awoken Slade eyed the yellow police tape threading the front door.

"I'm assuming that's the house," said Cork.

"All gift-wrapped for us.""Good thing you know the back way in."

"I still have the callouses," said Slade.

Cork stopped the car at the eastern corner and Slade jumped out. He jogged down the sidewalk to the alley behind Adamo's row. He ducked right into the alley and ran to the familiar yellow house, back fence, and oak tree.

He repeated his actions from two nights before – over the fence and up the tree to the high branch outside the bedroom window, now totally dark. Shining his flashlight's pin beam on the windowpane, he noted the slight crack beneath it. He edged as close to the window as the oak branch would support him.

He stretched his right leg to the windowsill and wedged the stiff toe of his bike shoe into the crack. By strenuous ankle lifting, hehe managed to raise the window all the way. He stood up on his tree branch and grabbed a flimsy higher one. With an untimely glance at the concrete patio twenty long feet below, he leapt over it, and caught the windowsill with both hands. He pulled himself up, then through the window and into the bedroom.

Cork appeared to be strolling on the sidewalk near the front door when Slade opened it, ripping down some of the police tape.

"What took you?" Cork asked.

"Very funny."

Cork dashed up the porch steps. Maneuvering his frame through the remaining yellow tape, he entered the house. Slade shut the door behind him.

Slade pin-lit the ground floor. The staircase rose directly ahead across a short corridor. It led to a closet door on the right and an open den on the left. The two men went left.

Slade's moving beam revealed a de-cushioned white sofa, two unmatching armchairs, and a forty-inch television atop a long empty bookshelf, its paperback and DVD contents spilled on the threadbare brown carpet.

"Bedroom's a mess too," Slade said. "I'd say you and Adamo had the same company."

"And they came up empty here as well, ahead of the police."

"They hit your place next. Either the Bad or the Ugly."

"Right," said Cork. "The Good would've used a search warrant - thenwrecked my house."

They moved right through the small dining room with a two-seat wood table, and right again into the compact kitchen. The refrigerator stood a foot forward from its obvious wall spot. The cupboards were open. Vegetable and soup cans lay on the stove and floor. The back door led out to the courtyard.

They recrossed the living room to the staircase. Slade's beam illuminated their climb. The second-floor corridor led to a bathroom door on the right and a closet door on the left. The master bedroom was across the hall next to the bathroom. There was a second bedroom door to the left of it. Cork and Slade went through it and into Adamo's art studio.

Slade moved his pin light from left to right. An antique wood desk faced the left wall with an open laptop and a stack of bills beside it, an empty easel on a tripod by the right wall, and a work shelf storing small multi-colored paint containers and paintbrushes. The half open back window dissipated the faint smell of turpentine while chilling the room.

Cork indicated the empty easel. "There stood the painting Adamo was dropping off at the gallery when they shot him."

"Not *Revelation*."

"No, though his killers must have thought it was – being fresh off the easel."

"Why would they think you had the right one?" Slade asked.

"For the same reason they attacked you," Cork said. "They think we know more than we do. And we had better justify their faith in us before they strike again."

He moved left toward the desk and the Mac laptop on it, his path lighted by Slade.

"Nice of them to leave his laptop," Slade said.

"They didn't want it virtually tracked to their lair. So, they just accessed it right here."

"Can you?"

Cork sat down in the desk chair and turned on the laptop. The screensaver showed a Renaissance portrait of a handsome, muscular, brunette young man – naked but for a white loin cloth and a mostly fallen red tunic – against a dark background.

"Now that's real art," said Slade.

"'John the Baptist'," said Cork. "Adamo doubtless admired Caravaggio as a fellow dashing, rebellious, probably queer painter. And they had one more thing in common. They both died young under suspicious circumstances."

Cork tapped a laptop key. The new screen page requested a password.

"How frustrating."

"It's nearly dawn," said Slade. "We don't have time to play Password."

"Whoever hacked this laptop did – and entered it."

"How would they have known it?"

"Password Key," Cork said.

"I left mine at home."

"You couldn't afford it. Neither can I. But the buyer of that drone could."

"What is it?" asked Slade.

"A portable device that searches for the most frequently sequenced keys on a keyboard and extrapolates any words or numbers that may form a password. We used one at the Bureau in my last two years there."

Cork looked at the half dozen bills by the laptop, and the black inkjet pen beside them.

"Of course, it helps to jot down the potential passwords for easy access," he said.

He flipped over two bills and studied the third.

"Like this for instance."

Cork plopped down a DC Power company bill with two hand-printed words crossed out in black ink, and a third word unblemished. Slade shone the light beam on it and read aloud.

"Chiaro-scuro."

"*Chiaroscuro*," Cork said with an Italian pronunciation. "The sharp contrast between dark and light. Caravaggio was an early master of the style. As you see –"

He indicated the laptop, where a different Caravaggio screen-saver had appeared – a cute, plump young man with a flowery head-dress, half out of his toga against a dark background.

"'The Young Bacchus'," said Cork. "Let's bring forth some light from the darkness."

He tapped a key, which brought back the password entry slot. He typed in *chiaroscuro*. After a long tensemoment, the icon menu appeared on the screen.

"Bravo," said Slade.

Cork clicked on the *Bank of America* icon. The BOA access page came up with the preset user word - *Caravaggio1610* - and the hidden preset password. Cork pressed enter. A bank statement materialized. Cork scrolled down the data.

Slade went to the window. The night sky looked lighter already. He turned to Cork.

"Whadda ya got?"

"Adamo's bank statement," said Cork. "He was indeed a starving artist – till last Tuesday, when he came into some money, via direct deposit."

"How much?"

"Two-hundred-fifty thousand dollars."

Slade let out a whistle.

"It would seem he sold a painting," said Cork. "After giving it his special brushstroke."

"The Apocalypse Mask ... Who made the deposit?"

"Your favorite group – Green Strike."

Slade groaned. "A commie outfit that uses bad weather to trash capitalism."

"They're a little extreme."

"That's like calling the KKK a little prejudiced," said Slade. "But why would they spend so much money on a painting?"

"Clearly someone thereknew its real value. And used the group as a front to buy it. A major donor perhaps."

"'That rich bitch.' Adamo said. Whoever she is – she made the deal for *Revelation*."

"But Adamo craved more than money." Cork said. "He wanted recognition as a world-changing artist. And that was something the Ugly could not afford to give him."

"So, they paid him off in lead."

"Misbelieving they'd redeemed their purchase. Only Adamo had switched paintings on them."

"And a lot of good it did him," said Slade.

"I'll go through the Green Strike donors list at home."

A flash of light drew Slade's eye to the window then the alley below it. An unlit police car was cruising slowly toward Adamo's back fence, revealed by the dawn's early light. Slade turned off the flashlight.

"Cops."

Cork slammed shut the laptop.

"They trip-wired it," he said.

Slade looked out the window. The patrol car stopped two houses short of Adamo's. No home numbers in back, Slade realized. A temporary break.. The cops would soon correct the error, guided by their partners out front.

"Let's get out of here," said Slade.

He led Cork out to the corridor and down the now clearer staircase. Rounding the left railing, Slade froze. Cork went past him toward the front door.

"Stop!" Slade said.

Cork did. A flashing red police car light passed across the upper door glass.

"This way!"

Cork followed Slade right through the living room, then right again into the kitchen. They heard banging on the front door.

"Police!" a male voice yelled. "Open the door!"

Cork grabbed the rear doorknob and tried to turn it. The knob didn't budge. More loud pounding sounded from the front of the house, followed by the same voice.

"We're coming in! Have your hands up or we'll shoot!"

Cork struggled against the doorknob without success.

"What's the penalty for breaking-and-exiting?" Slade asked.

Cork pressed a tiny latch on the bottom of the doorknob, which spun in his hand. He pulled open the door, revealing a three-step drop to the courtyard. He held the door open for Slade.

Slade moved toward it, kicking a white espresso cup on the floor. His brain pinged. He grabbed the cup, then its fallen twin off the countertop, and went out the back door. Cork did too, closing it quietly behind him. They heard the front door getting kicked.

In the small courtyard, Cork started for the fence gate. Slade ran after him and grabbed the back of his sweater, stopping him. Slade pointed at the right-side fence demarking the neighbor's back yard. Cork nodded.The partners hurried to the fence.

Slade interlocked his fingers and lowered them to Cork's knee level. Cork placed his foot in the cradle. Slade boosted him over the fence, then scaled the fence without help, the two coffee cups clanging in his pouch.

The neighbor's courtyard was the same size and shape as Adamo's, only treeless and with two green iron chairs minus cushions. One chair faced the alley gate, the other Adamo's fence. Slade nodded at the house.

"Just hope they're still asleep in there," he whispered.

gHe pointed to the chair facing Adamo's oak tree. Cork sat down in it. Slade handed him one of the expresso cups and took over the other chair. He held the mug like it was full of hot coffee, Cork copying him.

"'High Noon' sucks," Slade said, projecting his voice at the alley gate, away from the house. "Gary Cooper scurries all over town like a scared rabbit, begging shopkeepers and bankers for help against four outlaws. What kind of Marshall is he?"

A flashlight beam appeared outside the gate pointing at them through the boards.

"It's an allegory about McCarthyism," said Cork, anxiously eying the light beam. "Which was quite prevalent at the time."

"'Cause Hollywood was full of commies. It took John Wayne to run them out of town, and Ronald Reagan."

There was a knock at the gate. Slade stood up and approached it, talking the whole way. "Wayne made 'Rio Bravo' as a slap-down of 'High Noon'. And it's a much better movie."

He unbolted the gate lock and swung the door wide open on a mustached Black patrolman. The cop looked at Slade holding the ostensibly full espresso mug.

"Hello, Officer," Slade said. "Are we talking too loud?"

"No, sir. We got a call about a ten-sixty-two in progress next door. You see or hear anything suspicious?"

"Why, no. My buddy and I have been out here twenty minutes. It's been right peaceful."

The policeman looked past Slade to Cork, who raised his cup at him.

"Can I offer you some espresso?" Slade asked. "The wife brews a mighty fine cup."

Cork flinched but kept drinking air. Slade could almost hear his friend's teeth clattering on the cup rim.

"No, thanks," said the cop. "Sorry to disturb you guys. Have a nice day."

"You too, Officer. You men are doing a hell of a job out there."

The cop stepped back into the alley. Slade closed the gate. Cork appeared beside him exhaling through his mouth. Slade waited half a minute then reopened the gate, peering left into the alley. The patrol car was parked just outside Adamo's open gate, with no cop in sight

A light came on in the left second-floor window behind Cork and Slade.

"Who's out there?!" shouted a woman while raising the window.

Cork and Slade rushed out the gate, Slade closing it behind them. They power-walked left past the police cruiser and Adamo's fence, then broke into a run.

"Hey, Cork," Slade said in mid-run. "What's a ten-sixty-two?"

"Breaking and entering."

"Lot of that going around."

They reached the street, turned left, then started walking normally toward Cork's car.

# CHAPTER 27

Slade ran over the old wood footbridge to "Walk and Talk Like Angels" by Toni Childs. He usually noted the first landmark on his towpath course, but on this Monday morning with the cold sun succumbing to grey clouds, the run occupied only his body. Amy Gallup's phone call absorbed his thoughts. It had awoken him from a deep, exhausted sleep just before ten, her husky voice sweet, sad, seductive, and enchantingly Southern.

"There's a place three hours away from here, in the mountains. It's called Boone. My cousin owns a cabin there. Come winter, you can see for miles through the naked woods, the fallen snow sparkling like stars. They say there's a scientific reason for that, but I think it's a magic place, where fairies dance and lovers can hide from the world. I wanna hide there with you, Mark. I wanna lie by the fireplace and kiss you all over, and make you forget everything and everyone else."

"I could use some forgetting," he'd said.

"And me some new memories – you holding me, pressing me ..."

"Okay, I'll buy the place."

She'd chuckled and said, "I got a different contract in mind for you."

"I hope it's not iron clad."

"Don't worry," she'd said. "I put a nudity clause in the fine print."

"What about the main section?"

"Exclusive rights. Your down payment was more than satisfactory. God, I miss you!"

"Me too, babe. How's Gastonia?"

"Exciting as ever," she'd said. "The Goodyear Blimp flew over us this morning."

"Wow! And the grandparents?"

"Good. I'll be heading back to Chapel Hill tomorrow. You okay?"

"So far. There're some bad men after us. Cork thinks it's 'cause we're on the right trail."

"I'm so sorry, Mark. I brought this trouble down on you boys."

"It was worth it – to get to know you."

"Oh, my you're sweet. I love you."

"Amy …"

"I mean it, Mark. I wanna be with you right now. Let me come up."

"If I wasn't in this mess – might be different," he'd said, quoting John Wayne in *Rio Bravo*. "When it's all over, I may head south. Haven't seen the Goodyear Blimp in a long time."

"I'll make sure you won't forget it."

"Call you tonight."

"My folks go to bed real early. I'll call you."

"It's like I'm back in high school."

"Play your cards right, I'll show you my cheerleader moves."

Slade finished the run with a smile on his face. He reentered Yates Field House overtaken by a new idea. Had he found someone who could break Nina's spell? Or was that spell holding him back? Because something was.

He took a brisk shower and went into the sauna carrying his cellphone, earbuds attached. Ignoring the chubby student inside, he took a low bench and brought up the *CNN* website. He scrolled down to a frozen video shot of Nina Holt – damnably gorgeous in a stylish blue ski coat that didn't hide her cleavage, wand microphone in hand – standing before an all too familiar boulder in Rock Creek Park. The headline below read, *P.I. Kills Two Men in Rock Creek Park Shooting*. Slade clicked the arrow on the picture, and Nina came alive.

"Tom, I'm in Rock Creek Park right outside the National Zoo gate. It's the site of a deadly double shooting Sunday. According to the Park Police, two gunmen opened fire on private detective Mark Slade, a former Army Ranger and Afghan War veteran."

The screen picture split in two, to include an Army ID picture of Slade in uniform.

"Slade reportedly shot back, killing both men. Police have not disclosed either of their name nor any possible motive., but Mark Slade was also present at the Capitol Hill Sniper shootings last Saturday. And that may have some connection to the violence here."

The right screen picture of Slade vanished, replaced by a live view of toffish fifty-something anchorman Tom Carter asking a question.

"Nina, you have a history with Mark Slade, don't you?"

Nina winced but instantly recovered. "That's right, Tom. I knew Slade at Georgetown University. We dated for a while before he joined the Army and went to war."

"Well – maybe he'll give you the first interview. Thank you, Nina."

The Nina half of the picture vanished. Carter looked at the camera.

"In political news, the November election is fast approaching," he said. "And recent polls are looking even grimmer for the incumbent President. A new Rasmussen Poll now has him at double digits behind the man he beat last time, with just nine months to close the gap. Ann Whitaker is at the White House..."

The video froze again and switched back to the original full shot of Nina. Slade gazed at her for a little while longer, reviewing her obvious displeasure at Carter's personal question. She clearly hadn't expected him to broadcast their former relationship, and place extra career pressure on her. Of course he could help her out like Carter implied.

"That'll be the day," he said aloud, imitating John Wayne in *The Searchers*.

# CHAPTER 28

Slade descended the steep narrow staircase into the Catacombs BarThe décor was dungeon chic – cavernous stone walls with mounted faux-flame torches, round wooden tables with red-cushioned chairs, and a dark mahogany bar. Slade fit in wearing his blue tweed jacket over a grey-striped wool sweater and black jeans.

Two nubile collegiate waitresses, a redhead and blonde, in fashionably torn black silk dresses and tights bustled around the low-lit lounge. It was a third full of businesspeople and academics enjoying the start of happy hour. A preppy young brown-haired bartender filled their drink orders. Two lawyer-types sat at the left end of the bar. Slade took the stool on the far right.

"What can I get ya?" the bartender asked.

"Cuba libre, though I'm afraid Cuba won't be free for a long time."

"Too bad," said the bartender, mixing a rum and cola. "There's a Cuban hottie in my Russian Lit class I'd like to liberate."

"You'll need to be a Rough Rider."

The bartender looked blankly at Slade, setting a full glass in front of him.

"Guess they don't teach that in school anymore," Slade said. "The Rough Riders were a volunteer cavalry unit that served in Cuba during the Spanish-American War. Teddy Roosevelt led them in a famous charge up San Juan Hill. Least it used to be famous. Inspired me as a kid."

"Hmm. You a soldier?"

"Used to be."

"Thank you for your service. You know, I once thought about joining the Navy. Seeing the world and getting a free ride at GW. Then I watched that royal screwup in Afghanistan."

"Looked a lot worse from the inside."

"Whoa," said the bartender. "What do you do now?"

"Private eye."

"That any easier?"

"It's murkier. Mark Slade, Cork Detective Agency."

"Tim Collins. You working on a case now?"

"Yeah, of Einbecher at home," said Slade. "But a professional one here,"

"So, you didn't come in here to drink."

"No, but I'm flexible," Slade said, sipping from his glass. "I could use some info."

"Shoot."

"Another bartender here – Paretsky."

"Theo's dead," Collins said with a frown.

"I know," Slade said. "I killed him."

Collins gasped. "Oh shit! It's you!"

The two lawyers turned to Slade and the now nervous Collins.

"Look, man, I'm just a part-time bartender paying off my school loan!" Collins said.

"Relax, will you?" Slade said, glancing at the pair on his left. "I got nothing against bartenders. Your buddy tried to kill me. I'd like to know why. Can you answer a few questions?"

"Shoot," Collins said, then quickly raised his hands. "A figure of speech!"

"How well did you know Theo?"

"We worked together weekend nights. Didn't hang out. He was too obsessed with Climate Change. Said it would kill us all in five years unless we took radical action. Kept blaming the Republicans for blocking it. He said they wanted a climate catastrophe to bring on the Rapture."

"The Apocalypse," said Slade.

"What?"

"Nothing."

"He got so obnoxious – our manager had to tell him to quit harassing the customers."

"Did he have any regulars? Say an Arab-type, early thirties, short beard. He and Theo double-teamed me."

Collins shook his head. Saw his picture on the news last night for the first time. Along with yours."

"How about a rich chick? Might've had some private chats with Theo."

Collins reflected for a moment before answering.

"Come to think of it, there was one like that in here last weekend. Looked like an old-time movie babe. You know, before they got all scrawny and angry at men? This chick was total glam – fine threads, gold bracelet. Came in with some big red-haired dude with a crew-cut. He seemed more like a bodyguard than a boyfriend. They sat at that table." Collins pointed to a table near the right corner. "I remember it 'cause Theo asked me to cover for him while he went over to talk to the chick. That threw me, 'cause she was so way out of his league. But she waved him to a chair. And Mr. Crewcut came over and ordered a martini for her – with Jewel of Russia vodka."

"Jewel of Russia," Slade repeated.

"Pricey stuff. She and Theo talked for like ten minutes. I could tell it was nothing personal, especially when she handed him an envelope. She finished her martini and left with Mr. Crewcut. Theo came back here."

"Did you ask him what they talked about?"

"You bet. I was curious."

"And?"

"What else? Climate change. He said she's a big deal in the movement."

"What about the envelope she gave him?"

"He seemed mad I saw that. Said it was just Green Strike stuff."

"Describe her for me, Tim," said Slade.

---------------- ---------

"Forty-something, five-foot-eight, brunette, shoulder-length perm, high cheekbones, and a great balcony," Slade said, adding, "Bartender's words, not mine."

He sat in Cork's client chair reading from his cellphone notes, as Cork rifled through a short stack of printouts on his desk.

"He said he could ID a photo of her if we come up with one," Slade said.

Cork held up a printout picture of a stunning, busty brunette in a pink cashmere sweater. She perfectly fit Slade's description. Cork passed her picture to Slade, who appraised the gorgeous face.

"Wow, that could be her," said Slade. "She looks like *Zara, Demon Hunter*. Wait a minute. It *is* Zara – Joan Russell!"

"AKA Joan Gardner."

"AKA 'Rich Bitch'?"

"She matches your bartender's description," Cork said.

"Yeah. How'd you come up with her?"

"The Green Strike Emerald Patrons list, subdivided by DC residents, among them Mr. and Mrs. Adam Gardner."

"The millionaire lobbyist she married and quit showbiz," said Slade. "Holy cow - Zara, Demon Hunter. My voice changed watching that show. Joan in her skimpy leather outfit, beating up guys and ghouls. I guess the bartender didn't recognize her out of costume."

"Not surprising, since the series ended before he was born, and kids don't watch reruns like we did. Text him that picture."

Slade laid the printout on his lap and took out his cellphone.

"She was always a big greenie," he said. "I read all about her back in the day – when she was gonna be the future Mrs. Mark Slade. No wonder Green Strike got its hooks into her."

"I'd call it synergy – if she bought Adamo's painting through the group."

"And hired Paretsky and Arab Boy to mess me up," said Slade.

He took a photo of the printout on his lap then prepared to send a text.

"There's something you should know about Green Strike," Cork said.

"They're commies."

"Literally. We tagged them in the Bureau. A great deal of Russo-Chinese money flows through their coffers."

"Makes sense," said Slade. "Six years ago, America was energy independent, and Commieland's worst nightmare. Then Green Strike cried 'wolf' about global warming, using that weird little girl –"

"How dare you?!" Cork said in a Euro accent. "The Climate Crisis is real. But go on."

"President Oil got replaced by President Windmill through electoral skullduggery –"

"Which I'm ashamed to say my ex-firm engineered."

"And Ruskie gas became the only fuel in Europe."

"While America begs for oil from Venezuela and Iran," said Cork. "A Chinese puppet and a Russian one."

"You bet your ass Green Strike's a good investment for Commie World. They build ships while we build plug-in stations."

"But even they won't be able to stop President Oil from retaking power in November."

"The Apocalypse Mask can," said Slade. "Theoretically."

His cellphone pinged an incoming text. He looked at the message on screen.

"Good Lord," said Cork. "If the Russians or Chinese are the Ugly …"

"They got a gorgeous face to hide behind. My bartender just confirmed it. Joan Russell is Rich Bitch."

"Excellent."

"Think I'll pay Zara, Demon Hunter a visit," said Slade. "If I can find her Hidden Fortress."

"Be careful, Mark. She has dangerous associates. And she knows who you are."

"Puts her one up on my old girlfriends."

"In what way?"

"She already wants me dead," Slade said.

## CHAPTER 29

The Post Pub was a cozy oblong bar three doors to the left of The Washington Post Building's K Street entrance. Just before the end of the dayside shift at the newspaper, it was nearly empty. Slade sat in the right rear booth facing the door, a bowl of breaded onion rings on the table and a Dos Equis bottle in hand. He scanned the row of framed *Washington Post* front pages along the opposite wall: *Kennedy Orders Blockade of Cuba, President Kennedy Shot – Feared Dead, "The Eagle Has Landed" – Two Men Walk on the Moon, Nixon Denies Role in Cover-Up.* He was on *Nixon Resigns* when Phil Totter walked in.

Totter appeared dapper as ever in a gold cashmere V-neck sweater and khaki pants that contoured to his slim build. Long, graying brown hair topped his pale handsome face. Slade gave him a wave. Totter sat down across the table from him.

"You look the same, Phil," said Slade.

"It's getting harder to maintain that mirage. Damn grey hair is betraying me."

"Buy you a beer?"

"Make it Coke. We're on deadline."

"You and Walter Desmond."

"I still work under him," Totter said. "In more ways than one."

"He's the Washington Post Gossip King."

"Really 'queen,' but I'll seize the crown someday. I just need the right exclusive."

Totter looked intently at Slade. A cute short waitress appeared beside them. Slade indicated his companion.

"Coke."

The waitress withdrew. Totter appraised Slade.

"So, you're out of the Army for good, eh?"

"Yep," said Slade.

"But still shooting bad guys."

"Strictly return fire."

"Yes, so I read. Well, Mark, you're not only an old friend – you're a new celebrity. Which just happens to be my beat."

"And Nina Holt's right now."

"Right," said Totter. "I saw her report on the Capitol Hill Sniper, and your Rock Creek Park adventure. She's still quite beautiful. That has to sting."

Slade shrugged.

"You know, I was jealous of Nina at Georgetown," Totter said. "Having you for a boyfriend."

"You would've been less aggravating."

Totter smiled wistfully.

"Now she wants your sniper story too," he said.

"She won't get it."

"Will I?"

"When it's over, Phil," said Slade. "In exchange for another."

"Joan Russell."

"You can save me hours of online research."

The waitress returned, set a glass of Coke in front of Totter, and left. He took a sip.

"All you straight boys lusted after Zara," he said. "And you ruined Joan Russell's career. The role typecast her so she couldn't get much acting work later."

"She was great in *Executive Sweat*."

"She spent half the movie naked."

"The other half was pretty good too," said Slade.

"In any case, she landed on her feet. Joan Russell Gardner may be the most influential woman in Washington who's not holding office. Her husband has the money, but she basically controls it – and him. If you watch their joint appearances, you can see Adam defer to her in everything, like in a hostage video."

"Is she cucking him?"

"Off the record – yes," said Totter. "Currently with her tennis instructor."

"How cliché. But why 'off the record'? Sounds like juicy stuff – 'Zara's Newest Racket.'"

"That's cute, 'cept our managing editor doesn't want the Gardners tainted."

"'Cause he's a Dem starmaker," said Slade.

"You should've been a journalist. And you're right. Adam Gardner used to help get moderate Democrats elected. Joan fixed it so only far-left candidates have a place at the trough. Her passion is Climate Change, with Green Strike her fiefdom, courtesy of Adam's fortune."

"One of my attackers was Green Strike. He tried to wipe away my carbon footprint."

"You think Joan hired him?"

"Uh-huh. She met with him at the bar he tended. I'd like to find out why."

"Might be difficult," Totter said. "She's well insulated, mostly against conservatives and *Demon Hunter* fanboys. Never goes anywhere without her bodyguard."

"Big lug with a crewcut?"

Totter nodded. "Maurice Dubois. Ex-Mountie. Fired for bashing in the skull of an eighty-year-old trucker during the Canadian COVID protests."

"Dudley Do Wrong," said Cork. "Funny, Joan Russell's hitman was a Canuck too."

"Not so odd. Green Strike is a major player up there. The Prime Minister's a member."

"Canada's turned into our North Korea," Slade said.

"They even have a college in Quebec – the Green Strike Academy. Joan hosts a fundraiser for it every April. I could swing you an invitation to the next one."

"Way too late."

"Well, you're out of luck this week," Totter said. "She cancelled her only public appearance. An artist she was sponsoring was shot to death."

"Paul Adamo."

"That's right."

"What's the scoop on him?"

"Scoop? You think we have some kind of LGBTQ grapevine?"

"You knew he was gay," said Slade.

Totter grinned. "Good deduction. Paul was very popular in our community. Quite the swashbuckler. Devastated a friend of mine. Then, about three months ago, he dropped out of the club scene. Told Blake – my friend – he was in a relationship. Didn't say with whom. Any idea?"

"It'll be in my story," Slade said.

"I can't wait to hear it."

"I'd like to talk to your friend, Blake."

"He's in mourning. Might be attending Paul's funeral tomor –" Totter's voice trailed off then came back more excited. "Along with Joan Gardner!"

"And me," Slade said. "After all – it could've been my funeral."

# CHAPTER 30

"Paul Adamo did not believe in God," said the minister. "But he believed in evil."

A cold noon breeze blew through the tombstones of the *Eternal Peace Cemetery*. It was a small oval graveyard overlooking the Potomac on the Virginia side. Only a low cobblestone barrier separated the steep river drop from the cemetery's north edge. About three dozen mourners – many trim young men in dark overcoats – faced the river, and the grey casket with a flower bouquet on top suspended over an open plot.

"Not the spiritual evil that I confront – the earthly evil spread by this wicked country."

Even partly hidden by a black faux-fur coat and hood, Joan Russell Gardner looked provocative. The cowl maned her regally beautiful face. The coat failed to fully conceal her large bosom. Slade recalled Zara's brown leather top popping out of his parents' TV set in Wheaton, Maryland.

He stood five mourners to Joan's left wearing a black wool coat over his navy-blue suit, a maroon wool sweater, and his sunglasses. Examining her profile, he noted a male profile just past hers – a foot higher, a lot craggier, and topped by a brown buzzcut.

"Maurice Dubois," he said to himself.

On the opposite side of the coffin, the bespectacled minister continued his oration.

"Paul used his art to confront this evil – much as Christ did the Pharisees of his day."

"Jesus," Slade said.

"I had the chance meet this fine young man last month – in a climate conference held at my church, sponsored by our mutual benefactor, Ms. Joan Gardner."

Several heads turned to Joan, who remained impassive as a mannequin.

"I told him how much I admired his work. He told me how little he admired mine."

Some young men smiled or nodded knowingly.

"I said God condemned wickedness in both people and nations, and I cited Revelation."

"The Apocalypse," Slade muttered.

"Fallen, fallen is Babylon the great!
She has become a dwelling place for demons.
For she has made all the nations drink
The poisoned wine of her lewdness;
The kings of the Earth committed fornication with her,
And the world's merchants grew rich from her wealth and wantonness.
She shall be consumed by fire!

"Paul seemed to take these words to heart," continued the minister. "But he gave them his own spin. 'If there is a God, He could use some help,' he said. I believe Paul is now closer to the Lord than he ever expected to be. May his paintings light our own road into Heaven."

At the foot of the grave, a bent old man pressed a handheld remote. The coffin descended into the plot. Mourners started moving toward the parking lot, away from the river. Joan and Maurice remained.

Two young men deferentially approached Joan. Maurice stepped in front of them, shaking his head. Slade appraised his massive bulk in a black overcoat, calculating the bodyguard's three-inch height advantage and longer reach over himself. The young men quickly altered course. Slade took their place, moving closer to Joan.

"Ms. Gardner," he said.

Joan turned to him, giving him the full brunt of her beauty. She squinted as if trying to place him.

"Do I know you?" Joan asked in the husky voice that had thrilled him as a kid.

"Indirectly. We both knew the decedent. Not Paul Adamo – Theo Paretsky."

Maurice shifted his leg weight from left to right, a Savate movement Slade recognized. He stopped three yards back from Joan – outside Maurice's leg strike radius.

"Never heard of him," Joan said.

"How quickly you forget. The Catacombs Bar. Those Jewel of Russia martinis."

Joan cringed. "Who are you?"

Slade took off his sunglasses. Joan gasped, clearly recognizing him.

"What do you want?"

"To find out why you're hitting on me," Slade said.

"I don't know what you mean."

"Fine, lady. I'll go to the cops. You better hope they're Zara fans."

Slade turned to the parking lot and started moving toward it. Joan's voice reached him.

"Wait."

Slade stopped but kept facing forward.

"Please."

Slade turned around.

"I'll talk to you," Joan said.

"Without your Huskie," Slade said, nodding at Maurice.

Maurice sneered. Joan said something in his ear, and he gave a slight nod. Slade walked past four graves to the riverside footpath.

He looked left over the cobblestone wall at the fast-flowing Potomac. A small yacht was sailing downstream from under Chain Bridge.

Slade got a whiff of exquisite perfume. Joan appeared on his left at close to his height, due to the heels on her faux-leather black boots.

"I'm glad you're all right, Mr. Slade."

"No thanks to you. You hired Paretsky to mess me up."

"Just slow you down. I didn't want you badly hurt."

"Sorry to disappoint you, but I like my limbs in one piece," Slade said.

Joan took a deep breath that flattered her impressive chest.

"I was shocked he used a gun on you. I'm sorry."

"Sorry don't get it done, Dude," Slade said, quoting John Wayne in *Rio Bravo*. "Who was the other guy with Theo?"

"I don't know," said Joan. "I only hired him."

"What's your problem with me anyway?"

"You're after Paul's painting – *Revelation*. So am I."

"How do you know that?"

"A friend in the DOJ. He said you were good – you and your partner. I was afraid you'd find it first."

"Why? What's so special about that painting?"

"All I know is what Paul told me. It's the only thing that can stop what's about to happen."

"A conservative president."

"An environmental nightmare," Joan said with a lump in her throat, her husky voice quivering. "He'll reverse everything we worked for over the last four years. Clean energy that can heal the planet – solar power, wind power, alternative food sources. Instead, there'll be a thousand more pipelines and coal mines and cows all over the land, poisoning our air and water."

"Cows?"

"They're responsible for twelve percent of all global greenhouse emissions."

"And the Johnson County War," said Slade.

Joan ignored him. "All for what? Gas-guzzling dinosaurs. Arctic-level air-conditioning. Toxic food. It really will be the Apocalypse!"

"Wow," said Slade. "I always thought you should've won an Emmy. Especially for Season Two."

The lump in Joan's throat disappeared.

"Maybe I did pour it on a bit thick," she said in a steadier voice. "But I meant every word I said about the end of the world. I'll do anything to prevent it."

"Even murder?"

Joan's azure eyes focused on Slade.

"Not you, Mark," she said huskily.

"How about Paul Adamo?"

Slade noticed the wrinkles under Joan's eyes she never had as Zara. They made her seem more vulnerable if no less attractive than her former TV self.

"I didn't kill Paul," she said. "Or have him killed."

"He was shot with a silencer. Your drinking buddy pulled one on me. So did his partner."

"I swear I didn't know Ted had a gun, let alone a silencer. I met him at the Green Strike Academy in Quebec. He asked me to bring him to DC so he could help me organize the protests here. I found him useful. As for Paul, I needed him alive to give me his painting."

"You thought you had it. Only he'd pulled a switch."

Joan shook her head and waved off the accusation.

"There's another group of art lovers in the mix," Slade said. "You got accidents planned for them too?"

"Who?"

"Kudzu."

"Kudzu," Joan said. "What's that?"

"You should've said, 'Who's that?'"

"You are good," Joan said.

"Look, baby, I killed two men 'cause of you. And I hate looking over my shoulder for their replacements. I'd just as soon plug the source – you."

"You wouldn't hurt me," Joan said.

"How do you know?"

"You have kind eyes."

"They could watch you fry without blinking."

"They could watch me do many things, I think, but not suffer," Joan said, her sweet perfume supporting her argument.

Slade tried to remain intimidating. "Better hedge your bet. Talk about Kudzu."

"How much do you know?"

"You start."

"They're a secret force of right-wing extremists plotting to overthrow the government."

Slade groaned. "You mean like an Insurrection?"

"A real one this time," said Joan. "aAlso led by a powerful Republican."

"Sam Owen."

"Yes. We've got to stop them before it's too late. Not just for the country, for the planet!"

"Cut the Green Strike crap," Slade said. "The only global warming I'm worried about is from Chi-Com nukes. And if I see one more goon from your cult, we'll meet again. And I'll be a lot rougher next time."

Joan appeared unintimidated, in fact quite the opposite.

"I might like that, Mark," she said.

Slade's hard façade almost slipped. Joan noticed.

"Do you know where the painting is?" she asked.

Slade's brain pinged.

"I might," he said. "What's it worth to you?"

To his amazement, Joan's chest seemed to expand, and without Hollywood CGI. Her eyes narrowed seductively as she moved her face closer to his.

"You wanted me as a boy," she said. "I know the look. I see it all the time on much less attractive faces. Give me the painting, Mark. I'll make your boyhood dream come true."

Slade really wished he had the damn thing, and wondered what he'd do if he did.

"Did you make Adamo the same offer?"

"Yes," Joan said. "He declined it."

"He stayed true to his school. Though a quarter mil's not a bad second prize."

"Double that on delivery."

"Which never came."

"You can have both," Joan said. "The money and me. Here's my first payment."

She pressed two black velvet gloves to Slade's temples and moved her luscious mouth toward his. Her soft lips melted into his, her tongue probing pleasure nerves deep in his throat. For a moment, he felt like a teenager again. Joan withdrew her face, gazing carnally at him.

"What do you say, sweetheart?" she asked huskily, her bedroom eyes still on Slade.

"Still got your old Zara costume?"

Joan smiled lustily.

"Mm hmm," she said. "And it still fits."

"I'll give it some serious thought."

"703-261-9543," Joan said, sensuously enunciating each numbers sequence.

Slade punched the phone number on his mobile. After one ring, he hung up.

"Be seeing you," he said, and moved back into the cemetery.

Two shovel-bearing gravediggers were approaching Adamo's grave. Maurice was nowhere in sight. Slade didn't like the look of that.

# CHAPTER 31

"You told Joan Gardner we have the painting?!" Cork exclaimed.

"I intimated it," said Slade.

"I knew I should've bullet-proofed this house after the last break-in."

They sat in Cork's restored living room drinking bottles of Heineken dark – Cork on the sofa, Slade in the armchair with his jacket off. The wide rear window behind Cork showcased the sunlight-filtering woods on the downslope to Goldsboro Road. You could only see the road in wintertime when the poplar trees were bare.

"Whatever possessed you – other than her obvious charms?"

"It seemed like a good idea at the time," Slade said, channeling Steve McQueen in *The Magnificent Seven*. "And I figured it might speed things up."

"Yeah, our demise."

"We want the other players to show their hand."

"Not their gun hand, when they find out you were bluffing."

"At least we'll be dealing 'em in – the Good, the Bad, and the Ugly," said Slade. "Though Joan Russell sure doesn't fit that last description. She's hotter than a pistol."

"I can see where she wounded you," Cork said, pointing at Slade's mouth.

Slade brushed a pink smudge from the right side of his lip.

"I was saving that for the next sci-fi convention," he said. "*Demon Hunter* lipstick."

"Stick to Westerns."

"Okay. Joan knows about the Good and the Bad."

"The Bureau and Kudzu. Do they know about her?"

"I reckon they do," said Slade.

"Does she know what the painting contains?"

"Yeah. She let the A-word slip."

"Apocalypse," Cork said. "What else did she have to say?"

"That Kudzu plans to overthrow the government."

"Why would they bother, when their boy's about to take it over in November? Makes no sense. Unless –"

"He gets taken out first," said Slade.

"Politically speaking."

"Perhaps not," said Cork.

Slade chugged some beer.

"To protect him," Cork said, "Kudzu has to secure the Apocalypse Mask."

"By beating everyone else to the painting."

"so, the Bad needs it to save their once and future President – the Ugly to save the current one."

"What about the Good?"

"The Good," Cork said, and took a long sip of beer as if to wash down his next words. "I thought they were once – when I first joined the Bureau. They recruited me right out of Georgetown."

"I remember. And me the Army. What patriotic suckers we were."

"I had no idea how deep the rot went – till they went after the president. They hit him with everything they had. And what they didn't have, they fabricated."

"The Siberian Candidate," said Slade.

"And what *he* had, they suppressed," Cork said. "I questioned my superiors when they called it Russian collusion, yet I still went with the program."

Slade lowered the bottle from his mouth. "Why, Cork?"

"Not my finest hour," said Cork. "I told myself I had a wife to provide for and a baby on the way. Besides, I didn't vote for the man. In fact, I cheered his defeat. Then, Wilcox ordered us to raid his home, telling us to turn up something, anything, that would keep him from running again. A preemptive strike against the leader of the opposition, and his supporters - all seventy-five million of them."

"Welcome to Moscow."

"*Da*," said Cork. "The government enforcing one-party rule is the road to tyranny. It doesn't matter whether you support that party or not. Justice has to be blind. But the DOJ kept one eye open."

"The left eye."

"And it only got worse under the new regime. Pretty soon, we were targeting traditional parents and pro-life Catholics as domestic terrorists. By then, I didn't have to make the choice. Kathy made it for me. She forced me to quit the Bureau."

"Your partner didn't – Nichols."

"Poor Alan," said Cork. "Yes, he kept his job, but at great cost."

"Kathy."

"He'd already lost her when I left."

"You did the right thing," said Slade.

"Perhaps not. I should've stayed inside – exposed the whole rotten crowd."

"To whom?"

"That is the question, isn't it," said Cork. "The media is entirely on their side."

"CNN sure is. I got first-hand proof of that."

"Nina Holt. You never know, Mark. She might surprise you."

"She did once."

"Yeah," said Cork. "Sorry."

Slade held up his empty bottle. "Want another?"

"No thanks. I prefer to savor mine."

Slade stood up and walked to the kitchen. Cork's cellphone

beeped. He looked down at Kathy's pretty face above her text – a line from one of their favorite old movies, *Marathon Man*.

*Is it safe?*

Cork texted back.

*No, there be Nazis. Stay away. I love you.*

Two heart emojis popped up. Slade returned with an open Heineken and sat down.

"Well, if the polls are right, the cavalry is on the way."

"Yes," said Cork. "'Orange Satan' is poised to retake the White House. Once he does, he'll torch every agency that burned him – beginning with my former colleagues. If I know them, and I do, they won't go down without a fight."

"Neither will Joan Russell."

"Who, thanks to you, believes we have the painting. We had better watch our backs."

"I'd rather watch hers," said Slade. "But I know what you mean."

He began tapping the familiar drumbeat of *The Good, The Bad, and the Ugly* theme on the armrest of his chair – *tap tap tap, tap tap tap tap tap, tap tap tap tap tap, tap tap tap tap tap.*

Cork hummed the first five music notes. Slade concluded with the next three.

"*Wah wah wah.*"

The two men laughed.

---

It was full night by the time Slade got back to Adams Morgan. He found a parking space for his Mustang right on Euclid Street just a half block from his apartment building. He hoped the short, brisk walk wouldclear his head. He shouldn't have had that third Heineken.

Climbing the El Cid's too dark front steps, he noticed the porch ceiling light was out again. He continued toward the door. Extracting his key, he felt the old familiar chill in his spine, if on slight delay.

He whirled around just in time to glimpse the nightstick streaking toward his skull, too late to dodge the blow. Pain detonated in his brain. He fought it back, trying to remain conscious.

"My old friend's kiss is not so sweet, eh, joli garcon?" whispered a male voice with a French-Canadian accent. "The kiss of death."

Slade's legs buckled. He fell to the porch floor. Then every other light went out.

# CHAPTER 32

There was very little traffic on MacArthur Boulevard at 3:42 Sunday morning. Officer Raquel Valdez drove the squad car east on it, going seventy miles per hour with the siren off. In the shotgun seat, Cork hardly noticed his driver's lovely profile and prominent chest. He'd been in a daze ever since he got the wakeup call from Wallace. Cork had distilled the information down to three points – Mark's Mustang in the Potomac River, Mark possibly in it, a police car on the way to pick him up.

He took off his glasses and rubbed his eyes. They felt a bit moist. Raquel gave him a sideways glance.

"We'll be there in about twenty minutes, sir."

Cork dropped his hand. "Anything new on the car?"

"Not since the diver ID'd the plate."

"My partner's," Cork said glumly.

"There's no confirmation of a body. He might be okay."

"He isn't answering his phone. Wallace said the car is snagged on an underwater cable, interrupting TV service. Or it would have sunk to the river bottom.

"Yes, sir, we got lucky," Raquel said, quickly adding. "To locate it so soon."

Cork looked out the windshield, now passing the centennial-old service station on Sangamore Road, the last building on the Maryland side of DC.

"I drove your partner to the hospital last week," Raquel said. "Him and the girl witness, right after the sniper shootings."

"I remember."

"I liked – like him."

"Me too," said Cork.

"Sir, I know the sergeant on the scene. He trained me. I could ask him for an update."

Cork turned to the policewoman. He noted she was very pretty with a feline aspect to her Latin face. Funny what a man could notice even in the depth of despair.

"I'd appreciate that, Officer Valdez."

Raquel seized the car radio microphone and spoke into it without reducing speed.

"One Adam Thirty to Baker Four Hundred."

A female dispatcher voice answered.

"Roger, Adam Thirty. Stand by."

The radio crackled again, followed by a man's voice.

"Loggia here. Where are you, Valdez?"

"'Bout fifteen minutes out, sir. My rider's hoping for an update on his partner's vehicle."

"I'll call you on your cell. Loggia out."

Valdez's mobile rang. She answered it on speaker mode.

"Valdez."

"Hey, Raquel," said the same voice from the radio. "Okay, here's the dope. Diver's blowtorching the cable off the car. It's taking him a while. And he did confirm a body in it."

Cork's stomach tightened. Raquel saw it in his face.

"Description, sir?"

"Too dark and murky for a good luck, but brown hair."

"Thanks, Sarge. See you shortly."

Raquel clicked off the phone.

"Mark has blonde hair," Cork said.

"That's right, he does."

"Although … we went to Ocean City a few times. His hair looked darker wet. What would three hours in the river do?"

The K Street waterfront ran for two steel-pillared blocks underneath the Whitehurst Freeway. The west block contained a brownstone office building with two restaurants and a bar, all closed for the night. A construction site took up the east block, offering a temporary view of the Potomac – a disturbing sight to Cork as the police car pulled in, made worse by the intense crime-scene lighting.

Stepping out of the car, he shivered – whether from cold or fear, he couldn't tell. He put his hands in the pockets of his brown wool overcoat and approached the river. He took in two more marked police cars, an unmarked grey sedan, a black van, and a red firetruck. A pair of firemen stood by their truck drinking coffee or something stronger out of thermos cups.

Cork's eyes locked on a powerful green tow-truck, its rear close to the river. In the bed stood a large cylinder with a chain leading out the back. Cork visually traced the chain from the truck to the river, where it plunged into the brown water. He knew what was on the other end.

Carl Wallace appeared next to his right shoulder. Cork gave him a quick glance. He had on a black parka and a rabbit-fur hat, his stubble already a semi-beard. Cork resumed staring at the river and the immobile tow chain.

"They said any minute now," Wallace said.

Cork nodded. "I killed him, Carl."

"Bullshit," said Wallace.

"He didn't want this case. Not after the girl left him."

"Amy Gallup."

"I forced him into it," Cork said. "Just because I wanted to get Owen."

"If Senator Owen had something to do with this, then you were right to target him – and I'll get him."

Cork shook his head. "He's too powerful. They all are – the

Good, the Bad, and the Ugly. My arrogance made me think I could take them on – and Slade paid the price."

"I prefer a more modern Clint – Dirty Harry," Wallace said. "You might say he's my role model in bending the rules."

He slipped something into Cork's right coat pocket. Cork felt the folded paper without taking his eyes off the tow truck.

"What is it?" he asked.

"Our coroner's report on Greg Bradford."

"I thought Wilcox's people had the body removed."

"Minus a blood sample."

"You were ordered to hand over everything to the Bureau," Cork said.

"That one slipped my mind."

"What's in it?"

"It's what was in Bradford that counts. A fair amount of Zolpidem."

"Sleeping drug," said Cork. "That must've spoiled his aim."

"It was still good enough to splatter my two all over Second Street!"

"And almost Slade and me. But Mark was a fast-moving target. I wish to God he still was."

"You better give me everything you got."

"Have at it," Cork said. "Amy Gallup hired us to find out why Greg Bradford dumped her. We found out he was sleeping with Paul Adamo. Greg gave his boyfriend a love token – a top secret item he'd stolen from his boss, Senator Owen, which could supposedly bring down the country. Adamo incorporated this iteminto his latest painting, *Revelation*. Now the painting's missing and everyone's looking for it, including Owen, the Bureau, and Green –"

A loud mechanical hum interrupted him. He and Wallace turned to the tow truck, where the mighty winch in back was powering up. It began to spin backward, reeling in the chain behind it. Cork looked to the river and the slowly withdrawing chain. He could almost feel each click in his chest.

A large bluish object started to rise from the water, becoming a dripping blue car trunk. Cork wished he didn't recognize the Mustang, even when fully emerged on dry land. He could see nothing of the interior through the murky auto glass. The moment it came to a full stop, he started toward the car. Wallace's firm hand on his shoulder stopped him.

"Neil, wait."

"I have to know," Cork said.

"You know the procedure. You supervised a few of 'em."

Cork stood still. Wallace waved to the van. The side door opened and two young figures came out, a male and female, in white hazmat suits with masks and gloves. An identically garbed though maskless fifty-something Asian woman followed them out, her short hair in a headset. As her team neared the Mustang, she approached Cork and Wallace.

"Our ME, Janet Fong," Wallace said, then to Janet, "Neil Cork. The car belongs to his partner. We're hoping the body in it doesn't."

"We'll soon see," Janet said.

They watched the male forensic expert test the driver's door handle while hispartner stood by. The door didn't budge. Janet listened to her headset.

"Door's jammed," she said, then into her mic. "Sally, see what Gus can do about it."

The female technician stepped over to the tow-truck driver's door. The window came down, revealing a heavyset, bearded driver in a purple windbreaker. Sally exchanged a few words with him. A moment later, he exited the truck wielding a drill pistol. The male technician cleared his path to the Mustang. Cork wanted to scream, "Speed it up!"

Gus pressed a drill-tip to the door handle and turned on the gun. Four seconds later, the handle dropped. Gus reached into the gap and pulled open the door. Sally and her partner moved into the space, obstructing Cork's view of the car seat. Cork gave Wallace a frantic look. Wallace got the message and turned to Janet. She spoke into her headset microphone.

"Whatya got, Bruce?" she asked, then repeated his report. "Caucasian male, thirty to forty. Skull trauma, possibly lethal."

Cork's legs trembled but he remained upright. Janet looked at him with concern.

"You all right?"

Cork nodded. Janet spoke again into her headset mike.

"Hold it, Bruce. We're taking a look."

Janet approached the Mustang, followed by Cork and Wallace. Her team members stepped aside, giving Cork a clear view of the driver's seat – and the seatbelt-harnessed man in it. He was pale and bloated, with brown hair and wearing a navy-blue suitcoat. A bloody gash marked his left temple. Cork let out the breath he'd been involuntarily holding.

"Who's this poor bastard?" Wallace asked no one in particular.

"I don't know," Cork said almost mirthfully. "But he's wearing Mark's suit jacket."

"Why go to all that trouble?"

"To make us think Mark's dead, to buy time, to get what they need out of him."

"So, where the hell is Slade?"

"Hopefully not there yet," said Cork.

# CHAPTER 33

His shivering awoke Slade. He felt too cold to be in hell. Where were the damned flames of perdition when you needed them? He could use their warmth, as well as some light in the darkness.

He realized he was still alive, though not for much longer without body heat. He tried to rub his arms but found he couldn't move them, or for that matter feel them. Maybe he was already frozen stiff. Except he had a bad headache where the nightstick struck him.

Gradually his eyes adjusted to the dark, providing some perspective. He was sitting on the concrete floor of an empty barn, facing the shut sliding door. The icy breeze seeped in through the crack, further chilling him. Especially, he noted, his naked torso. At least he still had his pants on.

His arms were pulled back over his shoulders, the wrists bound behind something. Tilting his head back, he could see the narrow four-sided timber beam and brown rope cord responsible. The post rose some twelve feet above his head to support the front edge of a hayloft – a cross beam at the top of it. There were two identical posts on either side of him.

The barn door started to slide open. Slade lightly closed his eyes to appear unconscious, leaning his skull against the beam. He peered through his eyelids while struggling to reduce his shivering and steam exhalation.

Two human silhouettes entered and paused in the doorway. The figure on the left made a hand-pulling motion. A dim glow illuminated the barn from a bulb above the door.

The light bringer was a twenty-something male with a short beard, wearing a darkgreen hooded sweat jacket and blue jeans. His similarly dressed – only hood down – companion looked masculine at first glance with her buzzcut, makeup-free face, and flat chest, but her slighter frame gave her away. She held a thin black rod in her right hand.

As they neared him, Slade noticed the identical logo on the left breast of their jackets – two green lightning bolts against a grey background. He recognized the Green Strike logo from his crash research. Taking a second look at the girl's stick, a faint shudder escaped him. It was a cattle prod.

Maurice Dubois entered the barn, now wearing a green down jacket. He stepped between the youthful couple looming a foot taller than either of them. Suspecting an ex-Mountie would be harder to fool, Slade tightly shut his eyes.

An electric shock to the chest reopened them wide. The cattle prod hovered an inch from his face. He looked past it at the smirking Maurice.

"*Bonjour, garçon,*" Maurice said.

"I'm not your waiter."

"Means 'boy,'" the girl said with a malicious smile.

"Very good, Suzo," Maurice said.

Slade's brain pinged. He recalled Maurice's creepy whisper and accent right after he crowned him. *My old friend's kiss is not so sweet.* Slade played the hand.

"I'm flattered, Maurice, but I prefer kissing your boss."

Maurice winced, confirming Slade's suspicion. The bodyguard had a more than protective interest in Joan Russell, no doubt unrequited. He would resent Joan kissing him at the cemetery, and her offer of more to come. This insight didn't help his current predicament, but it might if he lived long enough. For now, Maurice was clearly enjoying his misery.

"Cold, Slade?"

"No, I always play *Revelry* with my teeth."

"Revelry?" asked the younger man.

"*Reveille*," Maurice said. "The morning bugle call for soldiers – and some Mounties."

Slade noted how he said the last part almost respectfully, as if missing his old *esprit de corps*.

"Give him a drink, Albert," Maurice said, pronouncing the name "Al-bear".

The young man drew a small oblong golden liquor bottle from his right coat pocket. Removing the cap, he tilted the bottleneck to the captive's mouth. Rum poured into Slade, warming his chest. Albert let him drink a good portion before pulling away the bottle.

"Thanks," Slade said. "Untie me and I'll be glad to pay for it."

"We will release you," Maurice said. "*Après* you tell us where the painting is."

"What painting?"

Maurice nodded to Suzo, who lowered the prod to Slade's chest. A thousand fire ants began to burn it. Slade writhed in pain.

"Not so near the heart!" Maurice snapped. "We do not wish to lose him – yet."

The prod shifted to Slade's right chest, as did the fire ants.

"*Assez*."

Suzo withdrew the prod.

"What is this?" Slade blurted while recovering. "Psycho 101?"

Albert chuckled.

"*Revelation*," Maurice said. "Tell me where it is."

Slade calculated quickly. Maurice hoped to present the painting to Joan Russell and remove her reason to make love to Slade. To accomplish this, he would torture the information out of him with the help of his Green Strike Youth Corps.

As an Army Ranger, Slade understood the hidden truth about

torture. Everybody broke from it. He'd never been captured by the Taliban but knew two Rangers who had. Both hard men, yet both had talked, revealing the complement and last location of his Ranger unit, Task Force Black. After which, one got his head sawn off by knife-blade. The other would have met the same fate, only the unit got to him first.

Slade knew the sooner you talked, the sooner you died. When in harm's way, he was always ready to apply the *Stagecoach* option: Save a bullet for himself. Maurice was obviously going to kill him. The fact that he had no idea where *Revelation* was wouldn't save him. So, he had to withhold that fact long enough to escape. Which meant delaying the questioning – at additional pain to himself.

"Hey, Maurice," he said. "How'd you ever make the Mounties? Those guys were legends. They protected Sitting Bull right after Little Big Horn. And they always got their man. That's criminals, Maurice, not eighty-year-old truckers worried about their livelihood. No wonder they kicked your fat ass out."

Maurice grimaced. Suzo lowered the cattle-prod to Slade's chest, and the fire ants resumed their meal. He managed to reduce his outcry to a long groan. When the ant feast ended, he turned gaspingly to Suzo.

"And you – Suzy. Cutting off your boobs didn't make you a man – just less of a chick."

Suzo emitted a weird guttural moan and pressed the cattle prod to Slade's groin. The fire ants attacked his testicles. He could barely hear Maurice yelling over his own groans.

"Suzo, *non*! *Assez*! Stop!"

After an eternity, Slade's pain diminished. His chin fell to his chest. A part of him wanted to pass out. Maurice's angry tone prevented it.

"*Stupide! T'aurais pu le tuer*!"

"We're going to anyway," Suzo said.

"*Après* he tells us where the painting is," said Maurice.

Slade's brain pinged, but he felt too nauseous to decipher the message. Maurice looked contemptuously down at him.

"You are dying, Slade. I can save you. But only if you talk to me. *Albert*."

Albert poured the last of the rum into Slade's mouth, then tossed the empty bottle on the hayloft overhead. Slade heard it clang on the wood. His brain pinged again. This time he got the message – a possible way out of this mess. It put another life at risk but gave him a fighting chance.

"*Revelation*, Slade. Where is it?"

Slade knew he had to endure at least one more shock session to seem convincing. He only hoped it would be above the belt.

"Go to hell," he said.

The electrode sizzled his chest. He stifled another scream.

"The next time will be *beaucoup plus* longer," Maurice said.

Slade attempted to look defiant. Afraid took less effort, but he remained silent. Maurice nodded. The cattle prod approached Slade's chest.

"Wait!" he whimpered. "Please."

The electrode stopped a chest hair away from him.

"I'll talk."

Suzo looked disappointed.

"Let me just say something first. My partner – Cork. He doesn't know I have the painting. There's no reason to hurt him."

"All we want is the painting," Maurice said.

"You're gonna kill me."

"*Oui*. But I will do so much faster than Suzo."

Suzo grinned.

"It's at my apartment building," said Slade.

"We searched your apartment."

With my keys, Slade realized.

"Not *in* my apartment," he said. "The maintenance man has it."

"*Le concierge…*"

"I saw what you guys did to Cork's place. So, I asked Jimmy to hide the painting for me." Sorry, Jimmy, Slade thought, but you're my only hope.

"And where did *you* find it?" Maurice asked.

"Adamo's studio."

"*Menteur*. We searched there as well."

"Not good enough. His easel had a false back."

Slade prayed Maurice knew less about easels than he did.

"And why did you not tell your partner this?"

"Cork wanted to expose the Apocalypse Mask out of principle. I wanted money – one hundred grand. Banging Zara, Demon Hunter was just icing on the cake."

Maurice frowned pensively. That last touch sold him, Slade thought. Maurice could appreciate lust for Joan Russell since he shared it. And Slade had just learned something else. Judging by his non-reaction to the reference, Maurice knew about the Apocalypse Mask. Which meant Joan probably did too.

"Where lives this *concierge*?" asked Maurice.

"He's got a small room in the basement."

Maurice turned to Albert. "Take two *étudiants* to his building and get the painting."

"Wait!" Slade said a bit too anxiously. "He won't give it to anyone but me."

Albert looked inquiringly at Maurice.

"Persuade him," Maurice said.

Albert nodded.

"Take this, Albert," Suzo said, handing Albert the cattle prod. "I got a spare."

Slade fretted. So much for Plan A, he thought, time for Plan B.

"Don't hurt him," he said. "I gave him a code phrase, in case I couldn't pick it up myself."

"A code?" Maurice said dubiously.

"Warp speed," said Slade. "Say, 'Warp speed.' You better shout it. He's kind of deaf."

Albert looked inquiringly at Maurice. Maurice handed him a remote car key.

"Take my *char*," he said. "And call me when you have the painting. Or if there is any problem."

Albert exited the barn. Maurice looked down at Slade.

"You have forty minutes to live," he said. "With your pretty face or not depends on if you told the truth."

He walked out of the barn, followed by Suzo. She pulled on the bulb string, darkening the barn. The door slid shut behind her like a coffin lid.

# CHAPTER 34

Yanking hard against the strap warmed Slade, though it didn't do his sore wrists any good. After about ten minutes, he realized the futility of the attempt – and that he'd wasted precious survival time. But he'd also taken the full measure of his restraint.

It was a strip of rope – not manila or polyester, he could now see, but hemp - wrapped twice around each wrist with a foot-long strip between them. For extreme discomfort, his arms had been tied over his shoulders and not behind his back. This was their mistake, and his best hope.

He planted both feet on the floor, grateful they'd left on his Cole Haan shoes. Pressing his skull to the timber beam, he used it to leverage his body into a reverse plank position. He worked his trapezoid muscles against the post, raising first the left then the right, over and over, his head sliding higher each time. Wood splinters scraped his back every inch of the rise to his feet.

Now came the toughest pullup he would ever try, possibly the last. He gripped the timber beam behind him with both hands at skull level. He jumped up kicking back his heels and caught the post between his knees. Gravity and pain combined to dislodge him but he remained aloft. He knew this would get a whole lot harder.

Knees squeezing the post, he raised his hands as high up the beam as he could – two inches. Again, he twisted his wrists to grip the beam. He loosened his knee hold and began to push up his body. His arms, neck, and back rebelled for one interminable inch but he climbed it, then once more scissored the post with his knees.

He kept repeating the maneuver – lift hands, push up, lock knees – each time with increasing pain. Willfully ignoring it, he continued to rise. Inches turned to feet, pain to agony, and still he climbed.

On his umpteenth rise, his hands hit the cross-beam between the post and the hayloft. He clutched it, temporarily reducing the tension on his arms and wrists. He could touch the hayloft bottom two inches above the beam, his arms weakening rapidly enough to knock him off his perch in a few more seconds. Taking a deep breath, he launched his legs straight up. His groin struck the hayloft edge.

He lowered his legs over the loft until his shoe tips touched the floor of it. He tapped his toes around the hayloft withwhat minimal radius they had. They made no contact with any loose object, not even hay. He increased their separation to the limit, his groin paying the price, but desperation trumped pain.

His left foot struck something that budged. He moved his shoe over the object then pushed it to his right shoe, trapping it between them. He pulled his legs down from the hayloft to reveal their catch – the empty bottle of Montecristo rum. He parted his feet and let the bottle drop. It shattered on the concrete floor at the base of the beam.

Slade let go of the timber post and slid down, the angle of his rope bind decelerating his descent. He landed hard on his feet, feeling fresh scars on his back. He hoped they weren't bleeding, which would betray his labors to any onlooker.

He glanced down at the broken rum bottle. A few of the pieces were conspicuously large, primarily the jagged bottleneck. Using his feet, he swept the glass behind the post in as compressed a pile as his leg reach permitted. He could do nothing about the smaller shards.

He lowered the rope while walking forward, until he lay flat on his back. His fingers began sorting through the broken glass behind the post Whenhis right hand touched the bottleneck. He clutched it like the lifesaver it would have to be.

He wanted to attack the rope bind right away but knew he had to use precious time sitting erect. Getting spotted in any other position would arouse suspicion. For precious minutes, he wormed his skull, then neck, then back against and up the post. He ended on his butt just as Maurice left him, but with one vital difference – the bottleneck in his right hand.

He placed the glass point against the hemp rope and pierced it. Shifting and twisting, he dug the glass blade deeper into the puncture hole. Much too slowly for comfort, he drove the bottleneck all the way through. Using its jagged edges, he began to saw outward from the hole and through the rope, which seemed as tough as rawhide. How embarrassing, he thought, to be done in by hippie cannabis.He kept cutting.

# CHAPTER 35

The patrol car pulled up in front of the *El Cid* apartment building. At nineteen minutes to seven on a Sunday morning, the porch light was still on without a soul in sight. Raquel Valdez turned to Cork in the passenger seat. He looked just as tired as he had on their way to the crime scene, only more alert now. His partner being a Missing Person instead of a corpse had had that effect on him.

"Want me to wait out here?" Raquel asked.

"No thanks, Raquel. I might be a while."

"Can I ask what you're looking for?"

"Any clue to Mark's whereabouts – or fate."

"Couple of uniforms already searched his place."

"After someone else," Cork said.

"Yeah. Lieutenant Wallace said it was a mess in there."

"Perhaps I can sort it out."

"Maybe I can help," said Raquel. "I am a cop."

"An off-duty one. Third Watch ended at five, didn't it?"

"Yeah."

"Go on home to your family."

"I'm single, Neil."

Cork thought he heard a suggestion in her tone. But then he'd forgotten what one sounded like.

"I'm not," he said.

Raquel nodded and turned to the building entrance.

"You got the key?"

"Yes, from your boss," Cork said, holding up a single door key. "Only to Mark's apartment, not the building."

"I'll badge the manager for you. She should be used to cops bugging her at all hours by now."

"No need for that," said Cork. "Some dawn's early jogger should be running out any minute. But I appreciate your personal assistance."

He gave Raquel a thin smile.

"I'm trying to make detective," she said. "Helping to solve this case might do the trick."

She drew a card from a thin stack in the cup holder and passed it to Cork.

"My contact data, if you wanna get a hold of me."

"Thanks, Raquel," Cork said, slipping the card into his left pants pocket.

"Good luck, Neil."

Cork stepped out of the police car and watched it pull away, fingering the lovely policewoman's card. What some men would do with this, he thought. Those who weren't married to Kathy.

He approached the El Cid entrance and climbed the four steps to the porch. It was well lit by the single roof lamp. He tried the door and found it locked. He sat down on the top step with his back to the right wall, waiting for someone to exit. Despite the cold, he closed his sleepy eyes.

"Is that him?" said a man's voice on his left.

Something urged Cork to barely react – possibly Slade's influence on him. He half opened his eyes, looking intentionally drowsy. Three young men stood on the sidewalk by the bottom step. They wore identical green hoodies. Only the trim-bearded man in the middle had his hood up. A man-bun distinguished one of his cohorts, a pearl earring the other. Cork noted the Green Strike emblem over the right breast on their sweatjackets.

He mumbled, "Double double, toil and trouble ..."

"Just some homeless guy," Trim Beard said.

"Damn nice coat for a bum," said Pearl Earring.

"Fire burn and cauldron bubble," Cork said.

"Dude's tripping," Man Bun said.

"Let's do this shit," Trim Beard said.

The three men climbed the steps past Cork's feet. He visually tracked them to the front door, displaying little outward interest. Trim Beard reached into his jacket pocket and withdrew a round key fob. He pressed it against the entry box until the door clicked. He pulled it open and went into the building, followed by his two sidekicks.

The door started swinging shut. Cork crawled fast across the porch and trapped it open. Chest down, he pulled his slim snakeskin wallet from his right back pocket and applied it like a door stop. He rolled left past the door and out of sight of anyone inside. He rose to his feet.

He tilted his head until his right eye could peer through the door glass. The Green Strike trio stood before the elevator – its down arrow lit – all three with their backs to him. Trim Beard lowered his hood to reveal a mop of black hair. The elevator doors parted, and the three men entered it. The instant the doors shut, Cork flung open the front door, scooped up his wallet, and rushed into the lobby.

The staircase door was to the right of the elevator at the back corner. Cork went through it. He descended two half flights of staircase to the basement and stopped before the exit door. He took out his cellphone, ready to speed-dial 911. He pushed open the door open just enough to peek right through the crack.

The basement was mostly a utilities corridor - about forty feet long and crossed by overhead pipes - with a white brick end wall. Past the elevator on the right were three doors, too dull grey to indicate apartments. The nearest, largest door appeared to be to the boiler room, judging by the clanging heater sound within. In front of the farthest door huddled the Green Strike three, talking too low for Cork to overhear.

Trim Beard broke the huddle and moved to the door. He knocked on it three times, his companions visibly tense. After a half minute of no response, he pounded the door. It opened inwardly.

"Who the fuck are you?" said a deep, masculine African-American voice.

A bulky Black senior in red flannel pajamas emerged in the doorway. His pot belly didn't detract from a still muscular build. Cork recalled Slade's account of his apartment building custodian, a punchy ex-boxer. The name came to him – Jimmy "Machine-Gun" Kelly.

"Hi, I'm Albert Miller," Trim Beard said. "We're ex-Army friends of Mark Slade's."

"Yeah? What floor's he on?"

Albert appeared at a loss. Man Bun touched the lower back of his sweat jacket, specifically something inside it. A gun, Cork anxiously deduced. He looked at his cellphone, preparing to tap the police emergency number shown.

"Sixth," Albert said. "Sixth floor."

Cork relaxed the grip on his mobile.

"So, why'd you wake my ass up?" demanded Kelly.

"Mark called me," Albert said. "He said he's in trouble – and badly needs what you're holding for him. He asked me to get it from you."

"I ain't holding nothin' of his," Kelly said.

"He told me you'd say that – so, he gave me the passcode you guys agreed on."

"What you talkin' about?"

"Warp speed."

"What?"

"Warp speed!" Albert shouted.

Kelly's right fist shot out, smashing Albert in the jaw. He flew backward between his two companions and slammed into the opposite wall. Machine-Gun Kelly stepped out to the hallway with his fists circling. He seemed to be in some kind of trance.

Man Bun pulled a black pistol with suppressor from the back of his sweat jacket. Before he could raise it, Kelly's right hook bashed his temple. Man Bun stumbled sideways toward the laundry-room door, dropping his pistol on the way, and fell face down on the floor.

If Pearl Earring had a gun, he didn't get a chance to pull it. A left hook turned his chin into a glass jaw. He went down quickly, either unconscious or dead.

The unsteady Albert drew a wand-shaped weapon from the right side of his sweat jacket. He swung it at Kelly, trying to tap him with the tip. Kelly blocked it with his left armand threw a punch to Albert's face. He crumpled to the floor in a motionless heap. Kelly glanced around for an opponent, his fists still circling.

He failed to see what Cork saw – Man Bun crawling toward his pistol. Cork shoved open the staircase door and charged into the hallway. As Man Bun's right hand touched the gun, Cork kicked it away. Man Bun rose to his hands and knees. Cork watched him for a moment, wondering if he'd killed Mark, then punched him in the cheek, sprawling him on his side.

Machine Gun Kelly did not appear grateful for his salvation. He moved toward Cork with lethal fists circling. Cork had little time to ponder the irony, hoping his logic would apply.

"Leave warp," he said.

The ex-boxer came two more steps nearer to him, almost within punching range.

"Leave warp speed!" Cork shouted.

Kelly halted. He shook his head several times as if clearing it of cobwebs. He looked down at Man Bun then confusedly up at Cork. Cork thanked God he'd been a *Trekkie*.

"Who are you?" Kelly asked.

"Neil Cork – Mark's partner."

"Cork … Cork Detective Agency. I heard of you."

"Good thing," Cork said. "You almost made me hard to recognize."

# CHAPTER 36

Slade had almost- cut through the hemp rope when the barn door slid open. As sunlight flooded in, he hid the bottleneck behind the post. Maurice entered wielding his “old friend”, the nightstick. He closed the door behind him and approached Slade, tapping his left palm with the baton.

To Slade’s relief, he paused three feet away and directly in front of the post, the bottleneck out of his sightline. Slade met Maurice’s eyes while continuing to slice through the rope strip, if less effectively with now constrained arm motion.

“You appear unknot happy to see me.”

“I always get a charge out you, Maurice.”

“*Albert* should have called by now. He has not.”

“Maybe he got busted for DUI. That rum of his was pretty strong stuff.”

Slade cut another slice of cord. The strap felt no weaker. How much of the damn thing was left? Maybe more than his life span.

“I believe you sent them into a trap,” said Maurice.

“The painting’s where I said it is. If Albert screwed up, send Suzy. She’s more of a man than him anyway.”

“I will go myself – but to the correct place. *Après* you tell me where that is. And you will talk, Slade. By the time my old friend is done with you – your mouth will be the only part of you still moving."

Slade said nothing, just continued to slice. Maurice took two steps forward and stopped, a curious expression on his face. Slade heard the crunching of glass under his shoe. Maurice moved aside his foot and inspected the floor between his shoes. Comprehension dawned on him. He gave Slade a venomous stare.

Slade's right foot shot up and kicked him in the groin. Maurice grunted, dropping his nightstick to cover his testicles. Slade knew he had one maneuver left to live. Tossing the bottleneck, he pulled the hemp strap against the post, his wrists on opposite sides of it. He strained with all his might to break the cord.

Maurice took a deep breath, his look of pain replaced by a sadistic one. He bent down and picked up the nightstick. Raising it back over his shoulder, he swung it at Slade's left ear. The club struck wood instead of flesh.

Slade rolled right, hands free, the cord which had bound them snapped in two. Scrambling to his feet, he turned to face Maurice. He raised his fists, showing the double layers of cord encircling each wrist. The now unsmiling bodyguard closed on him, wielding his old friend.

The nightstick came fast at Slade's left temple. His left forearm went up faster and caught the blow. It would have broken his wrist except for one factor – the strap wrapped around it. His restraint had become his armor.

He fired a right punch at Maurice's jaw, rocking his head, then sent a left cross to the same spot. Maurice retreated, waving the nightstick in front of him to form a kinetic force field. He swung the baton at Slade's face. Slade blocked it with his right wrist guard, once more feeling the sting.

He shot two left jabs at Maurice's jaw, followed by three fierce punches to his stomach. It was firmer than it looked – enough for him to recover fast and bash Slade's right collar bone with the night-stick. Slade ate the pain and launched a left cross at Maurice's right cheek, then the reverse to the other side. Maurice staggered back, again wielding his baton like a mad conductor.

Slade closed in, fists circling as he probed for a gap in the night-stick defense. Maurice suddenly spun right, his boot striking Slade's left rib. Slade winced both from the pain and his carelessness. He'd been so focused on the nightstick, he'd forgotten Maurice's savate movement at the cemetery. But he remembered the tae kwon do counter to it from the dojo in Seoul. He blocked the next left side kick with his right knee.

Maurice needed two seconds to regain his balance – Slade half as long to blast three left jabs at his jaw. Maurice only partially shook them off. He began raining nightstick blows on Slade, minus his previous force and accuracy. Slade met one hit after the other using his new wrist guards.

Maurice paused to catch his breath. Slade cut it short, throwing a brutal right punch at his chin. He felt the jawbone crack as Maurice screamed. The sound didn't concern Slade. Any passerby would think it was him howling from Maurice's handiwork. Maurice dropped the nightstick and clutched his jaw.

"Help!" he yelled. "*Aider*!"

The switch to French alarmed Slade, knowing it might bring in reinforcements for Maurice. He rushed the Canadian and leapt into a flying chest kick worthy of his old sensei, Master Choi. Maurice slammed against the wall and fell to his knees.

"*Aider*!" he croaked.

Slade dashed behind him, unwrapping the strip on his right wrist. He placed it around Maurice's neck and crossed the ends into a knot.

"Meet my new friend," he said.

He pulled apart the cord ends, garroting Maurice's throat. He counted to ten, then let the strap slacken. Maurice pitched forward to the floor, never to get up again.

Slade turned over the body. He unzipped and removed the ski jacket, which he put on himself. The sleeves were a bit too long, but it beat being Tarzan in winter. As he pulled up the zipper, the barn door started to slide open. He ran to the right side of it and pressed his back to the wall.

Suzo stepped in past him and froze, gaping at Maurice's corpse. Slade pushed the barn door shut behind her. She whirled around to face him, an expression of hatred overcoming fear.

"I'm sorry," Slade said. "Did I *shock* you?"

Suzo shrieked and spun right, her bluejeaned leg a missile. Slade blocked the kick with his left forearm. The impact stung him less than Maurice's footwork had, even minus his wrist rope. Suzo spun left, her other leg flying at Slade. His right forearm neutralized it.

"You kick like a chorus girl," he said.

Suzo went into a rapid-fire kicking spree Slade batted them away while closing in on her.

"Time for your beauty sleep, baby," he said.

He jabbed Suzo in the jaw. She crumpled to the floor unconscious. Slade sighed. He hated hitting a girl – even a tortuous bitch who wanted to be a bastard. He moved to the door, opening it just wide enough to survey the landscape.

Half a football field ahead, across patchy grass, stood a single-story white farmhouse with a timber porch, an orange door, and a gable on the right. Two green electric SUVs were charging up in the driveway, indicating probable residents. An equivalent distance past the house was a barbwire fence. Beyond it, sporadic trees increased in number the farther from the fence, clustering into a forest. A narrow access road on the right interrupted the woods. The fence gate blocking it was closed and barb-wired on top.

Slade quickly analyzed the risk factor which came down to the known versus the unknown. Getting past the farmhouse and through the fence would increase his likelihood of being spotted by an occupant. While the unviewable area behind the barn might offer either a less perilous escape route or a literal dead end.

Either way, he'd have to exit the barn in plain view of the farmhouse. His best betwas a forward run, past the house, through the fence, and into the woods, easier thought than done. He slid the barn door open wider and darted out.

# CHAPTER 37

He ran midway between the farmhouse and the access road, not tempted by the fence gate to his right. Passing the house's front porch at his left, he heard a man yell, "That's not Maurice!", followed by, "It's Slade!"

He maintained a steady pace to the barbwire fence, now thirty yards away. Nearing the barrier, he saw it was about his height with ninebarbed strands. His life depended on their flexibility. He calculated the best cross-point to be between the fourth and fifth wires from the bottom.

Reaching the fence, he tested the tautness of the lower strand. It bent down just enough for him to get through, he hoped. A rifle shot put an end to his flex test.

The bullet hit the grass behind him to his left. He dove to the ground, looking back at the farmhouse. Four green-hoodied figures came off the back porch, two bearing long guns. Slade reckoned he had thirty seconds before they could get an accurate shot at him.

He rose to one knee and stripped off Maurice's coat. Holding it in front of him, he charged the fence. He draped the coat over the strand he'd bent and pressed down. Carefully, he moved his right leg through the gap until it touched the ground on the far side.

With one foot on each side of the fence, he saw the two riflemen stop forty feet away and take aim. He fought the urge to force his whole body through the fence. Getting stuck would be worse than painful, he realized – in fact fatal. He had to risk the rifle volley. Both guns cracked. One shot puffed dirt in his eyes, the other pinged the fence post an inch from his head.

Shaken, he miscalculated his right leg maneuver. The lower barb ripped through his pants, slicing the skin underneath. Suppressing the intense pain, he extracted his lower half between the wires, then his torso. He rolled out on the opposite side of the fence.

With no time or chance to free his stuck ripped coat, he took off running toward the forest. Bullets struck the closest tree as he passed it. Green Strike was well named, he granted. He never thought he'd miss Greenpeace.

He ran into where the forest thickened and stopped, his groin aching too much to continue. Unzipping his shredded pants, he urinated on fallen brown leaves for what seemed like three minutes. As he finished, he heard a car engine on his right, getting louder. He could just see the access road through the trees, and the green E stopping on it. He started jogging left and deeper into the woods.

Two minutes later, he heard continual traffic ahead, indicating a regular street. He ceased his jogging and warily approached it, resisting the desire to run. His caution paid off when he heard car doors closing. The second EV, he realized.

Its riders would pick him off the instant he came out of the woods. These Green Strike punks had actually caught him in a pincer movement and, unlike in Sandland, without a weapon. He retreated toward mid-forest, looking out for the assailants from EV One, who should be closing in on him any minute.

He surveyed his immediate environment. Brown trees with bare branches, ground covered by dead orange leaves. His navy-blue pants – or the remnants of them – stuck out like a rainbow flag in Afghanistan. But a target could also make a good decoy, he knew. His grey boxers and bare legs would blend better with the majority of beech trees. He removed his shoes, then his torn pants, and replaced the shoes.

He scanned the trees around him. Two looked thick enough to conceal him – but only from one direction. The farm road being closer, Slade figured EV One's Green Strikers would get to him first.

Scooping up his pants, he carried them to the farther tree from the access road. On the back side of the trunk, a sharp bark jutted upward to his waist level. He spiked his shredded trousers on it and returned to the first tree. Looking back, he could see a navy-blue pants leg fluttering in the breeze as if on someone hiding behind the tree.

He pressed against his hiding tree, obscured from any frontal approach. The thought he'd be an open target for any shooter behind him concerned him, but he'd picked his poison. A moment later, he heard crunching leaves, thankfully in front of him. A similar sound followed. Two hostiles, Slade deduced, heading right toward him.

A pair of green-hooded men appeared parallel to his right shoulder. One paused close, between him and the other man. Both held Uzi Micro pistols, minus silencers. The farther man stopped short.

"Bill!" he whispered sharply, pointing to the tree ahead.

The man near Slade froze. Both Green Strike cultists stared at the tree ahead - and the navy-blue pants leg billowing into view. Bill opened fire then so did his partner. They blasted at the tree while advancing past Slade.

Slade snuck up behind Bill and threw a punch to his right kidney. Bill groaned and dropped to the ground, the pistol falling from his hand. His partner spun his gun toward Slade too late. Slade was already on him, grabbing his forearm with both hands. He launched his right elbow into the man's chin, breaking it. The man collapsed without his pistol, now in Slade's left hand.

The two riflemen emerged on the right some thirty yards away and five apart. They halted and aimed their long gunss at him. Slade fired his pistol left to right within a single second. The pair dropped simultaneously.

Slade picked up Bill's gun. Carrying a pistol in each hand like

*The Outlaw Josey Wales*, he approached the left rifleman's body. He recognized the dead man's gold brown scope rifle as a Colt Canada C20, the Canadian military standard for the past three years. Maurice must have scored a deal on them, he thought.

He started moving to the highway side of the forest. Twenty yards ahead to his left appeared a Green Striker raising a handgun. Slade shot him in the chest with his left pistol.

His right eye caught a green flash behind a brown tree. He picked off the green. The hooded body fell into plain view.

Slade continued his advance. Two more Green Strike cultists materialized thirty yards ahead, the one on the right firing a pistol. Four bullets pelted the dead leaves close to Slade. His right-hand gun shot back. The man went down.

His sidekick turned and ran away. Slade had a clear shot at the back, but the fleeing form looked female. He lowered his pistol slightly and fired. The runner tumbled.

Slade heard the sobs before he reached his attacker, who turned out to be male. He was pressing his hand to his bloody right thigh, the pistol beside him. Slade kicked the gun into a bush and continued toward the highway.

He saw it from the forest edge – a two-lane country road with no traffic at present. EV Two was stopped on the curb, the Green Strike logo on the front passenger door, hazard lights blinking. A long-haired cult member sat in the driver's seat.

Slade rolled out of the forest behind the vehicle. He noted the Maryland license plate. A diesel truck blew past him at great speed, apparently finding nothing strange in these parts about a man in his underwear crouched behind an EV.

Keeping low, Slade made his way to the driver's door. He clutched the handle and yanked open the door while standing up. Longhair looked afraid for the second before Slade jabbed him in the jaw, dazing him. Slade grabbed him by the hoodie and pulled him out the door to his feet.

"Sorry, Shortie," Slade said quoting Clint Eastwood in *The Good, The Bad, and the Ugly*.

He flung Longhair onto the road and took his place behind the wheel. He drove the SUV onto the highway, cranking up the heat. In the rearview mirror, he saw Longhair crawling toward the highway shoulder.

A signpost appeared ahead: *Olney – 8 Miles, Washington – 37 miles*. Slade now knew where he was. Out of the frying pan and speeding toward the fire.

# CHAPTER 38

"Putting you in danger had to be Slade's last resort," Cork said. "He staked both your lives on your reflex."

"Ain't been able to shake that kink in thirty years," Jimmy Kelly said.

"Today I'm thankful for it."

They stood in the boiler room of the El Cid apartment building, the noise of the large heater pump forcing them to talk loudly. Cork had an Uzi Micro pistol tucked behind his back, minus the suppressor. They kept looking down at the floor where the three Green Strikers sat side by side, their backs against a heater pipe, their wrists bound behind them by bungee cords. Man Bun and Pearl Earring were unconscious. Albert was stirring.

"We can still call the police," said Cork. "It'll spare you a lot of trouble."

"No, man, you're right. These punks would just lawyer up, while Mark gets tortured or killed. Up to us to make 'em talk."

"Have at it."

Jimmy grabbed Albert by the hoodie and pulled him to his feet. He leaned him against the pump, its heat awakening him. Cork got right in front of Albert. He'd done interrogations before, though none without FBI muscle.

"Wake up, Miller."

Albert closed his eyes, appearing to slip into unconsciousness. Jimmy tapped Cork on the back.

"Man, let me. I been snapped out of a lot worse."

Cork made room for the ex-boxer. Jimmy lightly yet methodically began slapping Albert in the face until his eyes opened. He looked angrily at Jimmy, confusedly at Cork.

"Where's Mark Slade?" Cork asked.

Albert tried to look tough but his anxiety showed. Jimmy increased it with a rap across his left cheek.

"Answer the man."

"I don't know any Slade."

"Sure, you do," Cork said. "He's your old war buddy."

Albert shook his head. Cork held up the grey key fob.

"Then how'd you get this?"

Albert said nothing. Jimmy jabbed him in the stomach, provoking a groan.

"Where is he?" Cork asked.

"Fuck you!"

Jimmy drew back his fist.

"Wait, Jimmy," said Cork. "We don't have time for this."

Jimmy dropped his arm. Cork drew the pistol and pressed the barrel under Albert's jaw, making him quiver.

"I'm ex-FBI," said Cork. "Got fired for shooting too many assholes. But to tell you the truth, I kind of miss the rush. Tell me where my partner is, or one of your friends will when they see you dying in your own blood."

"Normandy Farm," Albert blurted.

"Where the hell is –?"

"I'm disappointed in you, Albert," said a clear, distinctive male voice behind Cork. "Drop the gun, Mr. Cork. Unlike you, I have shot men before."

Cork glanced at Jimmy, who raised his hands. Cork dropped the pistol and turned around. He faced a small, plump, grey-haired Asian man in a black tuxedo, his left hand propping the door open. The Chinese features looked familiar, but the silencer-tipped gun in his right hand distracted Cork. The man stepped inside, letting the door close behind him. He looked at Jimmy.

"Untie him."

Jimmy began loosening the cord around Albert's wrists.

"Major Lao!" Albert blurted. "These men –!"

"Broke you without breaking a sweat," said Major Lao. "And Maurice told me you showed promise."

"But Major –!"

"Silence! Before you reveal more than my name and rank."

Albert rose unsteadily to his feet, Jimmy with less effort.

"Zihan Lao," Cork said. "Cultural Attache to the Chinese Embassy – with everything but your passport stamped Ministry of State."

"Your official memory is excellent, Mr. Cork."

"I remember the false diplomats we kept on round-the-clock surveillance."

"That was under your last President," Lao said. "We have much closer ties with this one."

"Sweetened by a bit of yuan."

"A great deal of yuan."

Albert picked up Cork's dropped pistol and pointed it at Jimmy.

"No, Albert," Lao said.

Albert reluctantly lowered the gun.

"What have you done to Slade?" Cork asked Lao.

"Far less than he has done to me. He killed three of our people, immobilized several more, and ruined a convenient base of operations."

"Normandy Farm."

"A suitably bucolic name, don't you think?"

"So, Green Strike is a Chinese op," said Cork. "Of course. The

Green Agenda is perfect for your team. Cuts real energy production – and doesn't work."

"Neither will your Seventh Fleet, once the President is done converting it."

"If he gets reelected."

"Naturally, we prefer the senile fool to the alternative – a barbarian capitalist who loves oil and despises Marxism, especially when so close to your shores."

"Cuba," said Cork. "You're setting up shop down there."

"That is the scenario I was assigned to advance. Slade may have doomed it – and me, with your assistance."

Lao indicated Albert and his still unconscious partners.

"Mark Slade tricked us," said Albert.

Lao ignored him and spoke to Cork.

"I am finished in this country, and mine, unless I can reverse my misfortune. I don't suppose you have the painting?"

"No," Cork said.

"Pity."

Lao raised his pistol. Cork tried to sound unafraid and settled for desperate.

"Don't be a fool, Lao. You can throw in with us. I'll connect you to my former crew. They'd love to have you."

"The weeds of socialism are better than the crops of capitalism," said Lao.

"Mao Zedong was a pedophile," Cork said, believing they would be his last words.

Lao moved his silencer tip to Manbun's head and fired, a puff of air the only sound. His second shot struck Pearl Earring in the same spot. Blood spouted from the holes in both foreheads. At least they didn't feel it, thought Cork, relieved to still be alive.

"Get the door," Lao said to Albert.

Albert remained frozen, gaping at his two dead partners.

"Albert!"

Albert hurried to the door. Lao turned to Cork, as did his silencer.

"After you, gentlemen."

Cork nodded at Jimmy. “This man has no part in this. Let him go.”

“Perhaps later,” said Lao. “Perhaps not.”

Jimmy gave Cork an appreciative nod. The two moved past Lao and out the door, held open by Albert, the gun in his left hand.

“To the elevator,” Lao said behind them.

Cork and Jimmy turned left. They walked to the elevator door and stopped. Albert pushed the single button. The lift doors parted.

“Backs against the wall,” said Lao. “And do not make a move. You especially, janitor.”

“That’s maintenance engineer,” said Jimmy.

He and Cork did as Lao told them. Albert pressed the first-floor button. The doors closed and the elevator car began to rise. Lao addressed Albert.

“Remove your silencer. Keep your pistol hidden but aimed at them.”

Albert unscrewed the suppressor and put it in the front pouch of his hoodie. Lao thrust his own silencer in his left coat pocket. The two men concealed their now shorter weapons with their free hands, still pointing them at Cork and Jimmy.

The elevator stopped and opened. Lao and Albert backed out of it with pistols raised. Albert kept the doors from closing until Cork and Jimmy had exited the elevator.

The El Cid lobby was empty, sunlight streaming through the glass front door. Albert played doorman once again. Cork saw a grey limousine double-parked across the street, hazard lights blinking. He could see none of its interior through the tinted windows.

“Step out to the porch,” Lao said. “And no further.”

Cork went out first, instantly feeling the chill. He halted at the top of the steps. Jimmy appeared by his right shoulder, the old boxer’s arm much thicker than his. Sunday morning traffic was light on Euclid Street, the double-parked limo causing minimal disturbance. A church bell peeled nearby.

“It tolls for thee,” thought Cork, recalling the John Dunne poem he’d loved until today.

Lao's voice at his back overcame the third chime. "Walk a straight line to the car. One step to either side and I'll kill you."

Cork and Jimmy descended the porch stairs in tandem. Stepping off the sidewalk onto the street, Cork heard a phone ring behind him through a speaker, indicating an outgoing call. He and Jimmy reached the dotted line dividing the two eastbound lanes. The phone rang again.

"Cao!" exclaimed Lao.

His curse seemed to do the trick. In front of Cork, the limo driver's window slid down, revealing a grey chauffeur's cap. The head under it yelled, "Warp speed!"

Cork glimpsed an eight-ball flying at his right eye just before it struck his temple. He spun and fell face down on the street, his head throbbing with pain. He heard gunshots, four or five, from both sides of him.

"Leave warp speed!" declared the same voice.

Cork managed to look to the left. Lao and Albert lay sprawled on the street near the dotted line, Lao twitching. Cork turned his head to the right and saw the limo driver's door open. A pair of black dress shoes touched down on the street at his eye level, two bare male ankles stemming out of them. He scanned up the bare legs to the grey boxers, the chauffeur's coat, the pistol in the right hand, all the way to the man's face. It was Slade.

Slade began walking toward him. Cork felt himself getting effortlessly lifted to his feet. He turned to the force responsible, Jimmy, then refocused on Slade, trying to clear his head.

"Am I dead too?" he askedsaid.

Slade smiled. "Not hardly," he said, quoting John Wayne in *Big Jake*. "I got you out of the line of fire. Sorry I couldn't come up with a less painful way of doing it."

He put his hand on Slade's right shoulder. Cork smiled back at him. A nearing police siren darkened the mood. Slade turned to Jimmy.

"Take off, Jimmy. You weren't here."

Jimmy walked away toward the El Cid porch. Cork looked down at Slade's underwear.

"We'd better get off the street," he said. "Before you get arrested for indecent exposure."

They started toward the apartment building, moving between the prone Lao and Albert.

# CHAPTER 39

Slade's living room was a bigger mess than Cork's had been. All the books and DVDs lay strewn on the carpet, along with most of the cushions except those on the sofa. Cork sat on the couch talking on his phone in speaker mode. He had to speak above the hiss of the accordion radiator in the back left corner, providing welcome heat.

"We're fine, Kate. Only don't believe anything you hear or read about us."

"Like what, darling?" Kathy asked anxiously.

"Our role in the wounding of a Chinese diplomat. Just so you know – he's a CCP spymaster. Mark shot him and a minion before they shot me."

"My God!"

"It may be a while before I can call you again."

The apartment door flew open and Carl Wallace blew in.

"Gotta go, honey, love you," Cork said, cutting off the call.

Wallace shut the door behind him, looking around the room. "Where's Slade?"

"Taking a shower," said Cork. "He badly needed one, and some first aid."

"Best throw in a lawyer – for you too."

"That bad?"

"Just got a tip from my fed insider. You're about to be swarmed by your old gang."

"So I gathered," said Cork. "Can't you arrest us first, Carl?"

"What good'll that do? Besides give Wilcox a laugh while pulling your butts out of jail."

"Is that why we've been left alone up here?"

"I told my crew to stick to the crime scenes till I questioned you," Wallace said. "FBI won't be so accommodating. Talk fast or I can't help you. What happened after Slade escaped that funny farm?"

"Three Green Strike members came here looking for that painting," said Cork. "I led them into the boiler room and managed to take the group leader's gun."

Wallace smirked but said nothing.

"Lao showed up and shot two of them- his own men - but he freed their leader. They forced me at gunpoint toward Lao's limousine. Slade was in the driver's seat. He'd noticed the double-parked limo with diplomatic plates and gathered there was devilry (it's a Sherlock Holmes phrase) afoot. He parked around the block, snuck up on the car, and pointed a gun at the driver. When the man lowered the window, Slade knocked him out and took his place."

"Witnesses said there was another guy at the scene," said Wallace. "A badass brother."

"Don't recall him," said Cork. "Must've been a passerby."

Wallace stared at him. Cork assumed an innocent expression.

"All right, I'll write it your way," Wallace said. "But I still can't help you with the feds."

"What about that funny farm?"

"Olney PD Chief said there was no sign of anyone there - dead or alive."

"Professional cleaning op," said Cork. "I suspect a Chinese laundry."

Slade emerged from the bedroom wearing blue jeans and a black sweatshirt. He gave Wallace a short wave. The policeman smiled for a split second then resumed frowning.

"We under arrest?" Slade asked.

"No, though we may wish we were," said Cork.

"Feds."

"They're on their way."

"You made a lot of trouble for them," Wallace said to Slade.

"I did 'em a favor," said Slade. "Got rid of Green Strike."

"And the Chinese Cultural Attache," Cork said.

"Oh, yeah," said Slade. "That one might be a little hard to explain."

"I can try," said Cork. "Lao was the missing link between the Good and the Ugly, working together."

"So, we were right," said Slade. "The Good's gone bad."

"And the Bad may be good."

"You guys are giving me a headache," Wallace said. "Can you stick to divorce cases from now on?"

"If there is a now on," said Cork.

"Yeah,your old pals want you out," said Wallace. "And DC's a fed town. You got no idea how much they've muscled in on this case, with the Mayor's blessing. By the way. We ID'd the corpse in Slade's car – Bruce Kagan, computer genius, forty-three years old."

"Fast work," Cork said.

"We got lucky. His prints were in the system. Seems he did a little freelancing for the CIA."

"Aw geez, not those spooks," Slade said. "We got enough trouble with the FBI."

"Theoretically, the Agency can't operate inside the country." Cork said.

"They can in Brazil," Wallace said. "Kagan's partner said it's what Langley had him working on."

"Brazil," Cork reflected. "They just had an election there."

"The commies won," said Slade.

"And banned the ex-president from running again," said Cork. "He claimed the electronic ballots were hacked."

"Sounds familiar," said Slade. "We're in banana republic land now."

“One more note on Kagan,” Wallace said. “His GU lab got burglarized a couple weeks back. He called the FBI instead of us.”

His mobile rang. He answered it.

“Wallace … Right.”

He hung up, looked grimly at Cork and Slade.

“They’re here,” he said. “I’ll see what I can do for you. Good luck.”

He hurried out the door, closing it behind him. Seconds later, it burst open, shoved in by a clean-cut young wrestler in a light blue suit and holding a pistol. His similarly clad, aged, and groomed teammate came in, also wielding a handgun.

Cork stood up next to Slade, both men raising their hands.

# CHAPTER 40

FBI Inspector Stuart Wilcox entered the apartment. He was a thin, fiftyish man with patchy brown hair and faint melasma patches on his high forehead wearing a black overcoat.

"Hello, Wilcox," Cork said dryly.

"Cork."

Cork indicated his raised arms. "Can we, ah?"

Wilcox nodded at the young agents. They lowered their guns. Cork and Slade dropped their arms.

"Have a seat," said Wilcox, indicating the sofa.

Slade and Cork sat down on the couch.

"You'll soon have to get used to much harder furniture," said Wilcox.

"Good one," Slade said, then in an aside to Cork. "This your ex-boss? He's a bigger tool than you said he was."

"Inspector Stuart Wilcox," Cork said. "FBI Counterterrorism Division."

"I did a little counterterrorism myself," said Slade.

"Yours was a lot more clearcut," Cork said.

Wilcox scowled. "You used to make waves in our section, Cork. Today, you caused a flood."

"I see the snakes didn't drown."

"Poisonous snakes to you. You two pygmies have provoked an international incident."

"Pygmies?" Slade said. "How racist."

"And heightist," Cork said.

"Shut up," snapped Wilcox. "Still a righteous bastard, aren't you?"

He turned to the closer agent.

"You know, Fuller? Cork here must've sent the Director a dozen memos citing infractions by our unit."

"A third of them by you," said Cork.

"What'd it get you? A dingy office on Florida Avenue. And soon, a dark cell in Guantanamo."

"Guantanamo?" Cork and Slade both blurted.

"That's for terrorists," Cork said.

"I think we've joined the club," Slade said.

"Why Cuba?" asked Cork. "Why not just throw us in a federal prison?"

"With all those dangerous pro-life Christians," said Slade.

"You both have too many strings attached," Wilcox said. "Slade's a war hero with suspicious soldier friends, not to mention his high-ranking father. And you, Cork, know a number of disloyal agents."

"I'm counting three right here," said Slade.

"We'll announce your new case took you to Cuba," "Very clever," said Cork. "Cuba's a Chinese client state. Beijing paid Castro billions for a base down there – while Lao enriched our President."

"Talk about the Manchurian Candidate," said Slade. "He's dancing to their tune."

"Degrading our military with green energy," said Cork.

"And turning it into a pussy force," Slade said.

"Only it all ends this fall," said Cork. "When Orange Man gets in and cleans house."

"The White House."

"Which controls the DOJ."

"Which controls the FBI," said Slade.

"The corrupt actors within it," Cork said, nodding at Wilcox. "Present company incepted."

"It'll be *The Wild Bunch* massacre all over again," Slade said.

"The Wild Bunch died in the movie," said Wilcox. "So will yout-wo.But not here in America.

"I see," Cork said grimly. "We won't be coming back from this, will we?"

"I'm afraid not," said Wilcox. "You'll make a daring escape from Gitmo,onto Cuban soil."

"We chopped down their Chinese money tree," said Slade. "Those commies ain't gonna kiss us for that."

"But they'll extract from you everything you know," Wilcox said. "And share it with us."

"I see," said Cork. "They torture us while you keep your federal hands clean -publicly at least."

"Privately, they're full of shit," said Slade.

Wilcox checked his watch.

"Your flight's at eight," he said. "Seven hours from now. You have one chance to miss it. Bring me the painting, Revelation."

"It's a deal," Slade said quickly.

"Not you, Slade. You stay here till departure time – to motivate your partner."

"That's no good," Cork said. "I'll need Slade to extract the painting. It's in a difficult location."

Wilcox shook his head. "He's an expert at evasion. His skills may rub off on you."

"I was bluffing, Wilcox," said Cork. "We don't have the painting – or know where it is."

"Then tomorrow you can join Slade on a nice Caribbean vacation, if he's still alive by then."

Cork looked at his partner with concern. Slade forced a smile.

"Go on, Neil," he said. "I'll handle the Good, like I did the Ugly."

Cork stood up and grabbed his coat off the bare armchair. The two FBI agents cleared his exit path. He walked past them and out the door.

In the lobby, two more obvious FBI agents - a Black man and a blonde woman – occupied the only chairs. They eyed Cork all the way out the front door.

# CHAPTER 41

Cork knew he was being shadowed the instant he left the El Cid. He hadoverseen enough FBI tails. He gathered his cellphone was doubling as a tracking device, another useful trick from back in the day. Walking rapidly, he made a left on the sidewalk to approach Columbia Road.

At the corner, he turned left again, and waded into the bustling Latin commerce. Throngs of tourists and residents patronized the small restaurants and clothing shops. Cork dashed across Columbia Road to the west sidewalk and continued heading south. At mid-block, he ducked into the Oasis Café, a favorite haunt of his and Kathy's.

The delicious meaty aroma hit him right away. A long glass counter on the right displayed empanadas, croquettes, ham, white rice, and black beans. A shorter counter across the back showcased jelly and guava pastries, and the cash register on top. In the right rear corner, a large coffee machine brewed black nectar. Four Latinas in yellow uniforms operated all the stations – a cute teen girl the cash register – serving the dozen customers ahead of Cork.

He got into the shorter coffee line then kept glancing back at the entrance. The next person through it would be a Fed, according to protocol. In front of Cork stood a gangly young Latino. Cork tapped him on the back. The boy turned to him.

"Pardon me, my phone's out of power," said Cork. "I'll buy your coffee if you let me use yours for one minute."

"Two coffees."

"Fine."

The kid handed Cork his cellphone. He did a quick search for St. Matthew's Church and its Sunday Mass schedule. The noon service had just begun. Cork pulled a card out of his left pants pocket. Looking at it, he entered a phone number on the mobile and wrote a five-line text. He gave the young man back his phone, interrupting his wistful gaze at Cashier Girl across the counter.

"The usual, Nico?" she asked, smiling at the boy.

"*Dos cortadas*," Nico said and aimed a thumb at Cork. "He'll pay for them."

"And one for me," said Cork.

"Three *cortadas*," Cashier Girl told the coffee-machine operator.

Coffee Woman measured the coffee while Cashier Girl rang up the total. Cork handed her a ten and stepped left out of the line. Nico barely made room for the next customer, preferring to chat up Cashier Girl. Cork heard the front door open and tensed.

A clean-cut young muscleman came in. His blue-and-white American University varsity jacket clashed with his grey suit pants. Cork recognized the type of Bureau agent that spent half his free time in the Hoover Building gym. Gym Rat joined the bakery line, towering over the mostly Hispanic customers. He didn't once look Cork's way.

Cork knew he couldn't lose the man without somehow handicapping him. Comparing their respective physiques, he found the prospect perilous. But he had to try or disappear with Slade in Cuba.

Cashier Girl placed a full coffee cup in front of him. Lifting the lid, he could feel its contents were too hot to drink. He carried the cup past the first few customers in the longer left line, blowing into it as he walked.

Gym Rat eyed the empanadas paying Cork no noticeable attention. Cork took a false sip from the cup and gasped as if from a lip burn. Gym Rat turned to him and Cork threw the coffee in his face. The man screamed, palming his face. Cork bolted out the door.

"*Llelo – rapido*!" he heard a woman shout as the door closed behind him.

He swung right on the sidewalk, running south. Hampered by pedestrians, he moved into the street, maintaining his speed. He ran the rest of the long block and made a right on Adam's Mill Road.

A line of parked cars obstructed his street path. He switched to the sidewalk on the run. Half a block farther, he slowed to a walk, catching his breath while approaching his destination – St. Matthew's Cathedral. The gothic steeple rose behind a generic new condo building on the right like a reminder of a higher truth. In the bell tower, Cork could see the brass bell he'd heard in front of Slade's place, which he feared had tolled for him.

A white Toyota sedan stopped before the marble church steps, the only space in sight with no parked cars. The front passenger door partially opened. Cork expected to see the now face-burned Gym Rat. Instead, an elderly Black woman in a worn red wool coat started to emerge.

Cork rushed up to the Toyota, crossing a narrow walkway on the right side of the church. He opened the car door all the way for the lady. She beamed at him.

"Why, thank you," she said. "Don't see many young men with manners."

She threw a glance at the driver who looked like her grandson, listening to headphones. Cork helped her clear the doorway while pulling his cellphone from his left coat pocket. He tossed it under the front passenger seat and closed the door. The Toyota shot forward, taking his cellphone with it and, he hoped, his trackers.

Gently taking the lady's arm, he escorted her up the church steps. He hoped his gallantry would camouflage him from any federal eyes. But on opening the bronze door, he gulped. The majestic cathedral was only a quarter full, with Mass already in progress. So much for blending in with the crowd, thought Cork.

He surveyed the adult Hispanic couples - several with children - and Black seniors standing up for the Penitential Act, led by a green-frocked balding priest. Cork lamented the near total absence of young people from the yuppie neighborhood around the church, aware of his own hypocrisy. Before he married Kathy, he rarely went to Mass.

His elder companion thanked him and went to join two other old women halfway up the center aisle on the right. He sat down in the pew three rows behind them, a wide distance from a sizable Latino family. The priest began the prayer, the flock reciting with him.

*"I confess to Almighty God, and to you, my brothers and sisters, that I have greatly sinned. In my thoughts and in my words, in what I have done, and in what I have failed to do. Through my fault, through my fault, through my most grievous fault. And I ask you, blessed Mary, ever Virgin, all the angels and saints, to pray for me to the Lord, our God."*

The congregation sat down and so did Cork. He checked his Rolex. Twenty-eight minutes till extraction, he noted – without knowing if it would even take place. But so far, no feds, he observed. Maybe sacrificing his mobile had done the trick. He checked the church doors – two in front opposite each other, two in the middle, and the main door behind him.

A tall, white-haired Black man in a dark grey suit stepped up to the podium donning a pair of spectacles.

"A reading from the Book of Revelation," he said in a deep, eloquent tone.

Cork sat up in the pew. No escaping the Apocalypse, he mused.

*"After these things I saw, and behold, a door opened in heaven. And the first voice which I heard, a voice as of a trumpet speaking with me, one saying, 'Come up here, and I shall show you the things which must come to pass hereafter.'"*

Cork prayed the hereafter didn't include a one-way flight to Cuba.

*"Immediately, I was in the Spirit. And behold, a throne was*

*standing in Heaven, with One seated on the throne. And He was like a jasper stone and a sardius in appearance."*

Cork pictured a sardius – an orange gem, the hair color of the presidential frontrunner. Might be a sign, he thought. The Apocalypse could be Election Day.

*"And there was a rainbow around the throne, like an emerald in appearance. Around the throne were twenty-four thrones. And upon the thrones, I saw twenty-four elders sitting, clothed in white garments, and golden crowns on their heads."*

Cork stiffened, an idea expanding in his brain.

*"And from the throne proceeded lightnings, thunderings, and voices. Seven lamps of fire were burning before the throne, which are the seven Spirits of God. The word of the Lord."*

"Thanks be to God," responded the congregation.

All except Cork, reeling from a miracle. He mentally detached from the rest of the ceremony – robotically standing, kneeling, or sitting along with everyone else, yet weighing his optional courses of action, and their probable consequences. Refocusing on the Mass, he stood up with the crowd for "The Lord's Prayer".

*"Our Father who art in Heaven, hallowed be thy name. Thy kingdom come, thy will be done, on Earth as it is in Heaven ..."*

A shaft of sunlight suddenly brightened the aisle floor on his left, indicating the open main door. Cork looked back to see Gym Rat coming up the aisle in his AU varsity jacket, a dark blot across much of his face. He accessed Nico's phone, Cork deduced, and his search for St. Matthew's Church.

*"Give us this day our daily bread, and forgive us our trespasses, as we forgive those who trespass against us ..."*

Cork watched Gym Rat move into a left-side pew six rows behind him. This time, unlike at the Oasis, he stared menacingly at Cork.

*"And lead us not into temptation but deliver us from evil ..."*

The verse held new significance for Cork.

*"For thine is the kingdom, and the power, and the glory, forever and ever. Amen."*

Exposing yourself to your target violated every shadowing technique in the manual. This was personal intimidation by a Bureau psychopath, Cork knew. Whatever his orders, Gym Rat wouldn't let him leave the sanctuary in one piece.

*"Peace I leave you, my peace I give you. Look not on our sins, but on the faith of your Church, and graciously grant her peace and unity in accordance with your will. Who live and reign for ever and ever. Amen. You may now give each other the Sign of Peace."*

Families and couples shook hands. Single individuals waved. Cork glanced back at Gym Rat, who gave him a sadistic smile – a far cry from the sign of peace. The priest raised the Host.

*"Behold the Lamb of God. Behold him who takes away the sins of the world. Blessed are those called to the supper of the Lamb."*

The celebrants kneeled, as did Cork, reciting, "Lord, I am not worthy that you should enter under my roof. But only say the word and my soul shall be healed."

The priest handed golden goblets to three female Eucharistic Ministers. He moved to the front of the center aisle along with one of the women, the other two went to opposite side aisles. A young Hispanic usher walked up the center aisle to the first pair of pews. He waved the communicants into the aisle, repeating the action with each subsequent row.

Two lines formed in the center aisle in front of Cork, the right communion line including his senior lady friend. When the usher appeared beside him, Cork stood and joined the line. He estimated a dozen people between him and Gym Rat's pew. Glancing back, he saw Gym Rat enter the left line.

Both lines advanced slowly toward the altar. The people ahead of Cork, after receiving the Host, moved right, then right again, and down the side aisle to their seats. Those in the left line went the opposite way. Reaching the priest, Cork cupped his hands in the traditional manner.

"The body of Christ," said the priest.

"Amen," Cork said.

He placed the wafer on his tongue and moved to the right.

Instead of turning into the next aisle, he rushed toward the side door. He looked back to see Gym Rat shoving people aside to start after him. Cork bolted out the door.

He emerged in the narrow walkway and ran toward the street. He heard the church door bang open , and knew Gym Rat was right behind him. Reaching the sidewalk, he darted right.

A silver Dodge Hornet idled at the foot of the church steps. Cork made for the passenger door like it was his escape hatch. But even as he reached it, he knew he couldn't open it in time.

A strong back shove flung him forward, blasting him against the passenger window. Through it, he saw the driver's door open and a blurry brunette step out. Twin vises gripped his shoulders and spun him around. He looked into the face of Gym Rat, his smile made creepier by the red burn mark all around it.

He slammed Cork backward against the car door. Pain shot up his spine. He launched two jabs into Gym Rat's stomach. It was like hitting a sandbag. He threw a right punch to the jaw. His fist got caught by a massive right palm.

Another hand grasped Cork by the throat and forced him backward against the car. The first hand joined its mate around his neck. He felt the air and life being choked out of him, his one final satisfaction – the charred skin on his killer's face.

"Freeze, Scarface!" yelled a familiar-sounding female voice.

Cork felt the pain and pressure ease on his throat and realized it was now hands free. Gym Rat stepped back, glaring rightward. Cork followed his look.

Raquel Valdez stood by the Hornet's right front hood. She wore a black alpaca sweater with two horizontal white stripes and a pair of blue jeans. She held a Glock pistol with both hands, the barrel aimed at Gym Rat.

"I'm FBI!" Gym Rat shouted.

"Good to know," said Raquel. "Hands behind your neck!"

Gym Rat angrily complied.

"Neil, you okay?" Raquel asked without taking her eyes off Gym Rat.

"Getting there," Cork said, rubbing his sore throat.

"Can you grab his gun?"

Cork closed in on Gym Rat and unzipped his AU varsity jacket. His facial mark seemed to glow redder. Cork withdrew a pistol from the shoulder holster -, a Glock 19M like he used to carry - and a phone from the right coat pocket. He stepped back, pointing the gun at its owner.

Raquel opened the Hornet's passenger door and extracted a set of handcuffs. Leaving the door open, she moved behind Gym Rat, his hands still on his skull.

"You're in big trouble, bitch," he said.

"That's Officer Bitch to you, *pendejo*," said Raquel, cuffing his wrists behind his back.

She circled back around Gym Rat to Cork's side.

"Going my way?" she inquired.

"You bet," Cork said.

He lowered the Glock and stepped closer to Gym Rat.

"You look like you could use a cup of coffee," he said.

Gym Rat seethed. Beyond and above him, the cathedral doors opened, held by two ushers. Churchgoers started to emerge. Descending the stairs, they slowed to view the big man with a marked face and wrists handcuffed behind his back.

Cork jumped into the Hornet, Raquel already at the wheel. The car shot forward. Cork smiled at Raquel.

"Sometimes there *is* a cop around when you need one," he said.

"Good thing you kept my number," said Raquel.

"Better than nine-one-one."

"I won't be responding to those calls for much longer. That's one angry fed back there."

"He's a little burned up," Cork said. "Left on Calvert."

Raquel turned left at the light, heading south on a wider avenue.

"I'm really happy about Slade," she said.

"Your joy could be premature."

"Whadda you mean?"

"Slade's on borrowed time," Cork said. "Take the quickest route to Alexandria."

"Great. Not just another jurisdiction – another state."

"A red state now."

"Right. Virginia cops think we're a bunch of softy libs. Blame us for their rising crime. And they're kinda right, thanks to our mayor."

"Good thing you're out of uniform," Cork said. "And may I say – quite fetchingly."

Raquel smiled and pushed her foot down on the gas pedal.

# CHAPTER 42

Slade picked up the last book off his living room carpet – a Bernard Cornwell hardback, *War Lord* – and squeezed it between the two other Cornwells on the shelf.

"You should leave one out," said Agent Crawford, observing him from the armchair. "You may want some reading material on your flight."

"I'll borrow your copy of the Little Red Book."

"Fuck you, Slade. We're patriots."

"So was Benedict Arnold, till he sold out the country."

"I can't wait to drop your ass off in Cuba," Crawford said.

A phone rang. Slade knew it wasn't his - still somewhere on Green Strike Farm. Crawford took out his mobile and pressed it to ear.

"Crawford," he said. "What? Who the hell is she? … All right. Bye."

He hung up and stood up.

"You got a visitor, Slade. Some hot chick. Might be your last conjugal visit."

Slade rose to his feet to stand on Crawford's right, both staring at the door. It soon opened, held by the second FBI man. Amy Gallup walked in wearing a frightened expression over her light blue crew-neck sweater, green flannel tartan skirt, grey stockings, and tan ankle-high boots. The other fed shut the door behind her.

"She's clean," he said.

"Looks pretty dirty to me," Crawford said gaping at Amy.

Slade fired a left jab at his temple, knocking Crawford against the bookshelf. His partner drew his pistol and pointed it at Slade, who raised his hands. Amy looked even more afraid.

Crawford detached himself from the bookshelf and closed on Slade, his lower lip bleeding. He threw a right cross at Slade's left jaw. Slade's head turned with the blow, his hands still raised despite the swelling pain

"Mark!" cried Amy.

Slade turned his face to her. She looked in greater pain than him. She took two steps toward him, moving past the fed with the handgun.

"Stop," the man said.

Amy halted, eyes moist, gazing at Slade. Crawford punched him in the stomach. Slade bent forward – air going out, pain coming in. He covered the source of it with his left hand.

"What kind of monsters are you?!" Amy screamed.

Crawford cocked back his arm for another punch.

"That's enough, Dennis," said his partner.

Crawford dropped his arm and stepped away from Slade. The other fed turned to Amy.

"Go ahead," he said.

Amy rushed to Slade. She put her right hand around his waist, her left hand on his chest.

"I got you, baby," she said.

She helped Slade onto the sofa. The two feds observed them, the gun wielder shoulder-holstering his weapon. Amy sat down on Slade's left. She pressed against him, stroking his shoulder though trembling herself.

"Mark, what's happening?!" she whispered anxiously. "These men – the girl who frisked me in the lobby said they're FBI."

"They are," Slade whispered back, his stomach healing faster than his jaw. "A rotten branch of it. But not rotten enough to hurt you."

"What about you?"

"I'll be all right. You got your phone?"

"Uh-uh. The woman took it. Said she'd give it back to me on the way out."

"What are you doing here, Amy?"

"I called you all last night," she said. "Kept getting your voice-mail. I had the awful feeling you were in trouble. And you are, baby. It's because of me, isn't it? I did this to you. Where's Neil?"

Slade glanced at the two feds, still looking at him and Amy. His brain pinged. He brought his mouth close to Amy's left ear as if romantically.

"Talk French," he whispered. "How'd you get here?"

"*En ma char*," Amy said expertly. "*J'ai conduit jusque de Chapel Hill.*"

Slade processed his poor French for a moment, translating it to, "In my car. I drove up from Chapel Hill." It took him a moment longer to formulate his next question.

"*Ou est tu char*?" he asked, his French pronunciation far worse than Amy's.

"*En bas de la rue*." Down the street.

Slade moved his mouth intimately close to Amy's ear, the two feds watching them.

"Leave the key under the seat," he whispered, kissing the ear. "And get away from it."

Amy turned her lips to his mouth and gave him a deep tongue-filled kiss. Crawford gawked at them. His partner's phone rang. He answered it.

"Fuller," he said. "No, sir, no trouble.."

He listened for half a minute more before speaking again.

"Understood, sir. Goodbye."

Fuller hung up and turned to Crawford.

"We gotta move Slade right now."

Slade silently cursed. Another brilliant escape plan down the drain. Once Amy left, he'd intended to take out the two feds and drop out the window.

"What's up?" Crawford asked.

"Cork lost our tail," said Fuller.

"What?! How?!"

"He hurt Holvak."

Crawford looked incredulous. "That twerp?"

"Bravo, Cork," Slade said quietly.

Amy clearly heard him.

"Cork's got pull around town," Fuller said. "Might give us trouble. They moved up our takeoff to five."

Slade groaned silently.

"Still Airstrip J?" asked Crawford.

"Yeah."

Crawford pointed at Amy. "What about the hottie?"

"Sharon'll watch her," Fuller said.

"No fair," Crawford said. "All right, Slade, get moving."

Slade stood up.

"No!" Amy moaned, clutching his left wrist as if hoping to hold him there.

Crawford said, "Don't worry, honey, I'll be back for you. But your boyfriend won't."

"You sick pigs!" cried Amy.

Crawford grinned. Slade gently detached his arm from Amy's grip.

"Stay alive," he said, quoting Daniel Day Lewis in *The Last of the Mohicans*, "No matter what occurs. I will find you." He bent down and gave Amy a fervent kiss which she vigorously returned.

"I love you, Mark," she said.

Slade stroked her cheek then joined his two captors.

"Can I grab a coat?" he asked, nodding at the bedroom.

"You won't need one where you're going," Crawford said.

Fuller opened the door. Slade exited, Crawford right behind him. They headed toward the elevator.

In the lobby, they were joined by a large Black agent and a hard-bodied blonde wearing a blue blazer with grey slacks. Sharon, Slade assumed. Through the front door glass, he could see Jimmy on the stepladder adjusting the porch lamp. The thought struck him right away. Jimmy didn't work on Sundays.

"The girl?" Sharon asked.

"Keep her here till you hear from me," said Fuller.

Sharon nodded and moved to the elevator. The Black agent opened the front door and went out, followed by Fuller. Slade felt a hand on his back push him to the door. He refrained from turning around and slugging Crawford. It would constrain him further and make breaking away harder.

He walked past Jimmy's ladder. The custodian remained focused on the porchlight.

"Hey, Fuller," Slade said to the man ahead. "How far is Airfield J?"

"Shut up," said Crawford behind him.

"I just wanna make sure we catch that five o'clock flight," said Slade.

A grey SUV pulled up to the sidewalk directly ahead. Fuller opened the rear right door. Crawford gave Slade another shove.

# CHAPTER 43

"Since we'll be sharing a prison cell, I ought to know more about you," Cork said. "Like where you're from. My guess is farther south than Mexico."

"Venezuela," said Raquel.

They were on the Woodrow Wilson Bridge crossing the Potomac River into Virginia. Raquel kept switching lanes in the heavy traffic.

"When did you come up?" asked Cork.

"Ten years ago, at seveneteen."

"Parents?"

"Just my mom. Dad didn't make it. He was a TV newsman in Caracas, and a major critic of Maduro. His car ran off a mountain road."

"SEBIN," Cork said.

"Secret police bastards."

"Our FBI is becoming just like them. Elements inside it."

"I saw that in Scarface back there," said Raquel. "Made it easier to smack 'im down."

"I'm trying to stop them."

"You can count on me, Neil."

"It could cost you your detective career."

"Then you can hire me."

Cork reflected for a moment.

"I could try you out," he said. "Are you good at following orders?"

"From people I respect."

The car pulled up to the security gate of a modest townhouse complex with brown brick residences. A heavy female security guard opened the booth window. Raquel rolled down her own window and showed the guard her badge. The metal arm ahead lifted. Raquel drove past it.

"She didn't recognize your DC badge," Cork said.

"The gold shield was enough."

They entered a complex of narrow, two-story, caramel-colored Tudor-style condos.

"Turn right past the playground," said Cork.

The car passed a small vacant playground with a triple swing set, a slide, monkey bars, and a seesaw. Cork pointed to a semi-hidden turnoff behind the playground. Raquel pulled into a dead-end road with four empty parking spaces. A footpath led from the playground toward the adjacent condo cluster. Raquel parked, nodding at the playground.

"No kids on a sunny Sunday," she said.

"They're all playing video games inside."

"Sad."

"My daughter won't be one of them," Cork said, adding, "If I get to see her grow up."

"You will, Neil. Unlike my dad."

Cork opened the car door.

"Let me come with you," said Raquel.

"No. It may be a trap. Wait twenty minutes. If I'm not back by then, take off."

"Anything I can do now?"

"Yes," said Cork. "Use your police influence to get the number of Jimmy – James – Kelly, custodian at the El Cid apartment building. Maybe he can let us know Slade's status."

"Will do. Good luck – boss."

Cork hurried onto the footpath. Walking rapidly, he reached the street on the other end. This side of the path felt somehow colder. Cork jogged across the street to the left of the townhouse group.

A narrow walkway ran behind and between two rows of homes, all marked by similar rear patios with wooden fences. Cork took it. Bypassing three decks on each side, he darted left to the fourth.

He clambered over the wooden railing and onto the terrace. Through the sliding glass condo door, he could see a cozy, clean living room dominated by a flat widescreen TV showing an inaudible football game. He knocked on the door four times.

A woman appeared in the dining room beyond the living room. She had short brown hair and a light purple sweatsuit on her slender figure. She looked at the patio door, worriedly at first then in unhappy recognition. After a moment's hesitation, she crossed the living room. She slid open the door but remained in the doorway.

"Neil," she said in an unwelcoming tone.

"I'm sorry, Linda, I had to come this way for a reason. I need to speak to Alan. Is he here?"

"He's upstairs getting dressed for the Redskins game."

Cork liked that Nichols still called the Washington team by its famous pre-woke name. He despised the name "Commanders" like his Western-loving partner, Slade. Either way, they'd made it to the playoffs versus the Philadelphia Eagles.

"Come in," said Linda stepping aside.

She closed the door behind Cork. He followed her through the living room to the far dining room. They made a left into the door-less combination kitchen and dinette.

The round breakfast table had three matching white chairs and one highchair in which a plump baby sat flapping a porridge-caked spoon. On the kitchen counter, a green-lit coffeemaker held a semi-full decanter – minus Linda's portion in a rose cup on the table. An empty blue mug awaited its fill. Cork smiled at the baby.

"This must be Tommy," he said. "Handsome devil."

His remark elicited a maternal smile from Linda. "He will be with more hair. Want some coffee? You look like you could use some."

"Please," said Cork.

Linda took down a blue mug from the shelf above the coffeemaker and filled it from the decanter.

"Cream and sugar?"

"Both, thanks."

Cork tried to sound casual despite the ticking clock in his head. And Linda seemed more tense than he. She placed the coffee mug on the table.

"""Alan'll be down any minute," she said. "Have a seat."

Cork sat down across from Tommy with Linda on his left. They uneasily sipped their coffee. Linda broke the ice.

"How's your family?" she asked.

Cork knew she never mentioned Kathy by name, having relegated it to Alan's past.

"Both fine," he said.

"How old's your daughter now?"

"Year and a half."

"That's nice," said Linda. "Tommy's nine months."

Cork smiled encouragingly.

"Hey, honey!" came Nichols' voice from the living room, followed by approaching footsteps. "I can't find my 'Skins sweatshirt. Did you finally throw it out?"

Alan Nichols appeared at the dinette entrance and froze on seeing Cork.

"Jesus Christ!"

"No, someone else they're trying to crucify," said Cork.

"Yeah, my superiors!"

"Only in rank, Alan. They're bent and you know it."

"What if they are?" Nichols relaxed slightly. "What can I do about it? I'm only a poor incorrupt official."

Cork studied his ex-partner. His belly appeared more prominent in a purple long-sleeved T-shirt above blue sweatpants.

"You can help me get them before they get me," said Cork. "And Slade."

"You said yourself, Slade's a nutcase."

"But he's my nutcase."

Nichols looked at Linda. She stood up and approached Tommy's highchair.

"Your sweatshirt's in the dryer," she said. "I'll leave it on the sofa."

"Thanks, honey," said Nichols.

Linda lifted Tommy and carried him toward the dining room. Nichols sidestepped out of her way. Entering the kitchen, he went straight to the coffeemaker.

"Wilcox said they were just going to interrogate you guys," he said, filling his mug.

"Yeah – in Cuba."

"What?!"

"They're spiriting us away to Guantanamo – where they don't have to show us no stinking badges."

"Black flight," Nichols said somberly.

"Pitch black," said Cork. "Eight o'clock tonight."

Nichols sat down on Cork's right looking glum.

"You know they tapped my cellphone, in case you called," he said.

"S-O-P," said Cork. "It's why I came in person."

"Did you bring my severance check?"

"A promotion perhaps," Cork said.

Nichols looked keenly at him.

"You're being passed over, Alan," said Cork. "You have seniority on Wilcox, yet he's your boss. As his flunkies will soon be. Because they play dirty, and you don't. Here's your chance to take them down and reap the reward, in a clean Bureau under new management. You can be part of it, if you play your cards right. One card in particular."

Nichols sat up straighter. "The Apocalypse Mask. You got it?"

"Not yet," said Cork. "But I know where it is. And I'll give it to you, if you help me save my partner."

"I'm open to suggestions."

"Is McKenna still a straight arrow?"

"Sure," said Nichols. "He gives Wilcox a lot of shit like you used to. And the Chief wants him out too. But he's a rock star to the younger agents."

"'The last of the G-men'. Tell Mac about the Black Flight. He can sound the alarm and ground it."

"If I do that," said Nichols., "Wilcox'll know it was me who sold him out."

"Just before he gets tossed out with every other bad apple."

"Only if the Orange Man gets back into the White House," said Nichols.

"The Apocalypse Mask will guarantee that. Whatever the hell it is."

Nichols appeared pensive for a half minute.

"You'd really let me have the thing?" he finally asked.

"And the glory."

"Okay, Neil," he said. "I'll make the call to MacKenn –"

A knocking sound startled both men – three raps from the direction of the living room. Nichols sprang to his feet and rushed out of the kitchen. Cork stood up, resigned to his recapture. He moved into the dining room, staring at the patio door.

To his relief, Raquel Valdez stood on the terrace all alone. Nichols opened the door for her, but she remained outside. After a brief exchange with her, Nichols waved Cork over.

Cork approached the open door. Nichols moved toward him. He gave Cork a nod as their paths crossed. Cork stepped out to the patio, closing the door behind him. Raquel looked anxious.

"I talked to Kelly," she said. "He said Mark got pulled out of there forty minutes ago."

"That's bad," Cork said.

"Gets worse. His takeoff's at five o'clock, not eight."

"Oh, no!" Cork gasped, looking at his watch. "That's ninety minutes from now."

He started pacing around the patio, lost in thought. Raquel watched him with concern. He halted in mid-step. He knocked on the door. A moment later, Nichols opened it. Cork handed him Raquel's contact card.

"Black flight's been moved up" he said. "Call that number ASAP, from a secure phone. If McKenna's in and I'm alive, I'll arrange for the handoff."

"Hope you make it, Neil."

"Me too," Cork said, and turned to Raquel. "Let's go rescue Slade."

He went over the patio railing and dropped to the grass. Raquel did the same if more gracefully. They jogged across the road. On the footpath. Cork slowed to a power walk, Raquel at his right shoulder. He talked on the move.

"Get Senator Owen on the phone. Cut all the red tape you have to but get me him!"

Raquel pulled out her cellphone, reducing her pace. Cork reached the Hornet well ahead of her. He crossed his arms on the roof and buried his forehead in them. He stayed like that until he heard Raquel's voice behind him, getting closer.

"Yes, sir," she said. "It is a matter of life and death."

Cork turned to see Raquel emerging from the footpath with the phone to her ear. She joined him beside her car.

"He's right here, Senator," she said, handing Cork the phone.

He gripped it as he spoke. "Senator – Neil Cork. I know where the painting is, and the damned Apocalypse Mask. If Kudzu's real, let's make a deal."

# CHAPTER 44

Airstrip J was a grassy unkempt field with an old aluminum hangar in a desolate patch of Prince William County. It lay conveniently close to the FBI Academy at Quantico (nineteen miles) yet much farther than the official Bureau airport. This allowed quick access by certain agents on more clandestine missions. In a bit of rare institutional humor, the veteran who authorized the airstrip had given it the famous initial of the legendary first FBI Director.

A nine-foot barbwire fence surrounded the area, accessible only through a double gate blocking the single driveway. To its left stood a white wood booth manned by a buff agent in a reddish ski jacket. Cork surveyed all this through the Hornet's passenger window in the six seconds it took to bypass the driveway. Raquel continued driving on the quiet country road.

"No plane yet," said Cork.

"Maybe in the hangar?"

"I'm surprised it's still standing. I wrote a memo about Airstrip J, questioning its function. Never got a response."

"Well, now you know," said Raquel.

"Yeah, Black Flights for vanishing passengers."

"Like your partner."

"He's probably in that hangar," said Cork. "Guarded by a dozen agents."

"That many?"

"Wilcox read his file. He knows how dangerous Slade can be."

"Lieutenant Wallace said he's a war hero."

"Now he's a POW," said Cork.

He pointed to an obscure crossroad forty yards ahead. "Pull over there."

Raquel made a right on the unmarked road and stopped halfway in the weedy lot bordering it. She and Cork removed their seatbelts. The sun was sinking fast. Cork could barely see the hangar a mile away across the barren field. He glanced at his watch.

"Four forty-seven. Thirteen minutes – if this Federal Express is on time."

Raquel nodded grimly.

"Doesn't look like the cavalry's coming to save Slade, if it even exists," Cork said. "Which makes me his only chance."

"And me."

Cork shook his head. "No, Raquel. You've done more than enough. Risking your career is one thing. Your life is irreplaceable."

"So was my father's. You said yourself, they're the same bastards who killed him."

"They aspire to be – and turn this country into yours."

"This is my country now," Raquel said.

Cork nodded. "Very well, then gallantry be damned."

"What's the plan, boss?"

"We wait till the plane is down and they're boarding Slade," said Cork. "Less time for them to react – more time for Mark to make his move. I suspect he's planning to already. We'll be giving him an edge."

He reached into the glove compartment and took out Gym Rat's Glock. He contemplated the gun in his hand.

"You know, I had a pistol exactly like this in the Bureau," he said. "Fired it just once, in basic training. Barely hit the target. And it wasn't moving."

"Mine were," Raquel said.

She extracted her gun belt from between the seats and gave the pistol a quick inspection. When she finished, Cork handed her his gun. She repeated the procedure on it. She returned the weapon with an approving nod.

They sat in silence watching the sun sink. Raquel drew a tiny silver crucifix from inside her blouse and fingered it. Cork could hear her whispering the *Santa Maria*. He translated it in his head.

The sound of a jet engine sound drowned out Raquel's prayer, faint at first but getting louder. Cork stepped out of the car. Looking up and left, he saw the small, sleek white jet descending steeply toward the hangar. He climbed back in the car.

"Amen," he said.

Raquel tucked the crucifix back in her blouse and started the Hornet. She made a U-turn then a left on the road to Airstrip J. Neither she nor Cork refastened their seatbelts.

# CHAPTER 45

Slade could tell the hangar hadn't housed a plane in years, resembling more a makeshift classroom. In the center of the space, three rows of portable metal chairs – eight per row in two sets of four – faced a whiteboard near the rear wall. Slade imagined the subject of the class – *How to Violate the Constitution and Get Away with It.*

He sat on the floor with his back against the right wall, between Crawford and Fuller, clearly the agent in charge. On the opposite side of Fuller sulked a large man with his left cheek bandaged. Holvak, Slade knew, the gorilla Cork had burned with the aid of a female cop. The lovely Officer Valdez, Slade deduced, having overheard Holvak's reluctant description of her.

Eleven fit, purple jacketed trainees" occupied the metal chairs, one a pretty Arab girl. Most of the men stared at their cellphones watching the Redskins playoff game. Slade could hear the announcer on the nearest phone, "It's the third quarter before the Super Bowl for one of these teams. Eagles – seventeen, Commanders -fourteen."

All eleven agents wore shoulder holsters, some more conspicuous than others. Too many to jump, Slade realized, especially with the hangar double doors shut. He'd have to seize his chance outside.

The roar of a landing jet drowned out the football game. Slade recalled the sound from various air bases in enemy countries. He never thought his homeland would be one of them.

Fuller, Crawford, and Holvak stood up near him. Crawford moved in front of him and gave his right shoe a kick.

“Get up, Slade. You don’t wanna miss your flight.”

Holvak grinned. Slade stood up, Crawford and Holvak circling behind him. Two men left their chairs and attacked the hangar doors.

“Move,” Crawford said, giving Slade the familiar back shove.

Slade vowed to break him of the habit, but he followed Fuller to the separating doors. He knew Crawford, Holvak, and Fuller would be getting on the plane with him but not how many others. To his relief, the rest remained in their seats, some already refocusing on the playoff game. His long odds had shortened.

The hangar doors opened on the grassy airfield seventy yards from the fence gate. Everyone but Slade looked to his right at the oncoming jet, he straight ahead at the gate. He calculated the long run to it and, unfortunately, the sentry booth guarding it.

The small white jet flew in low over the hangar and touched down sixty yards to the left . It taxied for thirty more, turned left, and came to a stop the hatch facing the hangar. The engine noise diminished to a low whine.

Slade appraised the aircraft. It was a white Cessna Citation with a black stripe rising from the nose to just above wing height, eight-passenger capacity, seven comfortably. He could handle that number, plus the short-haired Beach Boy-looking pilot in the cockpit.

His captors marched him toward the jet while the two doormen, one an inch taller than the other, reclosed the hangar. The pair then joined the flight group, frustrating Slade. He’d have to incapacitate five men, then make a run for the gate, probably under fire, and shoot it out with the booth guard. And these feds would be better marksmen than the Green Strike cultists. Slade hoped the fading sunlight would give him some cover.

He'd already weighed the morality of his plan, beginning with the trainees in the hangar. Maybe they were dirty, maybe just following orders. He’d try to avoid killing them except in self-defense. But every fed on this flight was dirty and deserved what was coming to him. Slade would live or die in America.

Holvak jogged ahead of the group to the jet. Slade mentally redrew his strike plan, positioning two men in front of him – Holvak and Fuller – and three in back – Crawford and the doormen. Holvak pulled open the hatch and lowered a three-rung plastic ladder.

Slade glimpsed the jet's white interior. It contained two pairs of plush seats facing one another, none in which he intended to sit. He neared the plane, tensing to jump Fuller, the smaller target of the two in front. Before he could reach him, Fuller went up the jet ladder and into the hatch. Slade felt a gun press against his back. He preferred Crawford's usual shoving.

"Tourist class now boarding," said Crawford.

Holvak chuckled. Slade approached the jet ladder. He couldn't see Fuller on the plane but hoped he was near the hatch, the easier to dispatch quickly. The instant he put his right foot on the ladder, he heard gunshots.

They'd come from far behind him. He felt Crawford's gun barrel detach from his back as Fuller reappeared in the jet hatch. Slade spun around. All six men stared at the double gateand the silver Hornet sedan blasting through it.

The car sped toward them taking more rear fire from the gate guard. The sound of distant gunshots didn't seem to penetrate the hangar. Its twin doors remained shut. Thank God for the playoff game, thought Cork, and good earbuds.

The two doormen pulled out their Glocks. Crawford swung his gun toward the inrushing Hornet, giving Slade his chance. He threw a hard right cross at Crawford's jaw, knocking him down and semi-out. The gun dropped from his hand.

Slade whirled to face Holvak, knowing he wouldn't get to him in time. The big man reached for his shoulder holster. Then his hand came up empty. He grimaced with his face bandage and began moving toward Slade.Slade shot a glance at Fuller, still in the jet hatch watching the Hornet stop twenty yards away. Holvak halted dhis advance on Slade to also look at the car. It all reminded Slade of *Tombstone* right before the Gunfight at the O.K. Corral.

On the far side of the car, the driver's door opened. Neil Cork emerged with arms raised.

"Don't shoot!" he shouted fearfully.

"Cork," Holvak muttered in Slade's earshot.

"Step away from the car!" yelled the taller doorman, his gun trained on Cork.

"I brought the painting!" Cork declared. 'It's right in the back seat!"

He cracked open the Hornet's rear door with his right hand, his left arm still up.

"Freeze!" screamed the shorter doorman, ready to blast Cork.

Cork raised his right arm, then caught sight of Fuller in the jet hatch.

"Fuller, tell them! I got the painting like Wilcox wanted!"

Fuller said nothing, apparently confused without orders.

"Walk around the car!" demanded the tall doorman. "Now!"

Cork moved to the hood of the Hornet, both doormen tracking him with their guns. The panting booth guard joined the pair with pistol in hand. Cork reached the hood, exposing his whole upper body.

Slade didn't look at Cork. He watched the Hornet's rear left passenger door open further, which could only be by someone crouching on the floor. Cork dropped behind the hood. Officer Raquel Valdez sprang up holding a pistol over the car roof, pointed at the doormen and booth guard.

"Metro police!" she yelled. "Drop your weapons!"

All three agents swung their guns toward her. She fired first, striking the tall doorman in the chest. He fell fast.

The other doorman and the booth guard opened fire. Bullets shattered the car glass as Raquel ducked behind the trunk. The two feds started blasting at it.

Cork's head popped up behind the hood as did the pistol in his hand. The shooters swung their guns to him as he fired off a full round. Several shots missed - one bullet chipping the grass near Slade's feet - but three hit their marks. The other doorman and the booth guard went down.

Slade saw the hangar doors start to open in the distance. He gave himself less than two minutes to evac his rescue team and himself.

"Start the car!" he yelled.

He saw Holvak probing the tall grass for Crawford's pistol. Slade charged him and leapt into a drop kick to the shoulder, knocking him down on his side. Holvak stood up fast to close on Slade, smiling under the bandage as if confident in his larger bulk.

He fired a punch at Slade's head, powerful enough to split it. The blow only scraped Slade's left wrist, which had shot up to repel it along with the right forearm. Slade blocked the volley of slugs seeking softer body parts. His right fist hammered Holvak's nose, breaking it. He shrieked. Slade let loose a sequence of precise punches to the jaw that soon knocked the big man out of his misery. Though he'd need another bandage.

"Come on, Mark!" yelled Cork.

Slade turned to the Hornet. Cork was in the passenger seat beckoning at him through the now glassless window. Fifty yards beyond the car, nine armed agents were charging at them like the Hurons in *The Last of the Mohicans*, only with two scope rifles and a submachine gun. Slade believed he had enough time to beat them to the car. Then he felt the old chill in his spine.

Glancing at the jet, he saw Fuller in the hatch taking pistol aim at Cork. Slade dove to the grass snatching up Crawford's pistol and fired four shots into the hatch. Fuller fell out of the plane to the ground chest down.

The Hornet started rolling forward, the swarm of fed trainees gaining on it. Slade took off toward it, gun in hand. Cutting in front of the jet cockpit, he glimpsed the Beach Boy pilot with his bare palms forward to signify his outsider status.

Slade caught up to the moving car and opened the right rear door on the run. He jumped into the seat behind Cork. The car picked up speed while plowing through the high grass. Cork and Slade looked back at the pursuers between them and the front gate.

"Hope there's a back way out," Slade said.

"It's chained," said Cork.

"We better unchain it," said Slade.

"I might be able to break through it," Raquel said.

They saw the double gate a half football field ahead and the narrow road beyond it. Raquel pressed her foot down on the gas pedal. Something blew inside the hood. The car slowed to a crawl, about to stop.

"They got the engine block," said Raquel.

"And us," said Cork.

"Turn parallel to them," said Slade.

Raquel turned the car left, putting it lengthwise to the oncoming feds. The three occupants abandoned the car and got on the right side of it – Slade behind the hood, Cork the carriage, Raquel the trunk. All three pointed their guns at the wave of feds rushing toward them.

"Raquel," Cork said. "Give yourself up. Wallace'll back you."

"They'll get me anyway," said Raquel. "Better here than in a fake car accident."

"True."

"Officer Valdez," said Slade.

"Yes, Mark?"

"I'd have you in my outfit any day."

Raquel smiled. The feds crossed the imaginary forty-yard line and got into shooting positions. The man with the submachine gun stepped in front of them. Slade pegged his weapon as a Heckler and Koch MP5/10, just before it opened fire.

Countless bullets riddled the Hornet's left frame, exploding the tires. The car sank, forcing Slade, Cork, and Rachel to duck down with it. The fusillade ceased.

"If either of you survive this," said Cork. "Give Kathy and Melanie my love."

"Your wife's a lucky woman," said Rachel. "I think her luck will hold."

"All I want is to enter my house justified," Slade said, quoting Joel McCrea in *Ride the High Country*.

"That you will, partner," said Cork.

Slade felt an oddly pleasant warmth at his friend's words. Peering over the car hood, he watched the submachine-gunner move in closer, a tactical mistake. Slade sprang up, fired once, and ducked. The submachine-gunnerdropped.

The other agents opened fire. Bullets pelted the car, keeping the three behind it pinned down. The moment the shooting stopped, Slade peered over the Hornet's trunk. He saw the two riflemen running to the right and left. He recognized the maneuver.

"They're gonna hit us from both flanks," he said. "Out of our pistol range."

He swiveled left, keeping the rifleman on his side in his gunsight. Raquel mirrored him on the right. The snipers paused fifty yards equidistant from the Hornet, then advanced past the car line. Slade and Raquel started blasting at them, their bullets falling short of the targets.

Raquel's pistol clicked empty. So did Slade's. They could do nothing more than watch their executioners point their rifles at them.

.

Cork saw the red laser dot strike Raquel's right breast, linger on it, then move toward her left breast as if violating her. A sudden rage overcame his fear. He pulled Raquel back and stepped in front of her. Aiming his pistol at the sniper, he fired once. The bullet fell far short of the rifleman but spoiled his aim, the red dot shifting to the car.

Slade looked straight at the other sniper instead of the target light on his own chest. He'd long been ready for this end. A crash noise to his left distracted him and the sniper. A black van was rolling over a fallen piece of fence and into the area between him and the sniper. The sniper fired at the van to the sound ofpinging metal. The van swerved right, emitting two shots out the back. The rifleman fell.

The van sped past the Hornet toward Raquel's sniper, who turned his rifle to it. The vehicle stopped thirty yards in front of him, the rear door flying open. Two men jumped out the back wearing black body armor, helmets, and goggles, and wielding Glock pistols.

One raider broke left, the other right to engage the sniper. The sniper fired first, striking Raider Two's left shoulder. Raider Two shot back, nailing the rifleman. He let the pistol drop and clutched his hurt shoulder.

Raquel's legs buckled. Cork caught her before she fell. She held on to his neck with both arms, trembling. They watched the raging firefight in front of them, along with Slade.

Raider One brought down two FBI trainees, his armor taking heavy fire from the rest – all except the frozen Arab Girl. He began retreating toward the Hornet. Slade snatched the pistol from Cork's hand and dashed into the battle. He shot a balding trainee in the right leg, then a bulky one in the left arm. He spotted the Black agent from the El Cid lobby raising his pistol at him. Slade shot him first in the right rib. The fed dropped to his knees pressing his bloody side.

Only the frozen Arab Girl remained standing. She dropped her pistol and raised her arms, looking terrified.

"On the ground!" yelled Raider One.

Arab Girl fell to the grass. Raider One turned to Slade.

"Get your team into the van, fast!"

Slade hurried toward the Hornet. He passed the wounded raider being helped into the van by an unarmored, ungoggled, redheaded man, obviously the driver. Cork and Raquel stepped out from behind the Hornet, he still supporting her. She paused to assess the car wreck.

"Five more payments to go," said Raquel.

"That car saved our lives," Cork said. "So did the driver. I'll buy you a new one."

"For now, get on the bus," said Slade, pointing at the van.

They moved to the van's open rear compartment. It was windowless and bare but for a yellow-cushioned bench along each side. The wounded raider sat on the right bench, a tourniquet on his right arm, his helmet and goggles off. Slade recognized Senator Owen's Indian bodyguard from police headquarters. The three rescuees took the bench across from him – Slade by the door, Raquel between him and Cork. Slade nodded at the Indian commando.

"How bad are you hit?" he asked.

"I'll live," said the Indian with a slight Southern accent.

"So will we, thanks to you boys."

The raider nodded. A moment later, Raider One jumped into the van, pulling the door shut. He sat down beside his partner The sound of distant police sirens could be heard getting louder by the second.

"Take off, Blane!" Raider One shouted.

The van started to move, picking up speed. Raider One took off his goggles and helmet, revealing himself as Owen's other body-guard with the large ears. The two groups faced each other across the van as the police sirens faded then died.

After several minutes, the van stopped. Raider One opened the back door on a cold dark evening. A dark unlit SUV idled behind the van, the shoulder of a ghostly road by an empty field. Raider One jumped out and held the door.

Senator Sam Owen climbed into the van wearing a caramel over-coat. He sat down in the vacated bench space across from Slade, Raquel, and Cork. The door closed and the van began to move.

# CHAPTER 46

Owen addressed the wounded raider on his right. "Need to go to the hospital, Tar?"

"No, sir. Doc Carter can fix me up."

"Good," said Owen. "That's one less security headache for me tonight. "Good job, gentlemen."

"Don't mention it, sir," said the Indian.

"You bet I won't," Owen said, turning to the trio across from him. "Sure hope neither will you three."

"The irony hasn't escaped me," said Cork. "I worked hard to flush out Kudzu, even off the Bureau clock. Yet tonight I owe them my life, and that of my friends here."

"I appreciate your dilemma, Cork," said Owen. "You made things pretty hot for us back in the day. Now we both need to cover up killing a half dozen FBI agents. That they were dirty, murderous agents involved in an illegal op might keep us safe until November."

"The election," Slade said.

"It's what I'm counting on," said Owen.

"Tell me one thing, Senator," said Cork. "Are you the head Kudzu?"

"More like the spine."

"Of course," said Cork, waving his hand around the van. "You couldn't finance an operation like this – of men and material – and keep it secret. You need an extra-government hand – make that anti-government."

"We just had a bad taste of the Government," Slade said.

"It's a little toxic," Cork said.

"It's radioactive," said Owen. "The whole damn thing. Most people can't see it 'cause the outer trappings are still there – White House, FBI, CIA –"

"Pentagon," Slade said.

"But they're all infested by parasites, with one hive mindset – destroy America as we know it. And phase one is complete – control the media, brainwash the people. Nothing to see here, folks. No twenty-million aliens crossing the phantom border. No crime-ridden city wastelands. No political dissent banned as disinformation or hate speech. No kids brainwashed to think they're racist, sexist, or the wrong gender, and our country a slaver patriarchy. And no secret deals with China and Iran threatening our national security."

"The majority voted for that," Cork said unconvincingly.

"No, Cork, they voted for the illusion of normalcy. You knew something was wrong when you left the Bureau. Some of us saw the cancer spreading long before that – one a billionaire you've heard of. And I had the political cloutTogether we formed the resistance."

"Kudzu."

"We've managed to delay the Marxist takeover of the country for a decade. But they're about to mount a real coup - not that clown show they engineered at the Capitol. We're the only ones who can stop it."

"Stop what?" Raquel asked anxiously.

"The end of the Republic," Owen said. "By the very process meant to guarantee it."

"The election," said Cork. "Election interference."

"Election disappearance," Owen said.

Cork, Slade, and Raquel stared at him.

"Any computer nerd can flip votes," said Owen. "The trick is to hide the cheat."

"Or mask it," Cork said.

"Exactly."

"Geronimo," said Slade. "After his raids, the cavalry couldn't track him – not even Nathan Brittles. His warriors dragged sagebrush behind their horse to cover the hoofprints."

"That was Bruce Kagan's invention," Owen said. "His algorithm cheats the voter count but then corrects the recount."

Cork said, "So, if a race result gets audited -"

"It will always pass the test. For every thousand votes Candidate A got – the audit will show all one thousand. But in the original rigged count – nine-hundred--eighty went to Candidate A – twenty to Candidate B. It'll make all the difference in purple states."

"But any deep dive will show that," said Raquel.

"Yes, young lady – if there is a deep dive."

"Only the election winner can force one," said Cork.

"Unless the winner's the loser," Slade said.

"Just ask the ex-president of Brazil," Cork said.

"And maybe the United States," said Owen.

"My God," Raquel said. "You mean –"

"It was the test run. He may've won. We'll probably never know. 'Cause the swamp creatures were already in control. They managed to shut down every investigation, silence any opposition, and throw challengers in jail. But then, they lost control of Congress and the biggest social media site. And they appear about to lose the White House."

"To the guy they tried to destroy," Slade said.

"Who'll exact his pound of flesh," said Cork. "To survive, they have no choice but to trigger the Apocalypse."

"They got eight months to do it," said Slade.

"Wrong, Mr. Slade," Owen said. "Implementation must begin in three days for the Mask to work right. They're desperate."

"That explains the Cuba gambit," said Cork.

Owen said, "We got wind of Kagan's invention from our CIA

mole,and Kudzu managed to grab the Mask. Unfortunately, my trusted LA, Greg Bradford, got the same notion, and snatched it from me."

"And gave it to his boyfriend," Slade said.

"Who turned it into art," said Cork.

"Explosive art," said Owen. "If it goes off, it'll destroy this country. And everyone here, including me, will be in prison or dead."

"After a little argument," Slade said, quoting John Wayne in *Rio Bravo*.

"So, you see, Cork, whatever you think of Kudzu, you have to give me that painting."

Cork took off his glasses and rubbed his eyes. Raquel squeezed his right arm. He turned to Slade.

"Mark?"

"Your call, Neil," said Slade.

Cork put on his glasses and looked at Owen.

"Everything you said is valid, Senator. But you're on the wrong side of the Constitution we both swore to defend. And that's a line I won't cross, except as a last resort to save the nation. I'll make a deal with you. I know a good man still in the Bureau. You can meet with him and me tonight. By midnight, either you or he will have the painting."

"You're risking a lot more than our lives, Cork," Owen said.

"I know," said Cork. "But that's the way it has to be."

Senator Owen looked frustrated. "Where and when?" he asked.

"Be in front of the Dirksen Building at ten. Officer Valdez will pick you up there."

Raquel looked pleasantly surprised.

"She'll drive you to the meeting place – not Kudzu," said Cork. "If any one of them show up, you're out. But I can promise you one thing. The Apocalypse Mask won't fall into the wrong hands."

"It may not fall into the right ones," said Slade.

"But I can still use your help, Senator," Cork said.

"What do you need?" asked Owen.

"A secure phone – absolutely untraceable."

"Tar," said Owen. "Give Mr. Cork your mobile."

The Indian held out his cellphone and passed it van to Cork.

"Call me by eleven, or Kudzu goes to red alert," said Owen. "And there'll be blood."

The van stopped. The back door opened, held by Raider One, revealing the same SUV behind the van. They were in the parking lot of a small shopping center, all stores shuttered for the Sunday night.

Senator Owen got out. Raider Two closed the door. The van started moving again.

"Where to?" inquired a voice from the front seat.

"The closest subway station," said Cork.

He leaned back on the bench and shut his eyes, guiltily aware of Raquel's luscious body pressing against his, but too tired to protest.

# CHAPTER 47

The van dropped off the three of them at Vienna Metrorail Station – the end of the Orange Line in Virginia. They entered the white concrete arch tunnel and turned left into the main station, Slade scanning the few other passengers. Cork bought three fare cards at the machine and handed one each to Raquel and Slade. They rode the escalator down to the outdoor platform and the subway train resting on the left-side track.

Slade noted only four other riders on the platform, all middle-aged men in Redskins wear. Homebound from a game viewing party, he assumed. He boarded the subway car first and took the left seat facing the opendoor. Cork sat down on his right in the first front-facing seat, Raquel beside him. They didn't relax until a female computer voice said, "Doors closing on the right," and the doors shut.

The train began to move, rapidly picking up speed. It would travel above ground for nine miles, paralleling the I-66 highway on the DC approach. Slade, whod been coatless since he was taken from his apartment, relished the heat. The group travelled in silence except for the computer voice announcing each station stop.

Somewhere between West Falls Church and East Falls Church,

Raquel's cellphone pinged. The caller ID came up *Unknown Number*. Raquel opened the text message and showed it to Cork. *Mac's in. Awaiting your instructions. A*. Slade looked inquiringly at Cork.

"The Good," Cork said. "Special Agent Bob McKenna, an FBI legend."

"Can you trust him?" Slade asked.

"About eighty percent."

"Let's bump it up to ninety."

"How?"

"Amy Gallup," said Slade. "I left her in fed hands. I'd like to see her again, safe and sound. If your boy's clean, make her part of the horse trade. No Amy, no deal."

Cork took out his Kudzu mobile. He typed a long text message and sent it to the number on Raquel's phone screen. The train went into the tunnel, from which it would not reemerge until Maryland.

"The next station stop is Ballston. Doors opening on the right."

The train began slowing to a stop in the white honeycomb station.

"What's *our* stop?" Slade asked.

"Yours and mine – Metro Center," said Cork. "En route to the Winger Gallery."

"Oh, not again," said Slade.

"What better place to unveil Paul Adamo's masterpiece. And the master piece."

"The Apocalypse Mask," said Slade. "You really know where it is?"

"I believe so."

Slade looked expectantly at Cork.

"Better you don't know – yet," said Cork. "That way if this *is* a trap, they won't be able to torture it out of you."

"No, just you."

"They won't take me alive."

"You got a suicide pill?"

"Yes – you," Cork said.

Slade nodded. "*The Last of the Mohicans*."

"A proper way to go, being your partner," said Cork.

"But only as a last resort," Said Slade.

"Stop it!" Raquel declared.

Cork and Slade looked at her distraught face.

"I can't believe you!" she exclaimed. "You talk about killing one another like it's no big deal, when it's obvious you two are brothers!"

"Cain and Abel," said Cork.

Raquel let out a chuckle despite her concern. Cork and Slade smiled at her.

"It'll work out, kid," Slade said.

The train began moving again.

"The next station stop is Virginia Square and George Mason University."

"What's my stop?" Raquel asked.

"Rosslyn," said Cork. "Blue line to Reagan Airport."

"Car rental?"

"An unwired car, to pick up Owen at the Capitol. Call Wallace on the way. Tell him everything that happened tonightonly leave out Kudzu. We took down the bad feds all by ourselves, just the three of us, okay?"

"Yes, Neil."

"Wallace can't save Slade and I if things go wrong, but he can follow our lead."

"And take some scalps," said Slade.

"All right," Raquel said.

"The next station stop is Virginia Square and George Mason University. Doors opening on the right."

Two stops later, the train pulled into Rosslyn Station, deep underground.

"Doors opening on the left."

Raquel stood up, seeming worried. She turned to Cork. "Neil, I …" she started to say.

Cork gently shook his head as if to dissuade her from continuing.

"I'd rather stay with you guys," she said.

"We'll be okay, Raquel," said Cork.

"Beers on me at the Dubliner," said Slade.

Raquel nodded somberly. The leftside doors opened beside her. She exited the car. Cork and Slade watched her through the left window, walking toward the north end of the station.

"That's not what she started to say," Slade said.

"I know," said Cork.

"What she meant to say?"

"Yes."

The subway doors closed.

"It's why you stopped her," said Slade.

"I have marriage insurance," Cork said. "My wife."

The train began to move, accelerating quickly.

"The next station stop is Foggy Bottom and George Washington University."

# CHAPTER 48

Slade bounded up the escalator steps at Dupont Circle Station. On reaching the top platform without getting swarmed by feds, he waited for Cork to ascend. They exited through the electronic gate, emerging on the east side of Connecticut Avenue, south of Dupont Circle.

They circled left around the row of fancy shops which included the Winger Gallery, and ducked into the alley behind it. Turning right into the small Winger parking lot, Slade noted the absence of the police tape, chalk outline, and Adamo's car.

He and Cork crossed the lot to the back door of the gallery. Slade watched the alley while Cork read a four-number sequence off his Kudzu phone screen then typed it on the code box.

"Winger gave you the code," said Slade.

"How could she refuse? If this works, her gallery will be the new Watergate."

"The downfall of a President."

"And the whole rotten crowd," said Cork.

The security box emitted a loud, long electronic beep then a click. Cork and Slade went through the door into a dark space, keeping close to the right wall. Slade shut the door behind him, marked *Emergency Exit Only*.

Cork turned on the flashlight on his Kudzu phone. He directed the beam to the near right wall, past the painting of the topless Eskimo boy to the light-switch by its bottom right. He flicked up the switch, illuminating the Paul Adamo Exhibit. As if magnetized, he and Cork turned to the two large paintings on the rear wall – and the vacant space between them.

"Now we shall touch the bottom of this swamp," Cork said dramatically.

"Shakespeare?"

"Arthur Miller, *The Crucible*. His response to the Blacklist."

"Like Carl Foreman's *High Noon*," Slade said. "'Cept the feds are the commies now."

"And their Blacklist a death list."

"Let's face 'em down like Will Kane, not a bunch of hysterical witches."

Cork examined the painting on the left with the two teen natives racing for salvation. Slade joined him, reading the title card aloud.

"*Utopia*. So, where's *Revelation*?"

"It'll turn up," said Cork. "Depending on who else does. Let's have a seat and wait."

They approached the two chairs to the left of the inner doorway. Slade took the seat by the door, Cork the other. Cork started writing a text, Slade finger-drumming on the right armrest – *Tap, tap-tap-tap, tap-tap-tap, tap-tap-tap-tap-tap-tap-tap. Tap-tap-tap, tap-tap-tap, tap-tap-tap-tap-tap-tap-tap-tap.* He began singing low and in tune, *The Ballad of High Noon*.

*"Do not forsake me, oh my darlin'*
*On this our wedding day*
*Do not forsake me, oh my darlin'*
*Wait, wait along."*

Cork sent the text and leaned back in his chair, looking at *Utopia* across the room.

*"I do not know what fate awaits me*

*I only know I must be brave*
*And I must face a man who hates me*
*Or lie a coward, a craven coward*
*Or lie a coward in my grave."*

"That won't be on your epitaph," Cork said, putting down the cellphone.

"Yours either," said Slade

"'Maniac' is more fitting."

"Ha. I'll take it, if it's at a ripe old –"

A long faint beeping sound interrupted Slade. It came from the security box outside. Slade sprang up, drawing the Glock from the back of his shirt. He moved to the left side of the door as it opened, pointing his pistol at the doorway.

Alan Nichols walked in wearing a vanilla-colored coat with a brown faux-fur collar. He saw the gun pointing at his head and froze. Seeing Cork stand up across the room, he relaxed. Slade lowered the pistol.

Nichols opened the door wider to admit Amy Gallup. She had on the same blue sweater, green tartan skirt, and grey stockings from the morning. Slade closed the door behind her. She gaped at him for a second then rushed to him. She threw her arms around his thick torso, pressing her cheek against his chest. He embraced her.

"Oh, Mark!" she gasped. "I thought I'd never see you again!"

"It was a good bet."

"I'm so glad I lost it," she said.

She gave Slade a deep kiss. He reciprocated for about five seconds then broke it off to meet Nichols' gaze.

"Mark Slade," Nichols said.

"Alan Nichols."

"Almost didn't recognize you without the fangs."

Slade smiled. "The Corks' Halloween party. You remembered my Dracula costume."

"I remember your biting that busty blonde's neck."

Slade noticed Amy's smirk and put his right arm around her shoulders.

"Thanks for bringing the girl," he said.

"My pleasure," said Nichols.

Slade led Amy toward the inner doorway and the two chairs beside it. He sat her down on the second chair from the door and took the other. Amy grabbed his hand, squeezing it tightly.

Cork joined Nichols in front of the painting marked *Utopia*. The two former partners shook hands.

"Thanks, Alan," Cork said. "MacKenna?"

"Just landed at Dulles. Left a major case in Nashville to come here."

Cork nodded. Nichols turned to the blank wall space reserved for *Revelation*.

"Where's the painting?"

"Well hidden," Cork said. "I want Mac and Owen to see where. Then they can vie for it."

"The big man himself," said Nichols. "So, you were right about your old obsession."

"Kudzu? Nah, that was just a fever dream."

Nichols studied his ex-partner. Cork gave him nothing more, moving closer to *Utopia*. Nichols rubbed his upper arms, appearing nervous.

Across the room in the chairs, Slade and Amy spoke just above a whisper.

"Where'd he find you?" Slade asked.

"Your apartment. I was praying you'd come back to it – and me."

"What about that FBI chick – Sharon?"

"She got a phone call that upset her," Amy said. "About some dead agents. And she left."

The firefight at Airstrip J, Slade figured.

"I was so scared for you," Amy said, her husky voice quivering. "That's when I knew – I love you, Mark."

Slade slightly stiffened. Amy clearly felt it in his hand, which she caressed.

"It was just talk before," she said. "Not anymore. You don't have to love me back. Just like me a little. I can build on that."

"I like you a lot, Amy."

"Next month is spring vacation," said Amy. "Will you come to Boone with me? I promise you the best time ever. Then we can get out of bed."

"Sounds perfect," Slade said.

Another loud beep distracted him. Cork turned inquiringly to Nichols, who looked more worried now.

"Can't be MacKenna yet," Nichols said.

"Or Owen," said Cork.

Slade rushed to the left side of the door and flattened himself against the wall, the gun in his left hand. A black silencer tip entered, followed by the pistol itself, held by a large man in a Green Strike hoodie. Slade pressed the Glock barrel to the right side of his hood and gripped the gun, a Beretta M9. The intruder instantly let go of it.

Slade waved him forward with the Beretta silencer, just as another extra-large green hoodie wearer came in, cowl down, hands bare. Slade pointed the Glock at his face, keeping the Beretta on the first man. Slade nodded for the new intruder to join his friend, which he did.

Cork and Nichols stared at the hooded duo. Slade spun the Glock to the door - and an incoming third person. Joan Russell entered in a long grey wool coat with faux grey fur open on a dark blue short dress over brown stockings. She saw Slade and his two pistols – one with a silencer pointed at her – she gasped.

"Don't shoot, Mark, it's me!" she cried.

"Come on in, Joan," Slade said. "And shut the door."

Joan nervously obeyed, her look of distress making her no less beautiful.

Slade said, "Hey, Alan, will you frisk those two goons near you."

Nichols approached the Green Strike men, and expertly padded their hoodies, spending more time on the man Slade didn't disarm.

"Amy, go stand by Cork," Slade said.

Amy rose to her feet and went to Cork's side. He put a supportive hand on her left shoulder, which she seemed to appreciate. Nichols finished patting down the Green Strike two.

"They're clean," he said.

"Sit your butts down on those chairs," Slade said, indicating the two chairs. "And don't let me a hear a creak out of 'em."

The two Green Strike men obeyed. Slade tucked the Glock in the back of his pants and turned to Joan while lowering the silencer.

"How 'bout you, Zara? Did you bring your meteorite sword?"

"Please, Mark, I'm unarmed," Joan said.

"You are now," said Slade. "What is it with you and these gunsels? Don't you love me anymore?"

"I do," said Joan. "I mean – they're protecting me."

"That's right, you lost your huskie."

"You – you killed Maurice," Joan said fearfully.

"I put him to sleep," said Slade, then turned to Cork. "I'm done here. Your show, Neil."

He moved to Amy's side. Cork approached Joan.

"To what do we owe this visit, Ms. Gardner? I don't recall extending you an invitation."

Joan appeared less intimidated by Cork than Slade.

"I got word *Revelation* was here," she said. "Or soon will be."

"From whom?" asked Cork.

"A friend."

"In the FBI," said Slade.

Cork turned to Nichols. "Alan?"

"I only told MacKenna," Nichols said.

"On what phone?"

"My next-door neighbor's. Retired lawyer. He loaned me his cell."

"Where'd you make the call from?"

"My condo –"

Nichols stopped himself as if realizing something.

"Bugged," said Cork.

"This ain't a private party," said Slade.

"But not yet a public one," Cork said. "The fed who overheard that chat may be in business for himself or herself."

"Half a million bucks is a good startup," Slade said. "Right, Joan?"

"One million now," Joan said.

"I knew I should've held out," said Slade. "I got distracted by the perk."

Joan appeared to almost smile. "Nobody called me," she said.

"Mac and Owen better get here fast," said Cork. "The sooner we're out of here the better."

"How long will it take you to produce the painting?" Nichols asked anxiously.

"I had better advance my presentation," said Cork. "You can report this to MacKenna."

# CHAPTER 49

Cork moved to the back wall. He stopped before the vacant space reserved for *Revelation*, directly between *Utopia* on the left and *The Unholy* on the right. Every eye in the room was locked on him.

"Paul Adamo was a mediocre painter, but a pure artist," he said. "He gave his unfinished work the perfect touch. Even though that touch was someone else's creation, stolen by his lover from Senator Owen's office. Paul realized this addition would be more valuable than his own contribution. And he accepted that – at first. He made a lucrative deal for the painting – one half million dollars, final payment due after it had hung here a week for all the world to see."

He pointed to the empty wall space. Nobody made a sound.

"But once Paul completed his work, like Pygmalion, he fell in love with it. He felt the two parts were aesthetically inseparable and couldn't bear to see his masterpiece divided and destroyed. So, he substitued *Revelation* with a lesser work. He was delivering it to this gallery when he was shot and killed. His murderer chose to save the quarter million dollars, doubtless to fight climate change."

"I didn't kill Paul!" cried Joan. "I told him I could wait a week to pay him!"

"Yes, Wwith Green Strike money," Cork said. "You're a true

believer, Miss Russell – thus a useful idiot to them. The decision to kill Adamo was made high over your head by the real power behind Green Strike, the Chinese Ministry of Justice, via their DC operative, Major Lao. They soon discovered they had the wrong painting. Then began a three-way race to find the right one, more precisely what it contained – the Apocalypse Mask – before its expiration date, two days from tonight. Mark Slade and I classified the seekers according to a classic western. The Good –"

He turned to Slade.

"The FBI," Slade said.

"The Bad –"

"Senator Owen."

"And the Ugly –"

"Green Strike," Slade said. "No offence, Joan."

Cork continued. "The Good and the Ugly need to activate the Apocalypse Mask to keep the Regime in power. While the Bad only has to prevent the activation – and let the American people choose the next President. With the Mask in his possession, Senator Owen had been running out the clock – until Greg Bradford pilfered it."

Amy winced at her dead boyfriend's name.

Slade and I came into this late," said Cork. "Courtesy of our lovely client, Amy Gallup. Yet we seem to have seized the prize."

"Where's the painting?" Nichols almost demanded.

"Right on this wall," said Cork, a hand sweep indicating the back wall. "For all the world to see. Paul Adamo got his wish after all."

"It's not there!" declared Joan.

"But it is," said Cork. "You see, Paul was impressed by the Book of Revelation. As taught him by a priestly acquaintance of yours, Ms. Gardner - a fellow climate alarmist."

"Reverend Sinclair," said Joan turning to Slade. "Paul's funeral."

Slade smiled with mock modesty.

Cork said, "To my embarrassment, it never occurred to me to reread the Scripture for inspiration. But by the grace of God, it came to me, appropriately in Mass – a reading from the Book of Revelation."

He approached the painting marked *Utopia*, reciting, "'And there was a rainbow around the throne, like an emerald in appearance.'"

"Like this for instance!" he declared, pointing to the green rainbow in the painting. "Behold the purloined painting, – to credit Edgar Allan Poe – in plain sight."

"Boy, talk about a revelation," said Slade.

He, Joan, Nichols, and Amy moved closer to the painting, as if toward a celestial light.

"What about the Apocalypse Mask?" Nichols asked.

"Knowing what we do about Adamo," said Cork. "It's precisely where it ought to be, to reflect both his ideology and sexuality."

"Somewhere over the rainbow," said Slade.

Cork began brushing the green rainbow with his right hand. Everyone reverently watched him. After about half a minute, his hand rested on the arch of the rainbow.

"Sorry, Paul," he said.

He dug his fingers into the area and slowly extracted a rectangular half-inch piece of green rainbow, leaving a white gap in the canvas. Holding the piece between his thumb and forefinger, he turned his hand around to reveal the back of a sliver Micro SD card.

"The Apocalypse Mask, I presume," said Slade.

Cork indicated the two sitting Green Strike musclemen. "This place has become a danger zone," he said. "I suggest we relocate right away. Alan, tell Mac to meet us at Metro Police head –"

His sentence was cut short by the Glock pistol in Nichols' hand, pointed at Slade. Amy looked shocked, Joan not at all.

"Drop the gun, Slade," said Nichols. "By the silencer. And keep your left hand up."

Slade raised his left arm. He took hold of the Beretta suppressor and laid down the pistol.

"Other hand up," Nichols said.

Slade raised his right arm to match his left one.

"Step back."

Slade took two steps back to Cork's right side.

"Great ex-partner you got there," he said to Cork.

Cork stared disgustedly at Nichols, who kept his eyes and gun on Slade.

"A friend in the DOJ," Cork said. " I take it MacKenna's not coming."

"Still in Nashville," Nichols said. "Joan, have your boys get his guns."

"Keith, Jerry," Joan said in the direction of her seated Green Strike men.

The pair stood up. Keith moved behind Slade, Jerry in front of him. Jerry picked up the Beretta off the floor. Keith pulled the Glock from Slade's back waist and handed it to Jerry. The two joined Joan, Nichols, and the distraught Amy. Nichols turned to Amy.

"You – with them," he said, nodding at Slade and Cork.

Amy walked nervously to Slade's right side. Nichols approached Cork with his left palm out, the pistol in his right hand.

"I'll take that, Neil," he said.

Cork clenched his right fist.

"Don't make me shoot you," Nichols said.

Cork opened his fist and handed Nichols the micro card, looking him in the face.

"Which came cheaper, Alan? The country or your soul?"

"Saint Neil," Nichols said bitterly. "Everything was always so clearcut with you. You didn't like the Bureau's mud bath? You had the skills to fly away and leave me behind, like a parrot in a cage. 'Alan want a bonus? Alan want a raise?' Eight years without a promotion, and no hope of one. They didn't even offer me the chance to go bad like the rest of them – because of you!"

"You were my partner," said Cork.

"Salt in the wound. Golden Boy Cork dragging me along with him. That's what everyone said. I didn't mind it so much. You were all right. And I had one great thing going for me – the only girl I ever loved."

"Jesus," said Cork.

"That's right, partner – Kathy. You had everything else. And you took her."

“I didn’t take her. We fell in love. And you did fine with Linda and your kid.”

“Fine,” Nichols said bitterly. “I’ll do a lot better with a million dollars. Come on, Joan.”

“Wait,” Joan said, indicating Slade and Cork. “What about them? They know about the Apocalypse Mask. They’ll expose it, and us.”

“They killed six Bureau men and wounded five,” said Nichols. “Wilcox will take care of them and the girl. I can make a deal with him for the Mask.”

“All right,” Joan said, slinking toward Slade. “Sorry, Mark. You would’ve liked me in my Zara outfit. And more of this.”

She moved her rich lips to Slade’s mouth and gave him a deep tongue-filled kiss. Amy looked upset. Joan rejoined her party.

Nichols stood by the exit door, Keith and Jerry behind him. He put his pistol inside his coat into an obvious shoulder holster. When Joan joined him, he started for the exit door.

“Do it, Jerry,” Amy said.

Jerry aimed the Beretta silencer at Nichols’ back, and fired what sounded like a puff of air. A red circle appeared on Nichols’ coat. He stumbled forward and palmed the wall near the door. He turned around, propping his back against the wall, his expression miserable yet unsurprised as if witnessing one more disappointment. He slumped to the floor, leaving a streak of red on the wall above him.

Joan looked shocked, as did Cork. But not Slade. He watched Amy calmly approach the shaken Joan. Joan’s fearful eyes darted from Amy to her Green Strike entourage.

“Jerry? Keith?”

“Cork was right,” Amy said, her southern twang a bit harsher. “You were a useful idiot.”

She crouched beside Nichols’ corpse and thrust one hand into his right coat pocket, her left hand under his coat as if checking for a heartbeat. She stood up holding the Micro SD card and turned to Joan.

“Now you’re a useless idiot,” Amy said. “Do it, Keith.”

“No!” cried Slade.

Keith launched a knife-edge blow to Joan's right clavicle. She spasmed, losing all motor control. She took two shaky steps toward Slade. He rushed forward and caught her, his hands under her arms. He let her body slide down, and gently laid her on the floor.

Her spasms ceased and she lay still.

"Why, Mark," Amy said. "I thought I was the only woman in your life."

Slade gave her a venomous look.

"I'd say suck my dick," he said. "But you already did that, bitch."

# CHAPTER 50

Slade stood up next to Joan's body and stepped back beside Cork, still glaring at Amy and the two Green Strike killers flanking her.

"Wow, Mark," said Amy. "You don't seem surprised by the new me,"

"I'm not," Slade said. "Not since I figured out you were the Capitol Hill Sniper and not Greg. You killed Greg."

"You might've mentioned that tidbit before now," Cork said.

"I was going to tonight."

"When, after she shot us?"

"I meantto hand her over to your FBI pal," said Slade. "My mistake."

"What gave me away?" Amy asked.

"Your French," Slade said. "You used the word '*char*' for car. So did Maurice."

"And?"

"It's '*char*' in Quebec. It's '*voiture*' in France. You didn't study French in Dijon your junior year abroad. You learned it in Quebec - at the Green Strike Training Academy - along with shooting weapons like Greg's rifle. And screwing men to their doom."

"You are good, Mark," Amy said huskily. "You're making me

real hot for you right now. But why'd you suspect me in the first place?"

"I was bothered by how Maurice got the jump on me in front of my apartment building. You knew about the lousy porchlight from your first visit there. Could've been a coincidence it was out when Maurice brained me. But nothing has been a coincidence. Including you and me – and Greg."

"Greg was your assignment," Cork said, realizing it just then. "In college. Quite an extra-curricular activity. Standard Ministry of Justice recruitment. Another student?"

"He was so beautiful," said Amy "An Asian god. No man ever touched me like Lee – till you, Mark."

"But you were already damaged goods," said Slade.

"He opened up a whole new world for me."

"The Eastern world," said Cork.

"Death to America," said Slade.

"I did whatever - whoever Lee told me to," said Amy. "Boys were so easy to twist up. The first two were just target practice. But Greg was my mission – a pretty long-term one. I was ordered to marry him."

"Logical," said Cork. "Greg had a bright political future ahead of him. With one major obstacle given his professional environment."

"For me too," Amy said. "The way he resisted me – I knew right off he was a fag."

"You hooked him anyway," said Slade.

"'Course I hooked him. I made Greg my bitch. He kinda enjoyed it. We got engaged, and he got the perfect job for us – aide to Senator Owen."

"A big shot on the Intelligence Committee," said Slade. "With many secrets."

"But then he dumped you," Cork said. "Pretty much as you described."

"I'd planned to get him back this summer," said Amy. "Then something happened that made it a rush job."

"Greg got the Apocalypse Mask and gave it to his new lover

instead of you," said Cork. "You needed to regain control of him fast. And for that, you had to find out who your rival was. Slade is right. Nothing has been a coincidence. Major Lao had a file on me. He knew I was obsessed with Sam Owen, and Kuzu, which made my firm the perfect weapon for delaying them. So, you came to us."

"And hooked me," said Slade.

"You were incredible," said Amy. "Both of you. Faster than we could've hoped."

"Which leaves just one question," Cork said.

"Why are we still alive?" said Slade, glancing at Joan's corpse.

"Sam Owen's a wary old fox," Amy said. "He'll wanna make sure you're alive before he comes in."

"Who said he's coming?"

"You did, Neil, to Alan." Amy nodded at Nichols' body. "Who told Joan." She nodded at Joan's corpse. "Who told Keith." She nodded at Keith on her left. "Who told me Owen would be coming here - without his Kudzu bodyguards, thanks to you."

"Good plan," Slade said to Cork.

"You intend to kill a United States Senator?" asked Cork.

"In self-defense," Amy said. "Owen came here for the painting, and so did Joan. You refused to give it to him, so he shot you, and Joan and Nichols. Joan's bodyguard had to shoot him."

"Now *that's* a good plan," Slade said.

"It's brilliant," said Cork. "With Owen dead, Kudzu dissolves. The Apocalypse Mask activates. The incumbent President wins. And the Regime survives. Could've worked too – were it not for the Unmask Card."

Amy looked unpleasantly surprised.

"Right, the Unmask Card," Slade said. "Owen mentioned that. What was it again?"

"The Kudzu device that will counteract the Apocalypse Mask. Greg took that too."

"You're lying," Amy said but with obvious concern.

"You can see it for yourself," Cork said. "It's in another painting. I can show it to you for a price – our lives."

"Your life, Neil, not Mark's," said Amy. "Masters' orders. He caused us too much damage. And he knows too much about the inner me."

"You're a dope, baby," said Slade. "Neil would never sell me out for –"

"Fair enough," Cork said.

"What?" gulped Slade, turning to his partner.

"I told you to quit screwing around and get married," Cork said. "A family makes you want to live at all costs."

"But I'm the cost," said Slade.

"You got us into this mess, chasing after her," said Cork, pointing at Amy.

"He's right, darlin', but I bet I was worth it," Amy said. "Where's that device, Neil?"

Cork turned to the side wall by the door. Slade kept looking at Amy and the Green Strike pair, Jerry's silencer pointed at him. Cork approached the painting of the cute Eskimo boy.

"It's a trick of the light," he said, his left hand indicating the furious sun at the top left of the artwork. "See that sun about to melt the world? It's Chiaroscuro – literally light from darkness."

Slade tensed. Cork's right hand surreptitiously flicked down the light switch by the bottom right corner of the painting. The room went black. Two sound-suppressed bullets struck the canvas where Cork had been a split second earlier.

Slade charged under Jerry's line of fire, tackling him at the waist. They both went down with Slade on top. He hammered Jerry in the face and felt him shut down. He groped the dark floor for the Beretta. A brutal kick struck his right rib, sending him rolling off Jerry in pain.

He kept rolling under his own power to the back wall, then sprang to his feet ready to meet Keith's next attack. He knew the kick would come from either side in the near darkness. A batlike mass flew at him on the left. His elbow shot up to block the shoe, taking a hard blow. His left forearm hurt, but he only needed his right arm in the next second.

He threw a hard punch to where he figured Keith's head would be, judging by his kick's trajectory. A solid hit on jawbone rewarded him. As his eyes adjusted to the gloom, Keith changed from invisible man to shadow. Slade realized the same went for himself.

Keith closed on him, his cupped hands circling martial arts style. Slade maintained the classic boxing stance. Keith fired a lethal right slug at his face. Slade blocked it with his left wrist then quickly did the same with his right, stopping a punch from the opposite side.

Keith jumped back. Slade knew what was coming and from where. He leapt left as a right roundhouse kick struck his rib at half force. It hurt like hell but didn't disable him as full impact would have. And it left Keith open to his counterattack – two rapid left jabs to the jaw, a right cross to the chin, two more left jabs, then a right-fist missile to the jaw. Keith went down and out.

The room light came back on. Cork crouched below the Eskimo Boy painting, his hand on the light switch, ready to flick it off. Slade stood over the fallen Green Strike men looking at Amy's beautiful smirking face.

"Well, Mark," she said. "You gonna kiss me or hit me?"

Slade couldn't resist. He backslapped Amy across the cheek, knocking her on her butt.

"Mark," said Cork.

"I'm not gonna hurt her," Slade said. "But she's lucky she's a girl."

Amy propped herself up on two hands, the blood drop on her lower lip oddly attractive.

"We'll leave her to Owen," Cork said. "Tell him what she had in store for him."

"No!" Amy cried, suddenly afraid. "Please, Neil. He'll hand me over to Kudzu. They'll make me disappear."

"Not from my heart, babe," Slade said.

"With good reason," said Cork. "You killed one of them – Jonathan Woods."

"I had to," Amy said, voice quivering. "He might've told you about the Apocalypse Mask."

"So, you tried to kill us," Slade said.

"I didn't want to!" Amy cried. "But you'd done your part, and found out too much! I love you, Mark! That isn't a lie."

"Sure," said Slade.

"Why the two cops?" asked Cork.

"I had to make it look like Greg went crazy," Amy said. "That he was the sniper."

"Who shot himself," said Cork.

"Yes," said Amy.

"You blew your boyfriend's jaw off," Slade said. "One hell of a breakup."

"Please, Neil," Amy said. "You can turn me over to the FBI -"

Slade made a scoffing noise.

"Someone you trust there," Amy said.

"Like you trusted Nichols," said Slade.

"I'll tell them everything I know about my superiors," said Amy.

"Even Lee?" Slade asked bitterly.

"Even Lee," said Amy.

A moan came from behind them. Cork and Slade turned to where Jerry lay motionless, the Beretta by his right hip.

"You're slipping, Mark, he's still alive," Cork said.

"And I left him his guns."

Slade rushed toward Jerry. He picked up the Beretta by the silencer and turned the man over, eliciting another moan. He pulled the Glock from Jerry's rear pants waist.

"Even the Bureau won't save you from Wallace," Cork said to Amy. "I know the man. He'll make you pay for killing his men."

"They can put me in witness protection," said Amy. "Hide me from Wallace and Major Lao's people."

"They just might," said Cork.

Amy rose unsteadily to her feet, watched by Cork. Slade stood up holding the two guns – then felt the chill down his spine. He turned around and approached Nichols' body, still propped against the back wall.

"But your information had better be pure gold," said Cork.

Slade crouched beside Nichols' corpse. He laid down the two pistols and reached into the dead man's coat. He shuddered. The shoulder holster was empty.

"Oh no," Slade said, turning his head toward Amy.

"Ya!" yelled Amy kicking up her right leg to smash Cork's chin.

He fell on his back. Amy pulled the Glock from under her skirt. Slade sprang backward toward the wall, his left hand snatching the Beretta. Amy fired at him twice. The first shot hit the wall just over his head, the second struck his chest. His Beretta silencer coughed in response. Blood spurted above Amy's right breast. Her gun hand fell but held on to the pistol. She looked dreamily at Slade. Slade switched the Beretta to his right hand, the silencer on Amy.

Cork rose on his hands, a purple gash on his chin. In his position, he could only see Amy, her breast wound telling him Slade won the duel.

"You got to me, Mark," Amy said weakly. "It really hurts."

"I'll remember you too, baby," said Slade, putting his left palm over his chest wound.

"Till your dying day?"

Amy's gun hand rose slowly, unsteadily.

"Don't do it, Amy," said Slade. "I will kill you."

"You already have."

"Drop it, Amy," Slade said, finding it harder to breathe.

Amy's arm straightened with the gun in her hand.

"Goodbye, darling," she said.

She started to squeeze the trigger. The gunshot rang loudly. Amy gasped, dropped the gun, and fell to her knees., She looked accusingly at Slade.

Raquel entered through the inner doorway. She held a pistol in her right hand, a tire iron in her left. She passed between Cork and Amy, and stopped on Amy's left. Raquel pointed the gun at Amy's temple. Amy looked afraid yet no less beautiful, her trembling right hand reaching for the dropped pistol.

"For Behling and Garcetti," said Raquel.

There was another gun blast. Amy pitched right to the floor. Cork moved closer to her body. He reached into her coat pocket and retrieved the Micro SD card.

"Neil," Raquel said grimly.

Cork felt a shudder. He turned his head to look behind him. Slade sat on the floor with his back against the wall, his chest bleeding.

Cork rushed to his side and knelt beside him. He stripped off his sweater and draped it over Slade's chest.

"Don't move" he said. "The cavalry's coming."

Slade opened his mouth to speak but coughed instead.

"Shut up and breathe," said Cork.

Raquel spoke into her cellphone with tension in her voice. "Send EMS. Two buses. Gunshot wounds. Five down, one up. Scene secure at my location."

She hurried to Cork's side, looking down at Slade with concern. His eyesight blurry, Slade he could barely see her and Cork, only hear them. Their conversation sounded distant.

"How is he?" asked Raquel.

"Not good," said Cork. "Where's Owen?"

"Out back in the car," Raquel said. "I saw the light go out and told him to stay put. TI thought for sure someone would hear me pry the door open. Then I heard the fight."

"And Amy's confession."

"Yeah. That's why I stayed hidden. I'm sorry, Neil, I didn't know she had a gun."

"Neither did I," said Cork. "Her henchmen had pistols, yet she lifted Alan's. I suspect she planned to kill them too, since they knew about the Apocalypse Mask."

Slade heard the faint sirens then Cork and Raquel's voice, now fainter.

"Tell Owen to get lost," said Cork.

"Right."

"Oh, and give him this."

"The Apocalypse Mask."

"Yes," said Cork. "To prevent the Apocalypse – or delay it for a while."

"I'll be right back," said Raquel.

The room turned darker for Slade. The theme song from *El Dorado* started playing in his head, sung by a deep male voice that might have been his.

*"The wind becomes bitter, the sky turns to grey,*
*His body grows weary, he can't find his way.*
*But he'll never turn back, though he's lost in the snow,*
*For he has to find El Dorado."*

For an instant he saw it – a golden city on a hill. Then it vanished along with everything else.

# CHAPTER 51

The nurse's face was Black, round, and pretty, even with thick rectangular glasses. She had her hair in a bun and her hand on his bandaged chest. Slade regretted he couldn't feel the hand. The nurse noticed him appraising her and smiled.

"I made it," he said.

"You sure did."

"How long was I –?"

"I'll get the doctor," said the nurse.

She left Slade to his thoughts. Okay, he wasn't dead. But was he free? He checked his wrists. No handcuffs, just the tube in his right forearm. There were zerno bars on the window, only daylight rain striking it. Dr. Ben Hooks appeared beside his cot.

"I want that nurse back," said Slade.

"Go to med school," Hooks said smiling.

"I guess I'm at yours – Howard U Hospital."

"Lucky me. I'm going into sports medicine, not combat wounds. But I volunteered to fix you up when the paramedics brought you in. How're you feeling?"

"Like I'm not here."

"It's the medication," Hooks said. "I added scopolamine - to reduce your slobbering during surgery."

"Scopolamine," said Slade. "That's truth serum. CIA used it in Sandland."

"Your secrets are safe with me."

"What's the story, Ben?"

"I operated 'round midnight – seven hours ago. Got the bullet out. Close call, buddy. That well-built chest of yours saved your life."

"And the fact that you're a better doctor than you were a b-ball player in school."

"Hey, you got cut from the team too," said Hooks. "Speaking of GU alum – Cork's out there. Up to seeing him?"

"Yeah. And thanks, Ben."

Hooks gave him a wave and left the room.

"High time you woke up," Cork said entering. "You get only one day of sick pay."

He wore a blue suit with a red-and-black striped tie, his coat tucked under his arm.

"Are we out on bail?" Slade asked.

"No bail. I had a long talk with Senator Owen. Well, he did most of the talking. He thinks he can keep the federal wolves at bay till Election Day. He said they fear the once and future President more than they hate us."

"What if they win in November?"

"Then we head for Belize and watch out for strange men."

"And beautiful women," Slade said sourly.

"I'll bring my own, and our daughter. But the Regime would have to win fair and square - without the Apocalypse Mask - and they're too long out of practice."

"So, we're heroes now."

"Spy smashers."

"Falling for one of them was brilliant detective work," said Slade.

"Hey, I trusted the wrong person too. Perhaps that's the price we pay to lead normal lives, leaving suspicion to Owen and Kudzu."

"You've come around, Cork."

"Not me," Cork said. "I find their extra-legal tactics troubling. But maybe, just maybe, they're needed. To save the system from worse men. By the way –"

He leaned closer to Slade, looking uneasy.

"Owen asked me to tell you – there's a place for you in Kudzu if you want it."

"Are you kidding? Those guys are fascists."

Cork grinned.

"Well then, we have a backload of clients. Though I hired a new detective in your absence."

"A hot Latina copper."

"She's on suspension from the force – for shooting Amy. I told Wallace she did it to save your life. Not quite true."

"True enough," Slade said melancholically. "She'll do.

He propped himself higher on the hospital bed.

"Nothing has been a coincidence," he said.

"One thing was," said Cork. "The lector reading precisely the right Scripture in Mass."

"You sure about that?" Slade probed.

"Perhaps not," said Cork with a smile.

"How's Kathy?"

"Great. I'm picking her up at the airport in an hour."

"Did you tell her about Nichols?"

"Yes," said Cork. "She, uh, wasn't surprised."

"Woman's intuition."

"I wouldn't say that too loudly. Your other visitor might disapprove – being the radical feminist type."

Slade's pulse rate increased. He watched it accelerate on the monitor screen.

"Tell her I died."

"Tell her yourself," said Cork. "I'm off to Reagan Airport. So long, Mark."

He exited. Nina Holt walked in wearing a tight grey skirt, a burgundy cashmere sweater, and a concerned look on her gorgeous face. She moved to Slade's left bedside.

"CNN must have a bureau in here," Slade said.

"It would be a good way to keep track of you."

"You never needed one."

"True. You were always there when I needed you."

"I still am," said Slade.

"I know. And it's difficult for me, Mark. Not you – you're so damn endearing. The whole concept of you. My *hero* – strong, stalwart, chivalrous – and primitive. If you only wanted to make love with me instead of babies, I could go for that. Though I've got to admit, the alternate's more tempting than it used to be."

"Why, Nina. What would your sisters say?"

"They'd excommunicate me," Nina said.

"Beats an exorcism."

Nina smiled. Nobody could smile as fetchingly, thought Slade.

"I hear a woman finally shot you," Nina said.

"Wasn't the first time," Slade said. "The first time hurt much worse."

Nina's eyes misted, blurring their green beauty.

"Pay no attention to me," Slade said. "They pumped me up with some truth drug. You better go before I say something I'll regret."

"Like what, Mark?" Nina whispered.

"Like I love you, Nina. I always have. And I always will. No matter how mean you get."

The mist in Nina's eyes condensed.

"I knew it," said Slade. "Damn drug should be illegal."

Nina bent over and kissed him lightly on the mouth.

"Get some sleep."

"You're not helping any," Slade said, quoting John Wayne in *Rio Bravo*.

Nina turned and approached the ward curtain.

"Hey, Nina," Slade said, raising his head from the pillow.

She stopped and whirled to him, half in and half out the curtain.

"Yes, Mark?"

"What about your exclusive?"

"I knew there was something I forgot," Nina said with a coy smile. "Guess I'll have to come back later."

She winked at Slade and slipped out through the curtain. He laid his head back on the pillow with an impish smile of his own.

# THANK YOU FOR READING THE WASHINGTON TRAIL!

We hope you enjoyed it as much as we enjoyed bringing it to you. We just wanted to take a moment to encourage you to review the book. Follow this link: The Washington Trail to be directed to the book's Amazon product page to leave your review.

Every review helps further the author's reach and, ultimately, helps them continue writing fantastic books for us all to enjoy.

---

You can also join our non-spam mailing list by visiting www.subscribepage.com/AethonReadersGroup and never miss out on future releases. You'll also receive three full books completely Free as our thanks to you.

Facebook | Instagram | Twitter | Website

---

**Looking for more great Thrillers?**

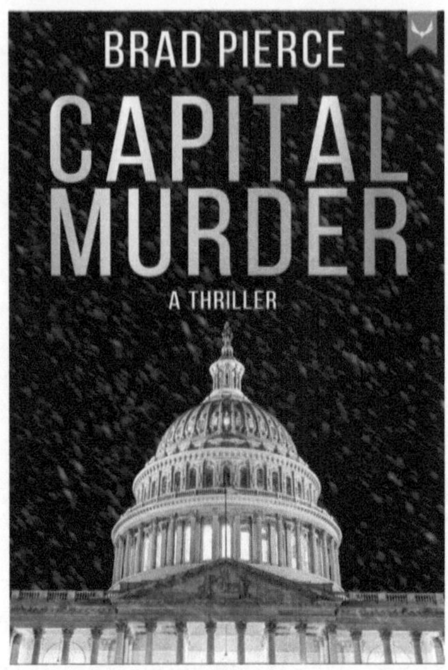


***A traitor in the Government. A Senator savagely murdered. A conspiracy years in the making.*** *As a massive snow storm paralyzes the US Capital, a secret congressional committee is handed evidence of the unthinkable. A high-level traitor in the U.S. Government selling secrets to China. Before they can act, one of their own is murdered. Enter Colin Frost, an ex-special forces operator. He and his highly-classified black-ops team have been hunting a dangerous serial killer across Afghanistan who is destabilizing the entire region. When they get the call to find the Senator's killer, they are startled to see the similarities between the murders in Afghanistan and the Senator at home. They instantly know the two are related and must get to the bottom of the conspiracy before more Senators are killed and the United States is irrevocably harmed. But Colin has a secret... His sister was murdered seventeen years ago, and the unsolved crimes of the past are too similar to the present conspiracy to ignore.* ***This snow-filled political conspiracy thriller by debut author Brad Pierce takes the reader through a dark mystery, decades-long conspiracy, and a personal journey of revenge and justice against a literal angel of death.*** Will Colin Frost succeed, or will he lose himself along the way?

Get Capital Murder Now!

***In a daring act of piracy, Yemeni terrorists have not only seized a special oil tanker but they've also captured a high-value asset.*** *With President Lewis desperate to save his biggest donor's assets and protect his deepest secret, he orders Director of National Intelligence Camille Banks to deploy her secret team to recover the asset. Garrett Knox, along with his hand-picked team members of elite operatives, must attempt the impossible: infiltrate the treacherous Yemeni mountains and bring the asset home alive. Battling hostile terrain and relentless attacks, Knox and company close in on their target only to have the tables flipped on them as a far deadlier plot emerges. The terrorists offer a chilling ultimatum—the asset in exchange for a notorious bombmaker in U.S. custody. With time running out and the world watching, Knox and his team embark on a pulse-pounding mission to retrieve the bombmaker. But when a shocking betrayal threatens everything, Knox must make an unthinkable choice to save Rico and save the president.* ***From the Oval Office to the explosive climax, Terminal Threat is a non-stop thrill ride packed with jaw-dropping twists. As a sinister conspiracy tightens its grip, will Knox's team prevail, or will the President's dark secrets destroy them all? The clock is ticking in this electrifying novel by R.J. Patterson.***

**Get Terminal Threat now!**

---

**For all our Thrillers, visit our website.**
**www.aethonbooks.com**

www.ingramcontent.com/pod-product-compliance
Lightning Source LLC
Chambersburg PA
CBHW030354310726
48979CB00001B/305

* 9 7 8 1 9 6 4 5 0 5 0 8 4 *